AT YOUR MOST BEAUTIFUL

HARPER
BLISS

At Your Most Beautiful

ladylit_ publishing

Other Harper Bliss Books

A Breathless Place
If You Kiss Me Like That
Two Hearts Trilogy
Next in Line for Love
A Lesson in Love
Life in Bits (with T.B. Markinson)
A Swing at Love (with Caroline Bliss)
Once Upon a Princess (with Clare Lydon)
In the Distance There Is Light
The Road to You
Far from the World We Know
Seasons of Love
Release the Stars
At the Water's Edge
The French Kissing Series
High Rise (The Complete Collection)

In the Pink Bean Series

At First Sight
More Than Words
Crazy for You
Love Without Limits
No Other Love
Water Under Bridges
This Foreign Affair
Everything Between Us
Beneath the Surface
No Strings Attached

Published by Ladylit Publishing – a division of Q.P.S. Projects Limited - Hong Kong
ISBN-13 978-988-74416-5-6

CHAPTER 1

A drop of sweat slid down Maya's neck. Then another. She pushed a strand of hair away from her face and expelled a deep sigh, but there was no one around to hear it. She could sigh as deeply and dramatically as she wanted, without Tommy responding with an exaggerated eye roll.

All was quiet in the garden. The surface of the pool was as unwrinkled as an untouched bed sheet. Only last weekend, Tommy and two of his friends had been splashing about loudly as eighteen-year-old boys do—bold and brash as though there's no other way to be at that age.

Two days ago, Maya had driven her son to LaGuardia Airport, where he'd boarded a plane for Paris. He would spend two weeks in Provence with his father and Heidi, followed by five weeks of backpacking through Europe. Seven long weeks without seeing her son. And that was only the beginning of her time without him—her time of no longer being a full-time mother.

Maya had spent plenty of weekends on her own since the divorce, but time alone when Tommy was due to return three days later was very different from time alone when he had just embarked on a seven-week trip, before leaving home for good.

Was this what the infamous empty nest felt like? Had she gone from one cliché—divorcée—to another—empty nester—as seamlessly as the decades had passed by and left her alone in this too-big suburban house at the age of forty-five?

She could only reply with another deep sigh. Maybe it was time to add another cliché to all the others she seemed to have become without noticing. Maybe it was time to open that bottle of pinot gris. She squinted at the sun. It was still pretty high in the sky. Wine o'clock would have to wait until the sun had dipped a fraction lower. Maya had some standards left.

A rustle drew her attention back to the garden. She wasn't expecting any company, so it probably came from next door. Maya's neighbor, Brooke, would probably be up for sharing a glass of pinot later, when the time was more appropriate. The rustle sounded closer. Maya sat up and wiped the sweat from her brow.

"I hope you're wearing sunscreen," a female voice that was not Brooke Hathaway's came from the garden next door.

Only then Maya remembered that the Hathaways had gone to their cabin in the Catskills for the weekend. She sat up straighter in order to see over the hedge that separated her property from the Hathaways'.

"Quinn?" Maya asked. Who else could it be but the Hathaways' daughter?

"The one and only." Quinn stepped into view. "Hi, Mrs. Mercer. Didn't you get the memo? Sunbathing is so last century, it's not even funny."

The girl next door was still as forward as ever, then. "I truly appreciate your concern for my skin, but I don't leave the house without a full coat of SPF 50."

Quinn shot her a bright smile. As far as Maya could see,

she wasn't wearing much more than a pair of flip-flops and an oversized tank top.

"I haven't seen you in such a long time." Maya walked over to the hedge. "How have you been?"

"I'm in-between apartments, so I'm staying here for a few weeks while I get my bearings." She pulled her top away from her skin. "The city's too hot right now, anyway." Had she just cast a longing gaze at Maya's pool? "I hear Little Tommy has flown the nest."

Tommy used to hate it when Quinn called him 'Little'. Maya nodded. "He's in Europe. Starting Stanford in the fall."

"No surprise there. I always knew Tommy would go to one of the big schools."

There are good schools on this coast as well, Maya thought. "What are you up to now?" Maya wanted to deflect the attention away from Tommy. He'd only been gone a few days. His bedroom looked as though he was still in high school and he'd be coming back any day. Although it had been a long time coming and Maya had had ample time to prepare emotionally for her son's departure, it all felt surprisingly raw and unnatural.

"This and that," Quinn said, just as her mother did whenever Maya inquired after Quinn's job. "Mainly photography these days, but, um, yeah..." She ran a hand through her curly hair. "The temperature might be more bearable here than in the city, but it's still damn hot."

Maya was getting the message loud and clear. Years ago, when Quinn still lived at home, and another brutal summer day had descended on Milbury, she would stand exactly where she was standing now, and cast longing gazes at the pool. Usually, Tommy was quick to invite her over for a swim, but Tommy wasn't here any longer.

"Come on." Maya nodded in the direction of the pool. "I can't bear to see you sweat like that any longer."

"Thank you so much, Mrs. Mercer."

"I think you're a little too old to still be calling me that. It's Maya."

Quinn deftly wriggled her body through the bushes, which were much denser now than when Quinn had last made her way through.

"You have my infinite gratitude, Maya." Quinn was already stripping off her tank top. Underneath, she wore the skimpiest bikini Maya had ever laid eyes on. "Seeing as my main career of late has been tending bar, I can make you a mean cocktail later to thank you." Quinn tossed her tank top to the side of the pool and shook off her flip-flops. Before diving in, she looked back and treated Maya to a glittering, sun-drenched smile.

Maya went back to her chair and watched Quinn swim a few slow laps. The mere fact of having someone to share her pool with, even if it was only for a short time, offered a potent distraction from her loneliness. The promise of that 'mean cocktail' was helping as well.

Maya tried to remember the latest news Brooke had given her about Quinn. No Ivy League for the neighbors' daughter, she knew that much. She'd also known Quinn was gay as she'd always been out. How old was Quinn now? Truth be told, Maya hadn't given Quinn Hathaway much thought at all. The girl barely came home. Brooke complained about it often enough, while Bill said she was just finding her way because she was still so young and what were we like at that age?

Now Quinn was swimming in her pool. If Maya partly closed her eyes and squinted, she could pretend it was her son enjoying himself in the cool water.

"Aren't you hot?" Quinn had swum to the side of the pool

closest to Maya, and rested her elbows on the ledge. Drops of water pearled on the skin of her arms.

"I'm fine. I'll go for a dip later."

"How are you holding up now that Tommy's gone?"

"Fine." It was nice of her to ask.

"It must be hard, though." Quinn tilted her head. "Tommy's always been such a mommy's boy." She grinned broadly.

"I don't think that's correct." If anything, Tommy was able to appreciate qualities in his father that Maya had never known the man possessed.

"That's because you can't see it. Because you're his mom." Still grinning, Quinn winked at Maya before her head disappeared under the water again.

Maya followed her with her gaze. She came up for air at the other side of the pool, where she leaned her head back and smoothed the water out of her hair with her hands. If Tommy was a mommy's boy, Quinn Hathaway was definitely a daddy's girl.

"Do you still have your dance school?" Quinn pushed herself out of the water effortlessly and sat on the edge, looking at Maya.

"I do." Thank goodness for that, Maya thought.

"Pity you didn't have it when I was younger. I regret not being able to dance properly." Did she just give Maya a once-over with that piercing blue gaze of hers?

"It's never too late to learn. I teach a seniors class, ages sixty-five and up."

"It must work wonders for your figure. You look amazing for a woman your a—" Quinn paused, and briefly drew her lips into a half-smile. "You really look amazing, Mrs.—um, Maya."

Heat rose to Maya's cheeks, and she was pretty sure it

wasn't caused by the sun. "Thank you," she mumbled. When was Quinn going to mix her that 'mean cocktail'?

Quinn stood and walked to the sitting area, leaving a trail of water behind her.

"Here. Use this." Maya tossed her the towel that was hanging off the chair next to her.

Quinn toweled off her hair, then wrapped the towel around her waist. For some reason, it drew Maya's gaze to her chest—maybe by way of her naked belly. As soon as she realized what she was staring at, Maya averted her gaze.

"Are you sure I'm not interrupting anything?" Quinn sat next to Maya. "With Mom and Dad gone, I was getting bored at the house. It's so quiet here. It's uncanny."

Maya didn't think it was quiet at all. There were birds. There was the dog from two houses down that yapped at the smallest noise. There was the hum of cars in the distance. But she guessed that compared to New York City, Milbury was very quiet. "Truth be told, I'm happy with some company."

Quinn nodded as though she fully understood what Maya was going through. She folded her hands behind her neck and let her head fall back, her chest jutting out so the sight of it captured Maya's attention again. If Maya didn't know any better, she'd think Quinn was doing it on purpose. On second thought, what did she know about Quinn? Not nearly enough to know if she was toying with her.

"When are you going back to the city?" Maya was suddenly very keen to know all about Quinn's life.

"End of the month." Quinn played with her wet hair. "I'm moving in with a friend." She shook her head. "Rent in NYC is murder."

"Where did you live before?"

Quinn expelled a deep breath of air. A shadow crossed her face. "With my girlfriend. Ex-girlfriend now. She kicked me out." She paused to paint on a wry smile. "Thank goodness for hotel Hathaway in good old Milbury."

"Sorry about that."

"Well, it was her place, so..." She ruffled her hair and a few drops of water fell onto her shoulders.

"Were you and..." For the life of her, Maya couldn't remember Brooke mentioning Quinn's girlfriend's name—or that they had recently split up. "Were you together a long time?"

"Coming up to a year."

Quinn had been with her girlfriend for almost a year and Brooke had never even brought it up in conversation with Maya, even though they had shared plenty of bottles of wine in that time.

"Did you ever bring her home?"

With her bottom lip jutted out, Quinn shook her head slowly. "Mom, um, didn't really approve of the relationship. Rach was older than me. She was my photography teacher. Too many red flags for Brooke to deal with." She shrugged. "Anyway, it's over now, so Mom doesn't have to worry about inviting her over for Thanksgiving."

"How much older?" It made sense now that Brooke hadn't mentioned Quinn's girlfriend.

"Rach is in her fifties. Big deal." Quinn pulled her feet up onto the chair. "She's also the fucking hottest woman I've ever met."

Maya bit her tongue to avoid telling Quinn off for swearing, and frantically tried to remember how old Quinn was. When had she graduated high school? She couldn't pinpoint the year, but surely Quinn was no older than twenty-five. Maya fully sympathized with Brooke on this, although this was not the time to let that be known.

"Did she break your heart?"

Quinn gave a one-shouldered shrug. "I don't know. We spent the last two months in this draining cycle of endless fighting and make up sex. I'm honestly glad it's over so I can focus my energy on something else."

Maya didn't know what to say to that. She was curious about this Rach, though. She was probably around the same age as Brooke, hence her disapproval of the relationship.

"It wasn't the age difference that caused the break-up?" Maya was probably pushing it, but she was curious.

"When the woman you love is thirty years older than you, it's going to have some consequences, I guess."

Maya tried to imagine Tommy bringing home a woman thirty years older than him—a woman older than Maya. Purely on instinct, the thought was almost unbearable. She didn't just understand Brooke's reluctance to acknowledge Quinn's former relationship; she fully agreed with it.

"Hey, it will only hurt for a while." Above all else, Maya was a mother herself and soothing words came naturally to her. "It may not feel like that right now, but it's reality." Young people hardly ever took older and wiser people's word for it. It was impossible. Some experiences had to be lived through before they could be accepted, let alone believed. "You're still so young. How old are you now?"

"Twenty-four," Quinn said. She dropped her legs, squared her shoulders, and took a deep breath. "My problem is that I just really, really, *really* like older women." She looked straight into Maya's eyes.

Again, Maya was at a loss for words. Not only because there simply was no quick response to this particular utterance from Quinn, but even more so because of the look Quinn was giving her.

Quinn chuckled. Maya wondered why she didn't find her more obnoxious, but she didn't. Even though Quinn made her feel a little uncomfortable, she didn't mind. At least she was feeling something other than the self-pity she'd been about to drown in before Quinn had caught her attention.

"How about that cocktail I promised you?" Quinn jumped out of her chair. "May I invite you to the Hathaway house?" She pointed to the bush she'd earlier made her way through. "Unless you want it pool-side. Then I'll just get the ingredients and I'll be right back."

"That would be nice." Something held Maya back from following Quinn to her house. "I shall wait here with growing anticipation."

CHAPTER 2

Quinn carefully placed the cocktail in front of Maya. Even though the glass was filled to the brim she managed not to spill a drop. It surprised her because Mrs. Mercer—Maya—was a real fox. How had she never noticed this before? It was also fairly easy to make her blush, although this drink would also help with that.

"Enjoy your paloma, milady," Quinn said. "It was all the rage at my previous place of employ."

"Looks delicious." Maya leaned forward to take a sip from the glass on the table and, while doing so, exposed a touch more of her cleavage. Quinn had to stop herself from ogling. She didn't want to embarrass Maya too much. Quinn would be out of here soon enough, but her parents would still be Maya's neighbors. She would still come back here every few weeks, or months, probably depending on who she ended up with next and whether her mother approved or not. "Hm. Yum." The guttural sound Maya produced pleased Quinn.

She sat and sipped from her own cocktail. It was damn good. And maybe it would help simmer down the restlessness in her blood. But this time of year, mid-July, when the days were hot and the nights hardly cooler, had always made Quinn frisky. Everyone, foxy neighbors included, dressed in barely-there clothes and showed off so much silky-smooth skin. The sun was everywhere and Quinn could still smell it on her skin when she lay in bed at night, too warm to sleep. And she no longer had Rachel to take care of things for her. She had herself, though. She knew what she would be getting up to after she had finished this cocktail. But not before she'd teased Maya a bit more.

Maya had flinched when Quinn had revealed Rachel's age. A lot of people had the same reaction—even some of the women Quinn hit on. But not the one who had just booted her out of her apartment.

"Glad you like it," Quinn said. "Because I sure would like another dip in your pool." When she put her mind to it, Quinn could make everything sound at least a little dirty.

"Any time." Maya looked relaxed as she leaned back against her chair.

"You might regret saying that."

"It's just me here. I told you, I'm glad of the company."

"When did you and Mr. Mercer get divorced?" Her mom must have told her, but Quinn had long forgotten. All she knew was that when she had left home for a failed stint in college six years ago, Drew Mercer still lived next door.

"About five years ago." Quinn couldn't detect any bitterness in Maya's tone.

"Was it a mutual decision?"

"Sure." Maya's voice was flat as could be.

Quinn chuckled in response. "Okay. You don't want to talk about it. That's fine."

"What are we doing talking about our exes on such a lovely summer day, anyway?" Maya took another sip. "Over such a delicious cocktail."

"You're right." Quinn relaxed in her seat. "To hell with them." She couldn't help but wonder what Rachel was up to now. Before she had started rustling around in the bushes, hustling for a swim, she'd been scrolling through Rachel's Facebook profile, an unfulfilling habit she'd developed since arriving home. Unperturbed by her age, Rachel would be out clubbing tonight. It was a given. Quinn made a mental note to avoid Rachel's social media tomorrow—as if she'd even remember when the time came.

"What's it like living in the city?" Maya asked.

"Expensive," Quinn said, because, apart from Rachel, money had been preoccupying her the most.

"I bet."

"But fun. I love the energy. The possibility. As if anything can happen with every corner you turn."

"You're not too bored spending time in good old Milbury?" Maya grabbed her cocktail and held it just above her chest. A drop of condensation fell onto the swell of her breast. This time, Quinn couldn't look away.

"It's good to take a breather once in a while." Quinn took another sip to lubricate the dryness in her throat more than anything.

"Gosh, to be twenty-four again," Maya mused, apparently impervious to Quinn's locked gaze on her chest.

"Weren't you a hot-shot dancer in your twenties?"

"Oh, yes. And I loved every second of it." Maya's voice grew more powerful, as though the memory stirred something in her. "Despite all the hours of training, all the sacrifice... to go out on the dance floor was always just pure ecstasy."

"Do you still dance?" Because that had also been the thing about Rachel, and the thought of her out in the clubs tonight, being watched by a myriad of other women stirred jealousy within Quinn. Rachel always had the smoothest moves, the coolest sway to her hips. She might be the oldest, but that never stopped her from being the hippest person in any joint she entered—baby dyke parties included. Quinn had loved to watch Rachel dance.

"Of course. I will only stop when I lose the use of my legs."

"Did you teach Tommy how to dance?" Quinn's gaze had traveled back up to Maya's face. The late afternoon light caught in her eyes, making them glitter.

"Of course. He might end up an accountant like his father, but at least he'll be an accountant who knows how to waltz."

"I'd love to see you dance," Quinn blurted out. It was true. Even when she simply reached for her cocktail, there was such elegance to the stretch of Maya's arm. But it might not be the best thing to say to her neighbor with whom she was having a chill and lovely time.

"Come to the studio some time. I'll teach you some moves."

Quinn hadn't expected that. "All right. I'll be there."

Over the rim of her glass, Maya eyed her. "What did you put in this, anyway?"

"Grapefruit juice, soda water, and some syrup. And a healthy dose of tequila, of course."

"It tastes deceptively light, but I can definitely feel it after only a few sips." Maya put her cocktail down, as though to make a statement.

"It's how we make them in New York City." Quinn couldn't stop a grin from spreading on her lips.

"So… why do you prefer being with older women? What's wrong with girls your age? I know it's none of my business, but blame *this*." She pointed at the contents of her glass.

Quinn chuckled. "I don't know. Maybe I have mommy issues, but I don't have the money to pay for therapy to find out."

Maya's eyes widened a fraction. "Before Rach, did you also date older women?"

"Before Rach, I didn't really have a clue about anything. I dated but... I don't know. It was different. It all seems so meaningless now."

"Are you okay, Quinn?" The sudden worry in Maya's tone made Quinn feel even hotter. "Did she hurt you really badly?" Maya canted her body toward her.

Quinn huffed out some air. "The situation wasn't ideal, but neither was breaking up. I guess these things always hurt. Although, according to Mom, it's all for the best and, in the long run, I'll be all the happier for it."

"And according to yourself?"

"I'll be fine. I just need some time." Quinn had always much preferred some light flirting to baring her soul.

"What is it that you'd like to do with your life? What's your passion?"

"Photography," Quinn said on a sigh. "In between bartending at night and waitressing during the day, I took a photography course. Guess who my teacher was?"

Maya shot her a warm smile. "Does their name start with an R?"

Quinn nodded. "As a result, when I'm lining up a shot, I still hear Rachel's voice in my head. I'm waiting for the day when I no longer associate taking pictures with being with her. That's what makes it so damn annoying. It's like the two are inextricably linked or something."

"Look at it this way, though. It's good that you have a passion. So many people never find the one thing they can't live without. Like I will never be without dance. I hope you will never be without a camera." Maya reached for her cocktail and took a sip. "In a few months, you'll be back at it, and you won't give Rachel a second thought." She narrowed her eyes. "Do you know how many dance partners I've had in my life?"

Quinn shook her head.

"Neither do I, that's how many. I've lost count. Save a few, people will come and go in your life. But what's in here." She put a hand on her stomach. "The thing you love, that will stay with you forever and guide you through the ups and downs of your life."

"Wow. I wasn't expecting a swim *and* life lessons today." Quinn's gaze was drawn to where Maya's hand rested on her stomach. She wore a see-through cotton dress over her swimsuit and seeing her hand pressed against her belly did something funny to Quinn's own stomach.

"Well, there you go. Sometimes life hands you something utterly unexpected. All you have to do is enjoy it."

"I will." Quinn figured that Maya most likely had no idea what life was offering her right now. "I am enjoying it." Quinn watched how Maya moved her hand from her belly to her hair, which she brushed away from her face with such gracefulness, it made Quinn a little more audacious. "I do have a more specific answer to your earlier question."

Maya responded with a slight lift of her eyebrows.

"Women in their forties and fifties, to me, are at their most beautiful." She tried to lock her gaze on Maya's. It was only hard for a fraction of a second. She needed eye contact for what she was going to say next. "Like you are, tonight."

The slightest puff of air emanated from Maya's lips, as though she was a touch perplexed but didn't want to show it. "I was going to ask you whether Rach had seduced you, but I think I know the answer to that question already."

"She was my teacher. Making the first move wasn't really an option for her, although she had little trouble with the second move." Quinn knew she sounded a touch conceited, but it was all part of the game. And wasn't that what this had turned into now? A flirting game with her neighbor? Quinn didn't have anything to lose. Maya hadn't chased her from her garden just yet.

Maya chuckled. "How did you go about it?" She reached for her cocktail again. Before knocking back the last of it, she peered deep into Quinn's eyes.

"Lingering after class. Asking some photography questions, followed by some non-photography questions. Inviting her for a drink with the group, then without the group. Things like that."

Maya nodded slowly, but didn't say anything. With a soft thud, she deposited her empty glass on the table.

"Can I fix you another?" Quinn asked.

"I think I've had enough." Maya looked as though she was thinking very deeply about what to say next. "But thank you."

"My absolute pleasure."

Maya blinked slowly, then gave the slightest shake of the head. "I'm going to get started on dinner. Feel free to have another swim before you go."

Before you go? Ouch. But what had Quinn expected? A dinner invitation? "Thank you for having me over, Maya. It was really lovely to get to know you all over again."

"It's been enlightening to say the least." Maya pushed her chair back. "See you around."

"I sure hope so."

Maya collected the glasses from the table and, without looking back, headed inside the house.

Quinn stared at the open door. There was always tomorrow. It was only Friday. Her parents wouldn't be back until late on Sunday. Quinn had all weekend for another dip in Maya's pool.

CHAPTER 3

Maya hadn't slept well. But she had nothing to do today except hope for a call from Tommy. She'd be happy with a brief text, just so she knew he was doing okay and getting along with Heidi and her teenage daughter.

Because there were no students around to teach during the height of summer, her dance studio was closed until the middle of August. Thinking about dance made her muscles tense up. A restlessness had taken hold of her flesh. She wanted to move her body. She wanted a strong partner who knew what he was doing to take her for a satisfying spin around the floor.

As she took a cup of tea into the garden, Maya admitted to herself that the reason she hadn't slept well was Quinn Hathaway. Her boldness had shaken her. She had flirted with Maya and there had been nothing covert about it. Unsure how to respond, Maya had left the scene of the flirting. She had fled inside her own house. Quinn hadn't taken her up on her invitation to use the pool again but Maya hadn't been able to draw a proper breath until she had heard Quinn rustle back through the bushes—apparently taking the driveway wasn't an option—and leave her property.

Maya couldn't remember the last time someone had looked at her the way Quinn had done last night. So brazen. So self-assured. Where did a girl—a girl who had very recently had her heart trampled on, for that matter—get such confidence to unashamedly flirt with a woman twenty years her senior? It was uncanny. Almost arrogant and perhaps a touch sordid. Whatever Quinn was implying was unthinkable. And yet, Maya had thought about it. As she lay sweating under her bedroom ceiling fan, she had given in to the thought. Briefly, but not without consequence.

What if Maya let Quinn seduce her, as she had seduced her photography teacher? Part of the thought was thrilling enough to allow another to follow. A snapshot of Quinn kissing her. The image of Quinn eyeing her, her gaze so hot, Maya would open her lips to her instantly and automatically. That was as far as Maya had allowed her thoughts to drift. She had to shut them down, even though they were, in the end, only thoughts. But still. They were wicked thoughts.

Maya had never really imagined kissing or felt any kind of sexual attraction to a woman before. But somehow, the fact that Quinn was a woman was not fazing her in any way. She'd been mesmerized by Quinn's forwardness. By what she'd said about Maya being at her most beautiful. That's what had struck her most of all. Because Maya had believed for years now that her most beautiful years were long behind her. The years when she was the belle of the ball no matter where she danced. The years when she trained more hours than any other dancer she knew because of the rewards that lay on the other side of the pain and the sacrifice. The years before Drew and Tommy that, sometimes, felt like another life.

Maya stared at the pool. She didn't have to close her eyes

to imagine Quinn sitting on the edge again, fat drops of water rolling down her gleaming skin. Maybe she was drawn to her merely because she reminded Maya of a version of herself she hadn't been in decades—although Maya's life at twenty-four had been the opposite of Quinn's. She'd traveled the country from competition to competition. She lived for what she did, for her passion. There was only ever dance and the occasional man to have some fun with, until Maya needed help with a complex tax issue and she'd met Drew, the most handsome accountant on the face of the planet.

But if it was Quinn's youth she was drawn to, that made her thoughts even more impure and sinful. Or maybe it was just a matter of how she spun it to herself. Because if thinking of Quinn was just channeling memories of Maya's own long-gone youth, there was nothing wrong with that. Reminiscing was harmless. It was fun, even, to consider the person she was then. So driven. So strong. So full of endless energy. These days, Maya only felt strong and energetic on the dance floor, and it only lasted for half an hour or so before she had to take a break, whereas before, she could have danced for hours on end.

She listened for sounds from the Hathaway garden. What was Quinn up to, all alone in her parents' house? Was she thinking of Rachel? Or was she planning her next move on Maya?

Maya hoped for the latter. Yes, the consequences of it were unthinkable, but it sure was nice to be flirted with, to be wanted by someone so gorgeous and vital. Because Quinn was gorgeous. Maya bet that teacher hadn't stood much of a chance once Quinn had set her sights on her.

She was only met with silence from the neighboring garden. Maya finished her tea, stripped off her sundress, and dove into the pool. She swam until her head was empty. Until she no longer associated the pool with Quinn's almost-naked body. The girl would be leaving soon enough, anyway. The imminent return of Bill and Brooke would also help Maya get her mind off any impure thoughts she might have about their daughter.

"Is it like heaven in there?" The voice coming from the other side of the pool made Maya nearly jump out of her skin, as she was climbing out of the water, even though the owner of the voice had been on her mind incessantly.

"Quinn." Maya looked around for her towel. She suddenly felt so naked. Damn. She'd forgotten to bring one out.

"I called to you from behind the bushes, but you didn't hear me." Quinn's crooked grin was all confidence again—but turned up a few notches since yesterday. "I heard you splashing about in the pool and the sound was irresistible."

"Could you do me a favor and get me a towel? They're in the first closet on your right when you go inside."

"Of course." As if in no hurry at all, Quinn sauntered inside the house. She hadn't bothered to wear a tank top today. Only the same skimpy bikini as yesterday and an abundance of glistening, smooth skin.

"Here you go." Instead of handing her the towel, Quinn draped it over Maya's shoulders. As Quinn reached up her arms, Maya's gaze was drawn to a tattoo on her lower belly that peeked out from underneath her bikini pants. When Quinn's arms lowered, the tattoo was covered up again, leaving Maya to wonder what it depicted.

"Feel free to jump in," Maya said, insinuating that a swim was all Quinn had come over for.

"Thanks. I will in a minute, but before I do"—she stood there with her hands on her hips, her blue eyes blazing in the sun—"I wanted to invite you to dinner tonight. To thank you for sharing your pool with me. And for your magnificent company, of course."

"You're inviting me to dinner?"

Lips pursed, Quinn nodded.

"That's really not necessary, Quinn. I'm more than happy for you to use the pool. You don't have to thank me."

"How else do I get to spend the evening with you?" She tilted her head and shifted her weight. How had this happened so quickly again? Maya wanted to scream yes and no simultaneously. How could she feel so uncomfortable and so flattered at the same time?

"Can you even cook?" Maya asked, unsure if her question would increase or deflate the tension.

"Not to save my life," Quinn admitted. "But we have a well-stocked freezer."

Maya burst out laughing. "So you were wanting to treat me to a meal your mother prepared."

Quinn shook her head. "My dad does most of the cooking at our house." She tutted. "Such gender-normative thinking."

"Must be my age," Maya quipped. "The times I grew up in."

"Okay." Quinn opened her palms to the sky. "I can't promise you a home-cooked meal, but I can promise you another hearty cocktail and some pleasant company."

Maya had to decide there and then if she was going to play along with this. Quinn might boldly claim her own company was pleasant—and it was, Maya had to give her that—but that didn't mean Maya had to say yes to any of this. "Why don't you just hang out here? I'll whip us up some dinner. You mix the cocktails." The thought of having dinner with Quinn at the Hathaways' house was several bridges too far. Maya had gone to countless dinners next door since she'd moved in, but never when Bill and Brooke weren't home.

"That's unacceptable. How am I thanking you if you're the one cooking?"

"Something tells me you'll find a way, Quinn." And there it was. The first drawbridge was lowered. Maya was flirting back—she had decided to play along.

"All right. I will." Quinn gave her a frank once-over. "It's a date." With that, she stepped out of her flip-flops and jumped into the pool.

As Quinn swam a few laps, Maya settled in a chair and watched her. Maybe she should have made plans for this weekend—the weekend Tommy took his first decisive step away from home. But Maya had believed she'd wanted to be alone this weekend. That she would go through some rite of passage, a sudden change; that, somehow, she'd learn to accept the situation if she was receptive to it. But this, she had not expected. A young woman in her pool. The girl next door inviting her to dinner. All these feelings spiraling inside of her until it actually gave her pleasure to relent. To say yes to Quinn. To look forward to tonight because she was sure of one thing: it would be anything but dull. Spending time with Quinn was the opposite of boring. Maya had to be on her toes, ready to respond to a quip here and some flirty banter there.

And in the end, it was just a bit of simple fun, because Maya knew where to draw the line. There were very firm boundaries she would never allow Quinn to cross, even though Quinn might very well be convinced right now, as she was enjoying Maya's pool, that those boundaries were only there to be obliterated.

That was how Quinn behaved. Like an unruly child. A wild horse that had only begun to learn the rules and bucked against its restraints. Maya found Quinn's wildness attractive. She was aware of that. But she had something that Quinn wouldn't come by for years: the kind of wisdom only acquired with age. That wisdom would always give her the edge. And the willingness to say no when it came down to it because, somehow, Maya knew what was coming. It hung in the air, like the damp heat of July, between them. She had allowed it to develop, and she would be the one to cut it short, but not before she'd had some harmless fun with the neighbors' daughter.

CHAPTER 4

Just as Quinn deposited an extra-strong margarita in front of Maya, her cell phone buzzed in the back pocket of her shorts.

She smiled apologetically at Maya before checking who was calling. "Oh, it's Dad." She walked to the far side of the garden.

"Hey, Pumpkin, how's it going? Do you miss us?" her dad asked.

"It might surprise you that your twenty-four-year-old daughter, who moved out of the house quite a few years ago, can be without her mom and dad for a few days."

"That does surprise me," her dad joked.

Quinn kept an eye on Maya while she listened.

"What are you up to?"

"Cooling off in Maya's pool," Quinn said, truthfully, although spending time with Maya had left her much more hot than cool.

"How's Maya now that Tommy's off on his big trip?"

"I don't know. Do you want to talk to her?"

"No need. I just called to check in with you. Send Maya

our love and tell her we'll have a barbecue next week. To take her mind off things."

"Sure, Dad." Quinn had her own ideas about how to take Maya's mind off things.

"Call me whenever you need to," he said.

"Thanks, Dad." Quinn ended the call and peered at Maya. Her cocktail stood in front of her untouched. She looked pensive. Perhaps a touch more tense than before. Quinn hurried back.

"How's Bill?" Maya asked.

"He didn't say, but I'm sure everything's fine at the cabin." Quinn tried to read Maya's face. "He said he'll invite you to a barbecue next week."

Maya gave a slight nod. "You told him you were here?"

"Should I not have?" Quinn arched up her eyebrows.

Maya just shrugged, her face still much tighter than Quinn liked to see it.

"Don't worry about my dad," Quinn said. "He calls me every single day. It's his thing. It's like he can't properly relax if he hasn't heard my voice."

"That's lovely." Maya finally reached for her cocktail. She took a sip. "And so is this. Thank you, Quinn."

"Has Tommy been in touch?" Quinn felt as though she should ask.

"He sent a couple of text messages, but I haven't spoken to him on the phone. He's not the type to call his mother every day."

"He's only just left." Quinn offered a smile. "I'm sure he misses you a lot as well, but it's different for him. He's discovering the world. He's in Europe." Probably nose-deep in a bottle of French wine, Quinn thought. She'd never been to Europe. She'd been too busy flunking out of college and then trying to make a life for herself in New York City without a proper degree to have a gap year in between—there hadn't been an in-between.

"I know. It's fine." At last, Maya smiled again. "I'm happy you get along so well with your dad. I hope I can have that kind of relationship with my son when he's older."

"My dad..." Inadvertently, a smile appeared on Quinn's face. "He has always been so vehemently against being disappointed in me. Like he's not capable of it, no matter how hard I try."

"He's a good parent, who has let you find your own way. I believe in that as well, although it's not always easy to not push your child in a certain direction. It happens without you realizing it."

"I haven't exactly found my way yet, but I'll get there in the end." That was what Quinn's dad always said.

"When did you come out to your parents?" Maya asked.

"I never really did. I never sat them down for 'the talk' and explicitly told them. It's like they've always known." Quinn twirled her glass around between her fingers. "My dad did tell me at a certain point, I think I was sixteen or seventeen, I don't really remember, that I was free to bring a girlfriend or boyfriend home whenever I wanted. That's actually how he said it."

Maya smiled softly. "What about your mom?"

"You know Mom. She's more uptight about everything. Especially about the age of my girlfriends." Quinn snickered.

"It's probably just fear. As parents, we want to make the life of our children as easy as possible and being in a same-sex relationship is often not the easiest path. Brooke is probably scared that you'll have a tougher life than if you were straight."

"Yeah." Quinn leaned back, chuckling. "I will never forget the look on her face when I introduced her to Rachel. She tried to smile but it didn't work and there's really nothing worse than a failed smile on Mom's face."

Maya chuckled along gently. "She loves you, that's all. She wants the best for you and she's still convinced she knows what is better for you than you know yourself. She'll grow out of it. Eventually."

"Doesn't matter anymore now, anyway. Rach and I are totally over."

"No chance of getting back together?" Maya asked.

"Zero." Quinn shook her head. "I don't even want to. I need to move on. I know that. But it still hurts."

"Yeah."

"How about you?" Quinn was genuinely curious. "You've been divorced for years now. I bet the single gentlemen of Milbury are lining up to take you out on the town."

"You'd be very wrong about that." Maya scoffed. "Men my age aren't necessarily looking for a woman in their own age bracket."

"In that case, men your age are all totally and utterly nuts, not to mention blind!"

"You would say that, with your proclivities." Maya's lips bloomed into a smile.

"Fair enough and yes, I would. On top of that, I would say it loudly and proudly."

"Men my age are much more interested in someone like you than they are in someone like me," Maya mused. "Young, blond, taut skin, girlish grin. The works."

Quinn knew Maya was right. She'd been tending bar long enough to know what the average man liked. "What about Mr. Mercer?"

"Drew did not follow the stereotypical middle-aged divorced man's path," Maya said. "His new partner is even a year older than he is. Imagine that. An entire year!"

"Wow."

"Not that he deserves a pat on the back for that," Maya said. "That would be setting the bar very low for middle-aged men in general."

"You haven't been on any dates in the past five years?" Quinn found that hard to believe, despite her own preferences, which she was overly aware of as this conversation progressed.

"I have, but it's all been so... unmemorable."

Quinn swallowed what she was about to say next—that maybe Maya had been dating people of the wrong gender. It wasn't a claim that was hers to make. And it might end the evening abruptly, which was a risk she didn't want to take. She was enjoying this pool-side chat with Maya too much to take too great a risk, at least for now.

"If I'm being perfectly honest, dating hasn't really been a priority. I've been so busy with the studio and making sure Tommy was okay after the divorce."

Quinn intuited it was one of those moments when her best contribution to the conversation was a prolonged silence.

"Now Tommy's all grown up," Maya continued. "So my priorities might change." She fell silent. The rattling of the ice cubes in their glasses was the only sound. "You weren't kidding when you said you make a mean cocktail."

"When you work for tips, it pays to be really good at what you do."

"Where are you moving to when you leave here?" Maya asked.

"Into a friend's place in Greenpoint. Her roommate's leaving at the end of the month. It's not too far from the bar, so it should all work out well in the end." Quinn didn't mention that without a monthly check from her parents, she wouldn't even be able to afford the tiny room in Andy's shabby apartment.

"I'm sure you'll find your feet, Quinn. You have that air about you. Like everything will be all right, no matter what."

"We'll see." Quinn drained the last of her cocktail. "Another?" It was Saturday evening and neither one of them had anywhere else to be.

"Let me prepare some dinner first." Maya peered at the remaining liquid in her glass, as though it would allow her to determine exactly how strong it was by doing so. "I may not make it into the kitchen after another one of these."

"Can I help? I chop a mean veg."

"Is that a euphemism?" Maya asked.

Quinn burst out laughing. "Absolutely not."

Maya sat there grinning broadly. "Why don't you have another swim. I won't be long. I'm just making a salad. It's too hot for anything substantial."

"I brought a bottle of white wine," Quinn said. "It's in the fridge."

"Filling my fridge with alcohol." Maya rose. "You'd better have only good intentions." She shot Quinn a quick wink and disappeared into the house.

Quinn took off her clothes and jumped into the pool. She hadn't minded that her parents had gone away for the weekend, leaving her alone for a few days. But she hadn't expected to be splashing about in the neighbor's pool at this time of the day, with a light cocktail buzz going on and the prospect of an evening of flirty conversation still ahead of her.

CHAPTER 5

Maya watched Quinn collect their plates as though this was her own house. She had that air about her that made her look at home. A quiet confidence that, at that age, Maya had only possessed when she stepped out onto the dance floor. For that reason, she told herself, she enjoyed watching Quinn's elegant, easy movement around the table. The gentle swell of her upper arms. The soft shine of her skin. Yes, that was what Quinn Hathaway was: a joy to behold and a joy to be around. Especially during this emotionally trying weekend for Maya. Quinn had succeeded in taking her mind off Tommy as though it had been her job to do so.

Maya followed Quinn with her eyes as she disappeared into the house. In the half-light of the evening, she could see her rinsing the plates in the sink. Quinn's lack of hesitation had something inspirational about it. Maya could twist or turn it any way she wanted, but Tommy leaving home had ushered in the next act of her life. Maybe she should approach it with some of that confidence that Quinn exuded.

"Can I make you another drink?" Quinn shouted from the kitchen.

"Let's finish the wine." Maya reached for her glass. She knew Bill kept some excellent bottles in his basement. She wondered what he would think when he returned from his weekend away and found a few of them missing.

It had startled her earlier when he had called Quinn. It had reminded her of who Quinn actually was, which was easy to forget when she and Quinn were together. That was the other thing about Quinn: she was easy to talk to, easy to be around, easy to watch. Earlier, when she'd been preparing dinner, Maya had eyed her through the kitchen window. The way she'd tipped her head back and slicked her hands through her wet hair had made something inside Maya twitch. She had no idea what it was. Maybe a sudden reminder of how deprived she had been of certain things—things that Quinn had somehow come to represent.

Quinn was still not wearing anything over her bikini top, completely unafraid to show herself off. And why would she be? Maya bet Quinn earned quite a few tips just because of how she looked—very girl-next-door but with an extra layer of natural glossiness. She had this spark about her that Maya had never noticed before. Or maybe it was the kind of weekend she was having that was adding the spark. How Quinn reminded her of herself when she was in her early twenties and had her entire life ahead of her. How she made her feel like she was so much more than a divorcée whose son was leaving home. Maya knew she was much more than that, but still, being around Quinn made it so obvious. Because Quinn clearly saw something in her and Maya's only response to that, apart from the necessary caution, was utter delight.

"I never understood why my parents always refused to put in their own pool, but..." Quinn fixed her gaze on Maya. "Today I'm very happy that they didn't." She pulled her lips into a grin. "Otherwise, I might have never made you those cocktails." She picked up her wine glass. "Thank you for letting me use your pool, Maya."

"You're welcome to use it any time you like." Maya looked forward to welcoming Quinn over and over again.

"What does the rest of your summer look like?" Quinn asked.

"I'm going to Puerto Rico later this month." Maya rejoiced at the prospect. "For a week of non-stop salsa."

"You'll be teaching Puerto Ricans how to salsa?" Quinn whistled through her teeth.

Maya shook her head. "I wouldn't dare. I'm doing a refresher course." Not that her salsa needed a lot of refreshing, even if she said so herself.

"I don't suppose you can show me a few moves?" Quinn sat there looking relaxed, except for her eyes—they were sparkling with some sort of secret delight.

"It's too hot," Maya protested.

"And it won't be in Puerto Rico?" Quinn flashed her tongue over her upper lip.

"Yes, but that's different. It's part of the atmosphere."

"Ah, right. I see." Quinn nodded as though she knew exactly what Maya was talking about. "The sweat. The heat. The well-toned men twirling you around the floor. It's not the same as your suburban backyard." She slanted her head. "Maybe later, after it gets dark." She gave the softest of chuckles. "Although there's honestly nothing that could make my day more than seeing you dance, Maya."

How did Quinn, with her mere twenty-four years of age, know so precisely what to say? By bringing up dance, she knew she was tapping into one of Maya's greatest passions. If she was hoping that Maya wouldn't be able to resist, she was betting on the right horse. Maya took a sip of wine and resolutely pushed herself out of her chair. "Come on. Get up." She walked to the side of the patio where there was more unencumbered floor space.

Quinn's smirk, which bordered on self-satisfied, didn't bother Maya in the slightest. Quinn might be very good at flirting—which was basically an exercise in intuiting what the other person wanted to hear in that moment—but Maya was very good at dancing.

"The basic steps of salsa aren't that difficult." She wouldn't say that to any other student—but Quinn wasn't her student. "Just watch." Maya counted herself down and then, much slower than she usually would, showed Quinn the steps. Despite the slow movement, a jolt of fresh energy coursed through Maya. It was what moving her body in this way did to her. Since she'd been able to walk, she'd loved to dance. She always had a beat going on inside her, a constant thumping in her blood that provided rhythm to her life, that accompanied her and, whenever she felt like it, which was often, allowed her to transform her gait into a dance step. "Why walk through life if you can dance through it?" she had a habit of asking her students.

She repeated the steps but didn't succeed in doing so slowly for very long. Maya was showing off now, perhaps, also, because when she danced, her age was of no significance. On any dance floor, she could easily pass for a woman ten years younger.

Then Quinn, without being prompted, mimicked Maya's steps. Maya did slow down then, to allow Quinn to watch the steps in more detail.

"One—two—three—four," she repeated and repeated, until Quinn was dancing the basic salsa step in sync with her. "Very good. You're a natural."

Teaching dance instead of competing hadn't meant that Maya had downgraded her life. She loved showing other people how to dance, how to find the beat of the music and move to it as though it was flowing through their body. It gave her such joy to watch her students improve after their first hesitant steps, because dance was such a universal language that everyone, if they gave it a chance, could speak and understand.

Maya stopped but encouraged Quinn to keep going. "I'll put on some music," she said. "Then we can dance together." Again, not something she would say to a student in a regular lesson, especially not a first lesson. But this was not a lesson either.

Maya brought out a portable speaker and hooked up her phone. She scrolled to a salsa music playlist and pressed play.

Quinn's feet had come to a stop. She looked only very slightly out of breath. She was barefoot, and wearing jeans shorts, and a bikini top which consisted of nothing more than two scant triangles covering her nipples, offering no support to the natural bounce of her breasts when she broke into a salsa rhythm. Quinn didn't seem to care about that one bit.

"Okay." Maya held out her hand to Quinn. "Let's try to make this work together." Quinn took her hand, and her touch gave Maya pause. She glanced at their joined hands as though it could be the start of something, before she pulled herself together. They were going to dance together. That was the only thing it would be the start of. "I'll move my left foot backward while you move your right one forward. All right?"

"Are you being the man?" Quinn asked, an inevitable grin on her lips.

"I'm leading," Maya said. "Those two things might have meant the same thing once but not anymore. I've taught plenty of same-sex couples."

"Lead away," Quinn said. "I don't mind one bit."

Maya raised their hands and put her other hand on

Quinn's hip. "Put your left hand on my shoulder." As she watched Quinn do so, she realized how expertly Quinn had played her. Was this what she had wanted all along? "Beginners keep their distance," Maya said in her stern teacher voice. Despite the small gap between their bodies, Quinn's hand on her shoulder felt hot against Maya's skin.

"Good thing I'm a natural," Quinn said in a surprisingly husky tone.

"Listen to the music." Maya ignored her quip. An interlude of dancing would snap her right out it—and would show Quinn who was in charge, even if it was only for a few minutes of this entire evening. Maya counted them down again.

It took them a few beats to slip into the same rhythm, but again Maya was surprised how swiftly Quinn got the hang of it. Maybe she really was a natural. Maya could hardly credit her own teaching skills as she'd barely done anything. She'd just danced for Quinn. And now she was dancing with Quinn and it was exhilarating to move to the music with someone else. To do it together. To hear the same beat and move their feet at the same time, as though their bodies were one. Oops. Inadvertently, Maya's hips had inched closer toward Quinn's, and her body heat radiated onto Maya's.

Oh, what the hell. Maya broke the very rule she'd just set of keeping their distance and touched her hips against Quinn's. It was simply much more pleasant to dance like this. The push and pull of someone else's hips as they brushed against hers was one of the ingredients that made the salsa so irresistible.

Maya had danced with plenty of women, having few qualms about touching them in this way, but with Quinn, like so many other things, it was different. It was more intense and subject to all sorts of innuendo. Even though Maya was leading the dance—and Quinn was doing a more than admirable job following her lead—and she should be feeling in charge, she didn't.

It wasn't just Quinn's hips pushing against hers when she moved toward her. Quinn's fingers dug gently into the flesh of her shoulder. Her other hand curled delicately around Maya's. Most of all, it was how Quinn, unlike most beginners, didn't feel any need to look down at her feet. Instead, she gazed deep into Maya's eyes and she found it impossible to look away.

"This is not your first salsa, is it?" she asked.

"It's my first one with you," Quinn replied. She grinned again, but softer this time. "You are such a gorgeous woman, Maya, but when you dance, you are absolutely exquisite."

Heat flushed Maya's cheeks. She should just say a simple thank you. After all, she had heard something along those lines a million times before. But when Quinn said it like that, it meant something entirely different. It wasn't just a compliment. It was a come-on. Maya's throat had gone so dry, she barely managed to scrape the word "Thanks" from it.

"You're very welcome." Quinn slowed their pace until their salsa turned into more of a slow dance. Their hips were still firmly pressed together.

Maya's body throbbed to the beat of the music, a beat they were no longer following. The next song came on and Maya was so entranced by Quinn's gaze, by the feel of her naked belly pushing against her, that she didn't even recognize it. This was the moment Maya needed to pull herself together and draw a clear line in the sand. If she let Quinn cross the next boundary, she had no idea where it would end. But how could she do that when she was enjoying this so much? Their feet had stopped moving in the salsa pattern. Their hips were swaying, not an inch of space between them.

Quinn drew a line with her fingers from Maya's shoulder, from where her hand had been earlier, over her clavicle, to her neck. Her thumb swept over Maya's jaw. Oh god, what was she doing? She brought her thumb to Maya's chin, hooked a finger underneath, and pulled Maya toward her.

"Quinn," Maya whispered, but her protest was so feeble, Maya didn't think Quinn had even heard her. And if she had, Maya saying her name like that might have easily been mistaken for encouragement.

Maya's pulse soared beneath her skin. Her heart slammed against her rib cage. She knew she shouldn't be doing this—she shouldn't allow Quinn to bridge the small gap between their lips—but that awareness wasn't nearly enough to stop herself. Still, she was the older one, so she should also be the wiser one. But who was she kidding? Maya had let this happen. She'd somehow fooled herself into thinking she would be able to stop it when it came down to it—if it ever did—but that was like being invited onto the dance floor by the most gorgeous dance partner only to be denied the actual dance.

Quinn's hand had descended to Maya's neck where it lay gently against her skin. Quinn looked at her, her face expressing nothing but desire to kiss Maya. Her lips were slightly parted. Her beautiful blue eyes narrowed. It looked as though she was waiting for something. As if she was leaving it up to Maya whether they would kiss or not—whether this would end right there and then or not.

Maya flicked her tongue over her lips before she leaned in, met Quinn's mouth with hers, and gave herself the gift of a reckless adventure.

CHAPTER 6

Quinn rested her palm against Maya's neck. She tried to exercise as much as control as she could muster and not let her other hand disappear into Maya's hair. She'd brazenly taken over Maya's lead earlier—in her very own arena, no less—but now she wanted Maya to feel as though she was in charge of what came next. Quinn wanted Maya—she'd wanted her from the very first dip in her pool—but that didn't mean she was hers for the taking. Quinn also knew that the step from dancing with to kissing another woman was a much bigger leap for Maya than it was for her. But Maya was kissing her. The first touch of their lips had been tentative, but Maya's doubts hadn't persisted for very long if the ferocity of her kiss was anything to go by.

Quinn had done all the preparatory work and left the road wide open for Maya to take that final step. And she had. As a result, Quinn's heart was doing a mad dance in her chest. Because she had meant what she'd said earlier. Maya was such a gorgeous woman and the way she moved would make any mere mortal swoon with desire.

Darkness was coming in slowly but it was still hot outside.

It was one of those sultry nights that only occurred in the middle of summer and that always felt different outside of the city. The air had a lighter quality here. The openness of the spaces around her somehow left more room for possibility. Or maybe Maya's beauty had more opportunity to shine in dreary old Milbury. But no, Maya would be equally exquisite in the city— she could easily eclipse the most breathtaking places in the world.

Quinn leaned into Maya more and now she let her hand meander through Maya's velvety mane of hair. There was a tenderness to Maya that Quinn seemed to crave. A gentleness that was perhaps hard to come by in the city. A quality that Rachel certainly didn't possess, with her leather jackets, pointy boots, and black sense of humor. Maya was the opposite of Rachel in many ways; although Quinn couldn't really know for sure, she sensed it. Maya wore her loving and caring heart on her sleeve, and Quinn needed someone like Maya now to offset Rachel's aloofness and sharp corners. Even Rachel's angular haircut was harsh. Kissing Maya would go a long way in helping Quinn get over Rachel. And who knew... maybe the stars, which you could actually see here if you stayed up late enough for the sky to go fully dark, had more in store for them tonight.

Maya's hands seemed stuck to Quinn's sides, as though she was afraid to make good use of them. Perhaps it was a touch intimidating for Maya to be holding a much younger woman in a scant bikini. Quinn decided to lead by example—the way Maya had done earlier when showing her how to salsa. She let her hand drift down from Maya's neck to just above the curve of her breast. Quinn stopped herself from flicking her thumb across Maya's nipple. Even though their kiss was deepening still, and Maya's hands were moving upward a fraction, Quinn was on very thin ice here. That the spell they were momentarily under could easily be broken—as easily as Maya suddenly coming to her senses.

Maya was the first to pull back from their kiss. Mouth slightly agape, she gazed at Quinn. In Maya's eyes, Quinn didn't see any intention to cut this short any time soon, but you never knew.

"Quinn." Maya gave a slight shake of the head. "I—" she started to say, then paused.

Hard as it was to not pull Maya close again, Quinn gave her the time she needed. She gave her the opportunity to come to her again if she still wanted to. Quinn wasn't here to convince Maya that kissing her again was a good idea. But she was definitely here for her if Maya decided that was exactly what she wanted to do with the rest of her evening, perhaps even night.

"We shouldn't—" Maya said, but instead of widening the distance between them, she looked down at Quinn's breasts, then even farther down. She brought her hand to just above the waistband of Quinn's shorts. "You have no idea how much I want to know what that tattoo says." She ran a fingertip over Quinn's sensitive skin, making every hair on her body rise up in anticipation.

"It's easy enough to find out," Quinn said, getting slightly ahead of herself, which she blamed fully on the dangerous position of Maya's finger.

She watched how Maya swallowed slowly. Even though they'd stopped kissing, the atmosphere between them had intensified.

"I'm not sure I should find out." Maya contradicted what she'd just said by hooking a fingertip underneath Quinn's shorts.

Quinn took a sharp inhale of breath. She didn't know what to say to that, so she didn't say anything.

Apparently, Maya had lost the need for speaking as well. She peered down at her finger. She pulled Quinn's shorts down a fraction to reveal the tattoo that ran low across the width of her belly.

The chuckle that followed surprised Quinn, although she'd had all sorts of reactions to her tattoo.

"It's too small. I need my reading glasses." Maya's finger stayed in the same position, holding Quinn's shorts slightly down.

Quinn's arousal skyrocketed. "Maya... " It was Quinn's turn to only have a breathless whisper left for a voice. "Please." Although a good distance remained between the tip of Maya's finger and the throbbing center of Quinn's body, it didn't make any difference. Quinn's desire was about to pass the point of no return. But she had to wait. Maya wanting to see her tattoo could be curiosity of a different kind.

Maya seemed to realize the effect the position of her finger was having on Quinn. "Maybe..." she said. "I'll find out later." She tugged Quinn closer, using the same finger, and kissed her again.

Although Maya withdrew her finger, Quinn was already anticipating what that finger could do to her. She was imagining what it would be like to see Maya naked in front of her. How heavenly it would feel to please her.

Maya had brought her hands to Quinn's cheeks, cupping them gently. She kept pulling Quinn in for kiss after kiss. Her tongue was impossibly soft against Quinn's, her lips pillowy and addictive.

When Quinn started kissing a path down her neck, Maya whispered in her ear, "Maybe we should go inside."

Quin nodded and happily let Maya drag her into the house. She followed her up the stairs, every cell in her body pulsing with hot anticipation. Although, of course, Maya could still change her mind. But Quinn decided she would make it impossible for Maya to do that.

Maya had confessed earlier that she'd only gone on a few unmemorable dates of late. This might not be a date but, no matter what it was, Quinn was determined to make sure that Maya never forgot about it.

CHAPTER 7

Maya stood outside her bedroom. It wasn't hesitation keeping her from opening the door. It was the frisson running down her spine, the delicious tension deep in her belly, the blatant desire she felt for this woman that stopped her in her tracks.

At least she wasn't the cliché of the middle-aged woman / empty-nester who started an affair with the pool boy after her son left home. She didn't know if an affair with the neighbor's daughter was better or worse. But it no longer mattered. Maya had stopped seeing Quinn as Bill and Brooke's daughter the instant their hips had touched earlier. If she hadn't, she wouldn't have led Quinn to her bedroom. They wouldn't be standing here right now.

Maya ushered them in. She might have shared the dance floor with other women, but she'd never shared her bed with one. Still, it wasn't her lack of experience that frightened her. It was the complete newness of it. The uncharted territory she was about to enter. She would worry about why she had let Quinn seduce her later. First, she was going to enjoy this.

Quinn came for her as soon as they'd set foot in the

bedroom. As though Maya had given her the final okay—and she had. She slung her arms around Maya's neck and pulled her close.

Quinn's rock-hard nipples pressed against Maya through the sheer fabric of her dress. Quinn ran her hands through Maya's hair and moaned softly into her mouth.

Kissing another woman was even more intoxicating than the cocktail said woman had prepared for Maya earlier. There was no scratch of five o'clock shadow. Quinn's kisses, though hungry and not restrained in the least, felt so much gentler than anyone else Maya had ever kissed. Quinn's lips were eager and soft and to be kissed over and over again. Her tongue was exploratory more than invasive. Her touch was delicate and intentional. It was all so overwhelming and utterly arousing. And maybe that surprised Maya the most.

Kissing Quinn was electric; a jolt of heat running through her, a blast that ran from her core to each tiny extremity. It was easy enough for Maya to tell herself it was her curiosity about being with a woman that was driving her lust. She had to gloss over Quinn being her much younger neighbor if she was going to go through with this.

Earlier, in the garden, Maya had been bashful. She hadn't known what to do with her hands. But now, in the privacy of her bedroom, she let her hands roam across Quinn's back, to the clasp of her bikini top with its two tiny pieces of fabric that revealed more than they concealed. When Maya was Quinn's age, she had worn exactly the same. A body honed and chiseled by hours and hours of dancing deserved to be on display as much as possible. Maya had never been modest about how she looked because she had always known very well where those looks had come from. They were a direct product of her hard work. These days, however, gravity was doing its depressing business of pulling parts of her body downward.

She noticed it every time she held up her arms to show her students how to carry their frame during the waltz. A small portion of the skin on her upper arms had started to slump. Maybe that was another reason why someone as young as Quinn was in her bedroom tonight. The vitality of her youth sparked something in Maya.

Maya unclasped Quinn's top, then brushed its straps off Quinn's shoulders. She broke away from their kiss because she wanted to witness the moment when Quinn's breasts were fully bared. Maya had been taunted by her near-naked breasts for two days now. She was the one who guided Quinn's bikini top through its final descent toward the floor. Her gaze was glued to Quinn's chest. Quinn's nipples were surrounded by a triangle of lighter skin and Maya had never guessed she would find tan lines so arousing.

As though drawn by an invisible force, Maya cupped Quinn's breasts. Her thumb swept lightly over her nipples. She was so overcome by the sight of Quinn's naked upper half that she barely noticed her own shortness of breath. The fire in her belly ramped up to a higher flame. A fire that drove her to inch closer to Quinn, lower her head and wrap her lips around one of Quinn's nipples. Quinn threw her head back, and brought her hands back to Maya's hair. She emitted a low groan that only revved up the fire in Maya's belly.

Maya no longer had any idea what was happening to her. She was not herself, that much was clear—it was also the only thing that was clear. That and how much she wanted Quinn. She let one hand drift down again, her finger finding Quinn's mysterious tattoo, and drawing a line along it.

Quinn's hands descended to Maya's shoulders, her fingertips digging into Maya's flesh, as she slowly walked them toward the bed.

Maya flicked her tongue one last time along Quinn's

nipple before letting go and pulling her own dress over her head. Maya took off her own bra before Quinn had the chance to do so. And then she was taken aback by a moment of timidity. Of course her breasts didn't look like Quinn's. That was, perhaps, a disadvantage of going to bed with another woman —comparing. But Maya knew better than to compare herself to a woman twenty years her junior. It was an exercise in futility that would only take away from her enjoyment. And Quinn had come on to her—had called her beautiful and exquisite and gorgeous. If Quinn liked older women so much, she must be well acquainted with the increased effects of gravity on their bodies.

Quinn put her hand on the arm that was covering Maya's breasts. She ran two fingers over Maya's skin. "I want to see you," she said. "All of you."

Just hearing those simple words was enough for Maya. She let her arm fall away and subjected herself to Quinn's soft gaze, her lips drawn into a small smile of delight, at least that's what Maya made of it.

"You're so beautiful," Quinn said, again, and laid her hands on Maya's breasts. She cupped them gently while she kissed Maya again, her lips and tongue reassuring Maya that every word she had just said could be nothing but the truth.

They fell onto the bed and then Maya experienced the delight of feeling Quinn's body draped all over hers. Quinn's knee between her legs. Quinn's naked breasts against her own. Quinn's lips traveling from her mouth to her neck, and then deliciously making their way to her breasts.

When Quinn closed her lips around Maya's nipple, a zap of electricity sparked between her legs. Everything about Quinn was so surprisingly soft. Maya had expected Quinn's young muscles to have a certain hardness to them when Quinn lay on top of her like this, but they didn't. It was all exquisite softness and enticing tenderness. Quinn sucked Maya's nipple deep into her mouth—and there was nothing soft about that action.

Maya looked down along her body, and saw Quinn gazing back at her, her eyes blazing with lust. All this desire on display, Maya thought, for her. She didn't stop to think how it was possible. She was far too busy enjoying the effect of Quinn's tongue on her nipple. It swirled and swept and licked Maya into a state of heavenly arousal that gripped her entire body. All Maya wanted was more of Quinn. More of Quinn's lips all over her, more of her hands, one of which slid along the side of Maya's other breast.

That was the other huge advantage of landing in bed with someone like Quinn. There was nothing else to consider but the here and now. Maya couldn't possibly allow her mind to drift further into the future because that would mean considering the consequences of her actions. The only consequence she was after was to have her acute desire quenched. To have her body suffused with post-orgasmic bliss. To be touched brazenly and deftly by someone who, very simply—no matter the reason—wanted her so much, she clearly didn't care about the consequences either. Together, it seemed, she and Quinn would ignore the hell out of the ramifications of what they were doing. They didn't exist yet and, as far as Maya was concerned, they never would. This would be the very definition of one night only. Anything else was impossible. Maya had to squeeze out every last drop of pleasure from the short time they had together. She had not another minute to spare for further qualms, for anything that would hinder her pleasure.

Quinn freed Maya's nipple from her lips and, her gaze still firmly locked on Maya's, blew some air over Maya's rock-hard nipple, the sensation making it even harder.

Quinn cupped Maya's breast firmly in her hand and then focused her attention on Maya's other nipple. Just her gaze on it made something twitch inside Maya again—pure, unbridled lust. A sensation that might as well be new to her, so long had it been since she'd felt anything even close to this.

Between her legs, her lips pulsed wildly against her panties. Maya wanted nothing more than to rip them off and tell Quinn she was ready—that she was hers for the taking. That was what it felt like when Quinn lay on top of her like that. When she sucked Maya's nipple deep into her mouth. She hadn't come here—talked her way into Maya's bedroom with all her youthful bravado and effortless charm—to gingerly show her what it could be like to sleep with a woman. Quinn had come here to ravage Maya. And this was only foreplay—something, Maya knew from her own experience, most men didn't bother with too much.

Quinn cupped Maya's breasts in her hands while she adjusted her position and slid between her legs. She kissed a wet circle around Maya's belly button while she swept her thumbs over Maya's nipples.

The closer Quinn's lips came to her panties, the more Maya lost control of her body. The fire in her belly, the heat in her core, the goose bumps on her skin. The way her mind had been taken over by desire only—no room left for anything else. She wanted Quinn so badly, so feverishly. She dug her heels into the sheets because all she could do was wait.

Quinn kissed Maya above the line of her panties—the same place Maya had caressed earlier on Quinn's belly. Quinn's hands drifted down. She placed one on Maya's belly, while she traced her fingertips down Maya's inner thigh. They danced along her skin, light as a feather, before Quinn drew a path inward and, ever so slowly, traced a line along the gusset of Maya's panties.

"Oh, Jesus," Maya moaned. Her clit pulsed with all the lust that burned inside her body. She glanced down, beyond the slope of her breasts and the hard peaks of her nipples, to Quinn who lay between her legs, teasing her, enjoying Maya's reaction. Then Quinn did it again. With the lightest of touches, she tracked a line along Maya's panty-covered lips, up to her aching clit, and drew a circle there, leaving Maya a quivering mess barely able to catch her breath.

Never in her life had Maya wanted to get rid of her panties so much. They were surplus to requirements, Quinn's ultimate means to tease her.

Then, just as Maya had hooked a finger into the waistband of Quinn's shorts earlier, Quinn did the same to her panties. She slowly pulled them down, but she couldn't get them off as long as she sat between Maya's legs. Clearly, she had no intention of removing them because she remained in position. Instead, she let her finger dip down, until it rested just above Maya's throbbing clit.

Did Quinn want Maya to beg for it? Did she long to see her face contorted with uncontrollable desire? When Quinn's finger moved only a fraction, a powerful spark of electricity ran up Maya's spine. Quinn was doing what she'd been doing all along. Expertly playing Maya, and she was in no position to pretend she wasn't enjoying it. Yes, she wanted more of Quinn, but she also wanted to enjoy these delicious moments before Quinn gave her the ultimate pleasure. Because not long after that, it would all be over. There would be no encore for the two of them. All they had was this night, these moments together. So Maya enjoyed the exquisite frustration building in her flesh, the delicate tension in her muscles, because—and this, too, was very different from when she'd bedded a man—she knew what was coming. Maya trusted that Quinn could get her there, although, rationally, she had no reason to. Yet, she did.

Quinn slid her hand out of Maya's panties and lifted it toward her mouth. She sucked her finger between her lips, then opened her mouth, and showed Maya as she swirled her tongue around it. With her other hand, she pulled Maya's panties aside, then dipped her wet finger inside again.

Maya let her legs fall as far apart as they would go—she was still plenty flexible, yet she knew that whatever she did, no matter how limber she was, it wouldn't make a difference. This was Quinn's show. This was the moment when she drove Maya beyond the edge of crazy.

Quinn's finger didn't stop this time around. Its glorious wetness circled around her clit, and Maya's hips moved upward to meet it.

"Aah," Maya moaned. "Oh, Quinn."

Her gasps of pleasure must have done something to Quinn because instead of letting her moistened finger work more of its magic, she slid her hand out of Maya's panties and swiftly maneuvered herself out from between Maya's legs.

When Quinn looked her in the eyes, Maya could see something uncontrolled in them too—the same unruly sensation that was coursing through her own flesh. Quinn started pulling down Maya's panties slowly, giving the illusion of being in control, but her motion was growing slightly wilder, and by the time the wretched garment had reached Maya's ankles, Quinn gave it one last quick tug and threw it behind her.

Amid the pleasure of anticipation, Maya also felt the satisfaction of Quinn succumbing to her own desires—desires created by Maya.

Quinn didn't resume her position between Maya's legs, however, but glued her hot skin against Maya's side. She kissed her on the lips while Maya spread her legs for Quinn again. Quinn broke from their kiss and swept her finger across Maya's lower lip before gently letting it slip into her mouth.

Maya sucked it between her lips, all the while looking deep into Quinn's eyes. She released Quinn's finger and drew in a breath while she watched Quinn's hand disappear between her legs.

Quinn drew another wet circle around Maya's clit.

The breath Maya had been holding came out in a desperate stutter.

Quinn might have looked a little lost in her own desire earlier, but she seemed fully back in control now. Why else would her touch only be so light? Sure, it was exquisite and even slightly satisfying to have Quinn's finger circle her clit, but it wasn't nearly enough. Maya wanted more. More of Quinn. More of her finger. More than her eyes looking down at her and her finger, which had felt so sensual against her tongue, moving so gently around her clit.

Then, Quinn drew her lips into a truly devilish grin, before her face slipped from Maya's view. Before she settled between Maya's legs again. Before she kissed the inside of Maya's thigh and her lips inched closer and closer to where her finger had been earlier.

Next thing Maya knew, Quinn wrapped her soft lips around Maya's clit, circled her tongue around it, and set every nerve ending in Maya's body on fire.

Every molecule of Maya's being ignited with pleasure. It was as though she could feel the touch of Quinn's tongue everywhere. Maya groaned with satisfaction, with knowing what was so imminent, with all the saved up desire she hadn't been able to expend, and with how utterly magical Quinn made her feel. Her hips bucked, her heels pressed into the bed, her hands were lost in Quinn's silken curls. All the while,

Quinn licked her and with every flick of her tongue, drove Maya closer to the precipice. That ledge she so desperately wanted to let herself fall off, beyond which a well of utter rapture waited, but Maya also wanted this to last. Quinn's full attention on her body, just as the lavish attention she had bestowed on Maya all weekend, was not something she wanted to part with so quickly. But Maya's stamina was no match for the deftness of Quinn's tongue and the strength of her intentions. She let herself be caught in the storm of delight that engulfed her, that prickled on her skin and glowed in her blood.

"Oh, Quinn," Maya moaned, because she wanted to acknowledge, for both of them, that this was all Quinn's doing.

CHAPTER 8

Maya pulled Quinn up into an embrace so tight, Quinn had a little trouble breathing. But she would catch her breath later. Her body was energized by what she had just witnessed. Maya Mercer enjoying a glorious orgasm. Quinn would never in her life forget the moment when Maya cried out her name as she came. It counted as one of the biggest wins of her twenty-four-year existence.

Maya huffed out some air and loosened her grip on Quinn a fraction. Quinn could feel how she lightly shook her head.

"Jesus, Quinn," Maya said. "That was fucking spectacular."

Quinn kissed Maya's cheek. "I only ever aim to please." She knew she sounded cocky. It was how she felt. Last night, alone in her bed, this was all she'd dreamed of, and now here she lay, in Maya's arms, not an inch of space between their naked bodies.

"Don't you feel any ambivalence?" Maya asked, on a small sigh.

"None." Quinn kissed Maya on the lips this time. "Why would I be ambivalent about something as beautiful"—She traced her fingertip along Maya's cheek—"as what we just did."

Maya chuckled. "You're such a sweet-talker."

"Not just a talker." Quinn kissed Maya's neck and inhaled her scent. She wanted her again already. She wanted to make this night count, although, already, in the back of her mind, Quinn was making plans to sneak out of the house the next night and the next—she'd be wanting a repeat performance of this for as long as she would be staying at her parents.

Maya placed her palms on Quinn's cheeks and pulled her nearer. She looked into her eyes. "I want you too, Quinn," she said, and Quinn almost dissolved into a puddle there and then. Maybe Maya had been with a woman before. Quinn didn't know because she hadn't asked, and she wasn't going to now. But whomever Maya had shared her bed with in the past, the fact that she was in bed with Quinn right now didn't seem to unnerve her too much. If she had any reservations at all, she hid them well behind the desire in her eyes.

Quinn nodded as another wave of lust rolled through her.

"Do I finally get to see that tattoo now?" Maya didn't wait for a reply, but pushed herself out of their embrace. She placed her warm hand on Quinn's hot skin, then slid it down to Quinn's shorts. Then she folded herself over Quinn's belly, as though she was going to do so much more than finally decipher Quinn's tattoo, unleashing yet another avalanche of arousal that tore through Quinn's muscles.

Maya traced a finger along Quinn's belly as she read out loud. "*Your secret's safe with me*," she whispered, then looked back at Quinn with a grin on her lips. "Maybe you can share that secret with me later."

Quinn flashed her tongue along her lips and nodded again. Maya's face was too close to where all the energy in her body converged—to the throbbing center between her legs—

for Quinn to explain now anyway. She was about ready to implode.

Maya maneuvered herself so she could slide Quinn's shorts and bikini bottoms off her.

For all her bravado of the past few hours and days, when Maya came to lay next to her and she felt the soft expanse of her naked skin safe and warm against her own, Quinn was momentarily overwhelmed. Despite the raging fire beneath her skin, she needed to take a pause. This wasn't just about the thrill of the conquest. Of finding herself in bed with a gorgeous, semi-forbidden woman. Quinn genuinely liked Maya.

She could hardly claim to have any feelings for her that were anything else than generated by lust, but Quinn did care for Maya. She'd been someone on the periphery of her life for a very long time. She wanted the best for Maya. She wanted her to have better than unmemorable dates with uninspiring middle-aged men. But more than what Quinn might want for Maya in that moment, she felt her desire reflected back at her, and was there ever anything more delightful than another woman wanting you just as much as you wanted her?

Maya ran a finger over Quinn's tattoo again, as though her hand was drawn to it magnetically. Rachel most certainly had been fascinated with Quinn's tattoo as well. But no. No thoughts of Rachel right now. Rachel was the past. Maya was the now. And who knew what the future might bring? Although Quinn had a very good idea what the very near future had in store for her. More desire. More pleasure. More Maya.

She spread her legs for Maya and the simple act of doing so lifted her to a higher level of arousal. Because soon it wouldn't just be air caressing her there. It would be Maya. Whether it would be her tongue or her fingers, Quinn didn't much care. As long as it was Maya, who had danced for her so sensually, and who had flirted with her, and made her feel so desirable, so utterly wanted, that Quinn could hardly remember why Rachel had dumped her.

Maya leaned in and kissed her. Their tongues flitted in and out of each other's mouth.

Quinn ran her hands along Maya's back, she held on to her hips, dug her fingertips into the strong muscles of her thighs. Quinn had meant what she had said to Maya the day before. As far as she was concerned, Maya was at her most beautiful right now. A woman who had already lived a large portion of her life but still had decades in front of her, with all the wisdom and grace she had already accumulated. A woman who could teach Quinn a thing or two, like how to dance a proper salsa in the back garden. A woman whom Quinn had delighted with her tongue mere minutes ago. A woman whose hand was drifting down Quinn's thigh.

While their tongues kept dancing, their mouths so eager for each other, Maya's fingertips slid along Quinn's sex.

Quinn moaned into Maya's mouth. She was so ready for her. So thoroughly wet for her. But Maya didn't immediately slip a finger inside. Instead, she lightly circled Quinn's clit, making her muscles tense.

Maya broke their kiss and looked at Quinn.

Fuck, Maya was so beautiful. Her eyes so dark, her hair so full and perfectly wavy and even in the half-light of the bedroom, her effortless elegance was still so evident, as though she simply had no other way to carry herself.

In another life, under different circumstances, Quinn thought, as Maya's finger kept skirting along her clit, this could be something. If Quinn had met Maya somewhere else, if she wasn't her parents' neighbor, Quinn would go after her like nobody's business. Then, all thoughts in her head came to an abrupt halt, because, ever so slowly, Maya pushed a finger inside. Quinn's breath stalled in her throat. Her already tense muscles constricted further in delicious anticipation. Maya's finger moved inside her and it was as though the motion dislodged something at Quinn's center. It undid all the tension she'd created between them—and inside herself—over the past two days. Because of course Quinn had put on a display, in her skimpy bikini, when she pushed herself out of the pool slowly, when she presented Maya with a cocktail that was a touch too strong. Quinn could let go of all of that now. She let her muscles relax. She let herself be exactly who she was—a woman enjoying the attention of another woman. And what a woman Maya was.

Maya added another finger and ramped up the intensity of her strokes inside Quinn. She gazed deep into Quinn's eyes.

With the smidgen of clarity she had left, Quinn stared back, and the way Maya was looking at her multiplied the effect of what her fingers were doing a thousandfold. Because there was no doubt that Maya was enjoying the hell out of this. The evidence of that joy was plastered all across Maya's face.

"Oh, fuck," Quinn groaned. "Oh, Maya."

Hearing her name must have spurred Maya on because she brought her thumb into play. As though she'd never done anything else in her life, she edged it along Quinn's clit every time she drove her fingers deep inside.

Maya leaned in and kissed Quinn lightly on the lips while her fingers delved deep inside of her and her thumb drove Quinn a little bit crazier with every minute movement it made. But it was the gentleness of Maya's kiss that finally tipped her over the edge. It was Maya's hot breath on her cheeks. Her nearness and the intimacy it created between them. Maybe, subconsciously, Quinn had expected things to be less intimate between them, but ever since their hips had connected while dancing, all distance between them had dissipated.

Quinn believed it was for that reason that when she came at Maya's fingers, with a hard tremor in her muscles and an unexpected lump forming in the back her throat, she knew she would never forget how Maya had made her feel. She knew she would want to recreate that same sensation over and over again. Because it wasn't just physically satisfying, it also healed something deep inside her. The wound Rachel had left her with when she'd told her they should no longer see each other. That there was no future for them together. Their difference in age had been an easy enough excuse, but Quinn knew it wasn't the only and possibly not the real reason they had split up—because the real reason was that Rachel had stopped loving her the way she once had. It was only now, in Maya's arms, that she could finally accept that and know that, one day, she would be loved again.

Quinn's eyes fell shut as her climax rolled through her body. When she opened them again, she witnessed the sweetest smile she had ever seen. It was so kind and heartfelt that it made Quinn wonder if it was that smile and the comfort it offered, that she'd been looking for all along. She wanted to capture and bottle it so she could carry it with her always—turn to it when needed—as she picked her life back up after Rachel.

Quinn could only smile back and enjoy the warmth that ran through her, that penetrated the most unreachable chambers of her heart, and assured her that, in the end, everything would be all right.

Maya gently retracted her fingers and, as she did, her smile changed. "Can you believe I've never done anything like this before?"

"Not for a single second," Quinn replied.

Maya chuckled. "I don't mean in the sense that I might be a natural at it." She gave a gentle shake of the head. "I just mean... I don't know. Before this weekend, I never really gave it much thought. And I certainly never expected it to be so... absolutely amazing."

"Being with a woman?" Quinn pushed herself up on her elbows. "Trust me, it very much depends on the woman. And you are an utterly divine woman, Maya."

"Am I?" Her smile changed into one of mischief now, assuring Quinn that this was going to be a long night of satisfying discovery.

"Fuck yes." Quinn pulled Maya near because she wanted more of her, she wanted more than to just look at her, she wanted to be sure that she wasn't imagining that this night was far from over.

"Wait," Maya whispered in her ear. "Tell me about your tattoo first." She put her head in the crook of Quinn's shoulder and ran her finger over Quinn's lower belly again. "What does it mean?"

Quinn curled her arm tightly around Maya—as though, if it were up to her, she wouldn't let go of her any time soon—and said, "It's from a Bianca Bankole song that goes, 'But my darling, always know your secret's safe with me.' I figured the whole lyric was too long. I only have so much skin." She paused. "When someone sees it, it's usually in an intimate setting like this, and I thought it was a funny idea at the time." She couldn't suppress a smile.

Quinn could feel Maya's body shake softly as she chuckled against her. "Wow." She craned her neck so she was looking into Quinn's face. "That's actually quite beautiful. And I love the way you celebrate your sexuality with such confidence."

"Thank you." Quinn was taken aback again. Maybe she would have to rethink her plans for sneaking out of the house to spend the night with Maya again. There was something special about her, and Quinn didn't want to run the risk of getting hurt again—not so soon after Rachel.

"Thank *you*, sweetheart," Maya said, her gaze kind and her tone as sweet as the term of endearment she had just used. "You have no idea what you've given me tonight."

"An orgasm and a great deal of ambivalence."

"There's that." Maya's finger slid up from Quinn's belly to her chest. "Speaking of." Maya's finger circled Quinn's nipple. "I think can handle a bit more of both."

CHAPTER 9

As soon as Maya woke, she went to war with herself. Part of her wanted to ignore the ambivalence that had increased exponentially throughout the night, throw her arms around Quinn, and do it all over again. But the other, much more prevalent and rational part of her, hoped Quinn wouldn't be there when she finally dared to open her eyes. The grown-up, wise woman that Maya knew she was, but most decidedly hadn't been last night, wished that last night had never happened because then she wouldn't have to deal with the awkward aftermath.

But when Maya opened her eyes, Quinn was there. She was still sleeping. She lay on her back, every inch of her glorious skin exposed to the heat that already hung in the bedroom despite the early hour. It was going to be another sultry hot day.

Maya's gaze was drawn to Quinn's tattoo. It was impossible not to look at. But she couldn't give in to any of that any longer. She had allowed herself to give in last night. Now was the time to face the music.

When had Quinn said Bill and Brooke would be returning? Maya hoped there wasn't some emergency that made them come home early. Imagine if they arrived while Quinn was still in her bed? The thought was so unbearable, she nearly woke Quinn and asked her to leave there and then. But she wanted to look at her a few moments longer.

She didn't exactly regret what they had done—it was impossible to regret the avalanche of satisfaction that had engulfed her throughout the night. Even though she was still lying in bed, she could already feel it had changed something in her body. Her limbs felt looser. Her shoulders were less tense. She knew that the next time she danced, her hips would sway a little wilder and the curve of her back would be more pronounced.

Every single second she had spent with Quinn in bed last night had been memorable and exquisite, and Maya was glad for the memories they had created, but that was all they were and could be now. Memories.

As though the intensity of her thoughts created a shift in the air, Quinn stirred. Eyes still closed, she stretched her arms above her, her chest protruding. Maya knew she should look away, but she couldn't. Her eyes were glued to the triangles of lighter skin around Quinn's nipples. She had to stop herself reaching for them with her hand or her lips.

No. She had to stop. It was Sunday morning. Bill and Brooke would be home soon. Quinn would return to just being the neighbors' daughter. There simply was no other choice.

Quinn opened her eyes. "Morning, gorgeous," she said. Instantly, she broke into a smile and turned on her side. "Did you get some sleep?" Her hand sneaked close to Maya's belly, but mercifully she didn't touch her.

Maya had no idea how, despite her very best intentions, she would react to a touch from Quinn.

"You exhausted me." Maya silently instructed herself to get out of bed, but her body failed to cooperate. "So, yes."

Maya could see Quinn's gaze drift from her face to her breasts and it felt as arousing as a touch. Why hadn't she covered herself properly?

Quinn brought her hand to Maya's hip. "You don't look as though you still need your beauty sleep. You already look so beautiful." Quinn shuffled closer. "It should be illegal this early in the morning."

"Ever the charmer." Maya swallowed hard.

"It's not charm." Quinn started tracing a fingertip up and down Maya's hip. "Not with you."

"Quinn." Maya put her hand on top of Quinn's so she could keep it from moving. "We have to stop this now."

"We have all day. Mom and Dad won't be back until late tonight."

"That's not the point." Did Quinn really expect them to have a careless day of canoodling by the pool? "I won't say that last night shouldn't have happened, but it does need to stop. *Now.*"

Quinn jutted out her bottom lip and narrowed her eyes into an expression of utter sadness.

"Look..." Maya allowed herself a quick squeeze of Quinn's hand. "Last night was wonderful. It will always be a wonderful memory for me. But I need to get back to myself now."

"I believe you were more yourself last night than you've been in a long time."

"Quinn," Maya said on an exasperated sigh. "One night with me does not equate to you knowing me. The simple truth is that you don't know me very well at all. You don't know how I live my life and what my principles are." Maya let go of Quinn's hand.

"Fair enough, but..." Quinn put some distance between

them. "I don't have any great or unrealistic expectations of this, Maya. I'll be out of your life soon enough. But I believe in seizing the moment and this doesn't necessarily have to end right now. I'll be around a few more weeks. Maybe we can have some more fun together."

"We can't." Maya was somewhat flattered by Quinn's desire to do what they'd done last night all over again. "Not when Bill and Brooke are back. That doesn't work for me. It's already such a mind fuck."

"They won't know. They will never know."

"Quinn, I'm serious." Maya looked at her intently. "Promise me you will never tell anyone about last night."

"Not anyone? Ever? That seems a bit extreme." Quinn arched up her eyebrows. "It sounds as if you want to erase what happened."

Maya shook her head. "I don't want to erase it, but I also don't want anyone to know about it. This is a small town and news travels fast. I have a son. I have a business here. I can't be the woman in her forties who slept with the neighbors' twenty-something daughter. Can you understand that?"

"Of course, but... no one in this town will ever find out."

"Promise me, Quinn. No one. Ever. This will be our secret for eternity."

"I promise I won't tell a soul. Ever." Quinn retreated farther.

Deep down, Maya knew it would perhaps be a promise neither one of them could keep because life was long and who knew what the future might bring? But, for now, having Quinn's reassurance that she would keep quiet about them did assuage her fears—not that she was expecting Quinn to run home and tell her parents.

"I appreciate that." Maya looked at Quinn, who suddenly seemed a lot less like the brazen woman who had asked for a swim in Maya's pool. The fact that she was still fully naked made her appear more vulnerable than sexy now that the boundaries between them were redrawn with actual words.

"I was already making plans to throw pebbles at your window after dark." At least Quinn managed a smile.

Maya couldn't help herself. She shuffled closer to Quinn and threw an arm around her. "Listen to me, Quinn. We had an amazing time together and we'll always have that memory." She kissed her lightly on the cheek. "You are going to have an amazing life because you are a wonderful woman, I know that much. You are a true delight to be around and you made me feel things, well... I think you know how you made me feel." She held her a little closer. "But this has to end now." Maya needed to emotionally disentangle herself from their night together and the feelings it had stirred in her as soon as possible, but that was not information she wanted to share with Quinn. "Thank you for understanding that."

Quinn wrapped her arms around Maya and pulled her close. "You're one hell of a cougar, Maya," she whispered in her ear.

They exchanged one final, almost chaste kiss, before Quinn freed herself from Maya's embrace and exited her house—and Maya's life.

CHAPTER 10

TEN YEARS LATER

Acton Academy was one of Quinn's best-paying clients, so she treated herself to a taxi to the Upper East Side instead of lugging her equipment around on the subway. In the back of the cab, she checked her Instagram account. A satisfying number of likes awaited her on the latest Photoshop creation she had posted online earlier that morning. One of those likes, she couldn't help but notice, was from Morgan.

Quinn exhaled audibly. Why did Morgan insist on liking every single thing she posted? It was a rhetorical question because Quinn knew the answer. For some absurd reason that Quinn would forever fail to understand, Morgan didn't want to leave her husband for Quinn, but she did want to remain this unbearable version of online friends.

As usual when faced with a social media like from Morgan, which was basically all she'd been able to offer Quinn, even when they'd still been together, Quinn's finger hovered over the 'block' button. Also as usual, she couldn't bring herself to tap it. Instead, she put her phone away and gauged the traffic ahead. She should make it on time which, for Acton, meant with at least fifteen minutes to spare.

Quinn didn't like to keep the people from Acton Academy waiting. They not only paid handsomely for the time she spent taking the actual pictures—a portrait of a new teacher today—but also for the hours she spent turning the picture into a magical work of art on the computer. The hallways of their building, financed mostly by the well-to-do parents of their students, were lined with Quinn's work and it was always such a treat to go back and have a triumphant stroll through her very own art.

Quinn was not the type to overly prepare for a photo shoot. She had always been more of a woman of action than research. Besides, no amount of research could ever fully prepare her for the kind of person she would find in front of the camera. People acted in all sorts of bizarre ways when a lens was aimed at them. Quinn's trick to make them feel at ease was to show them some before-and-after shots of previous projects. Because she had worked hard on her skills and could therefore present her subjects with some spectacular pictures, this approach usually worked like a charm. It was a way to relieve the pressure on the person whose picture was being taken, and not many people ever minded that, especially when living in the madness of New York City.

Quinn paid the driver, got her gear out of the trunk, and waltzed into Acton Academy as if she owned it. Appreciation for her work had that effect on her. She also believed that walking into a shoot with not-to-be-ignored confidence enhanced the chances of it being a smoother ride. She was the photographer so she was in charge and it was her job to create a relaxing atmosphere. So many people believed that being a photographer was easy. That all you had to do was push a button on a camera and apply a filter afterward. Maybe for some people, that's how it was, but for Quinn, it was an art form.

Taking someone's portrait was an intimate act that required a vibe that couldn't be created in the blink of an eye —or with the push of a button.

She smiled at the portraits she'd made of the other Acton Academy teachers as she walked through the hallway. Mr. Stephenson flying above his piano, only tethered to it by his fingertips, as if the ecstasy of making music made him float into the air.

"Quinn," a voice followed by the quick pitter-patter of heels came from behind her. "You're early. Wonderful."

Quinn greeted Indira, whom she'd gotten to know well over the years she'd worked with her.

"You know the drill," Indira said. "We'll set up in the dance studio." She led Quinn up the stairs to an obscenely large room with the shiniest polished-wood floor Quinn had ever seen.

A woman stood silhouetted in front of the window. A shape Quinn would, even after all those years, still recognize anywhere.

The woman turned and the face that had haunted her dreams—and fantasies—for much longer than she cared to admit, was now directly in front of Quinn. The woman whose name she'd had to keep to herself for ten long years. Quinn gasped and her body froze.

"This is Maya Mercer, our new dance teacher," Indira said. "Maya, Quinn will be taking your picture today. She's a wizard with the camera as well as the computer for post-production so you have nothing to worry about."

After the initial shock of seeing Maya again had subsided, Quinn studied her face. Maya looked just as stunned as Quinn felt. Clearly, Indira hadn't given her much detail about who would be photographing her today.

"Quinn and I know each other." Maya was the first to

speak. "Her parents were my neighbors when I lived in Milbury."

"Well, then," Indira said. "You'll get on like a house on fire." She turned to Quinn. "I know you like to be left alone while you work so I'll leave you to it."

Quinn managed a nod. She couldn't take her eyes off Maya, who was wearing a bright red dress and matching lipstick. Already, a dozen ideas of how she would make Maya look in the final version of her picture popped up in the back of her mind. But Quinn couldn't grasp any of them. Her brain was too perplexed, too busy processing that Maya was standing in front of her, in the flesh. She might be ten years older, but she still looked as gorgeous as she had done that night.

"Quinn, I—" Maya said, tilting her head slightly. "I had no idea."

"You're the new dance teacher at Acton," Quinn stated the obvious.

Maya huffed out some air. "Didn't your mom tell you I moved to the city?"

Had her mother told her? Quinn didn't think so. She might have, but it could have been one of those things that her mother said that Quinn hadn't really listened to—although the mere mention of Maya's name would have perked up her ears. Quinn hadn't been home in a long time, although she spoke to her parents regularly—her dad still called her every single day, but Quinn didn't always pick up. She did make sure to always text him back because she didn't want him to needlessly worry about her.

"You live in New York?" Even though Quinn had absorbed the first shock, she was still having trouble processing what Maya was saying. She blamed the red dress that clung to her body like a second skin.

"Yes." Maya put her hands on her hips. "I know you can't tell by looking at me, but I'm a grandmother now. I wanted to be closer to Tommy and his family."

Quinn chuckled. "Well, fuck me." She brought her hand to her mouth. "Sorry. That kind of language is not tolerated at this school, nor should it be." She gave a slight shake of the head. "Maya Mercer." She sunk her teeth into her bottom lip. "Let me assure you that you *really* can't tell by looking at you."

Maya beamed her a wide smile. "How are you, Quinn? Still, chasing...um..." She made a show of scratching her head. "What was it that you called me back then? A cougar?" She burst out laughing. "Please, tell me you've gotten over that phase and you're with a nice girl your own age these days."

Quinn believed the best response to that was to simply laugh alongside Maya. "I'm on a job," she said, after a few beats. "It would be inappropriate to discuss my love life." She was dying to find out more about the status of Maya's love life, though.

"Of course." Maya nodded at Quinn's camera and equipment. "Shall we do this?" She glanced back at Quinn. "I'm so happy that you actually became a photographer."

"A long time ago, someone I can't possibly mention urged me to follow my dreams." Quinn should start setting up her lights, but she seemed frozen to the spot, gorging on Maya's delightful presence.

"Why can't you mention them?" Maya sounded coy enough for Quinn to conclude that she knew exactly who and what Quinn was referring to.

"It's a promise I made."

"Looks like they were right, though. Whoever they might be."

"At least about one thing." Quinn painted on a smirk.

"Are you going to take my picture now?" Maya asked.

"Yeah." For the life of her, Quinn couldn't wipe that smirk off her face. Not only had she not expected to see Maya again, but she most certainly hadn't expected her to still look so smoking hot. Although, in the end, it really wasn't a surprise that she did. Perhaps what had really happened was that Quinn hadn't allowed herself to think about how beautiful Maya would look now. Nor had she ever allowed herself to entertain the possibility of running into her like this. For all those reasons, the surprise was all the greater, and perhaps powerful, for it now. "You look really good, Maya. Being a grandmother suits you."

"Thank you." Maya took a step toward her. "How about a hug for your old neighbor? Or is that inappropriate too?"

Quinn could only shake her head.

CHAPTER 11

Maya could not believe she was about to throw her arms around Quinn Hathaway. How long had it been? So many years, Maya had lost count. Just like she had, over time, lost touch with Quinn's parents, even though, up until quite recently, they had lived next door to her.

Maya pressed herself against Quinn's body. There was no rush of familiarity—how could there be?—nor of nostalgia, but there was something. The memory of the night they'd spent together that one hot summer had always stayed with Maya much more prominently than she'd expected—or wanted. In a way, it was one of the reasons she'd moved to New York. Not because Quinn lived there, but because of what Quinn stood for in Maya's mind. Maya wanted to experience once again the rush of freedom she'd felt during that night ten years ago.

Quinn was the first to let go—she was on a job. But so was Maya. She was a teacher at Acton Academy and that involved having her portrait taken. The first time she'd walked into the building, it had been impossible to ignore the art on the walls. Maya had instantly loved the quirky pictures of the other teachers for their playfulness and magical quality. She'd come to appreciate them even more once she'd gotten to know the teachers they depicted, making her wonder how the photographer could have captured so much of their subject's personality. She couldn't wait to see what Quinn would make of her.

"I still can't believe this," Quinn said, as they broke from their embrace. "You must tell me about Tommy and this grandchild of yours in much more detail."

The mere mention of her grandson made Maya's chest swell with pride, the way only a grandparent's could. "I'll show you a picture after we're done."

"Please tell me you're free to go for a drink after this." Quinn unzipped a large rectangular bag. "So we can have a long-overdue catch-up."

Maya nodded and watched Quinn as she set up two large lamps and a green backdrop. She looked so different from when Maya had last seen her, yet also still very much the same. So much could change in ten years of a young person's life. Tommy was only twenty-eight and he was married with a child now. Maya could only imagine the ways in which Quinn had changed from that brazen young woman asking for a swim—and so much more—into the person she was today.

"I love the dress," Quinn said. "You look absolutely stunning."

"I bet you say that to everyone whose picture you're about to take." From her years as a professional dancer, Maya was used to posing for judges and post-competition pictures alike. She hadn't been nervous about this photo shoot in the slightest. In fact, she'd looked forward to it. It had been a while since she'd painted on her most professional smile—the one she'd already perfected in the mirror as a young girl dreaming of a career on the dance floor.

Quinn chuckled. "Only the ones who look as gorgeous as

you." Quinn winked at her and in that wink, Maya could see so much of the woman she had become. She was confident, born to take a city as ruthless as New York by storm. Earlier, she had seemed slightly thrown by being confronted with Maya, but she had regrouped. Perhaps Quinn found comfort in operating her equipment and setting up the shot. Either way, Maya enjoyed watching her work and seeing Quinn in her element.

"Let's do some static shots first," Quinn said. "If you could stand in front of the green screen, please."

Maya did as instructed. She smiled for Quinn, which wasn't a hardship at all, while trying to suppress the memories that were surfacing from the deepest recesses of her mind. Maya had seen all of Quinn that night. She'd seen her vulnerable side. As though it had happened mere days ago, Maya could still remember what she'd looked like the first time she came. A frisson ran up her spine. She turned up her smile, making sure it was reflected in her eyes.

Quinn's face was obstructed by the camera—Quinn liked to take pictures in a way Maya hadn't seen for years, with her eye glued to the viewfinder—so Maya focused on Quinn's body. Her gaze was drawn to the dark lettering on the outside of her wrists. A white-hot jolt shuddered through her body as she remembered Quinn's other tattoo—the one on her lower belly.

"Do you think you have some moves for me?" Quinn asked, pulling Maya from her reverie.

"Of course." Maya was happy she managed to sound so self-assured, despite the memories of that night swirling around in her brain.

Quinn beamed her a full-wattage smile. "Remember when you last danced for me?"

Maya shook her head, although of course she remembered. Every second of the time she'd spent with Quinn had proved impossible to forget.

Quinn looked as though she didn't believe Maya. "I don't suppose you're teaching these kids how to do the salsa?"

"Acton is more ballroom-oriented," Maya said.

"Okay. Maybe you could stand in a waltz-like pose?" Quinn grinned at her. "Although I would have loved photographing you doing some Latin moves."

Maya tightened her core, extended her neck, and leaned her torso back as though she was dancing a waltz.

"Beautiful," Quinn said.

Maya didn't know if she meant her or the pose.

They tried out a number of different positions, one of which included Maya dancing a solo quick-step, her feet light as a feather, like she was flying from one end of the room to the other.

"I think I have all I need." Quinn put her camera to the side. "Would you mind if I took a quick pic with my phone to send to Mom? Maybe a selfie of the two of us?"

"Sure." All those years later, Maya could no longer see the harm in that.

Quinn grabbed her phone and walked over to Maya. When she held the phone up to take the snap, Maya could make out the word on her right wrist. *Acceptance* it said.

"Smile," Quinn said, drawing Maya's attention away from her tattoo.

Maya looked into the lens and put on her smile.

"Would you like me to send that to you as well?" Quinn was looking at her phone screen.

"You would need my number for that."

"I was going to ask for that either way so I can send you my work before I submit the final version to Indira. I like the people in my pictures to be fully happy with what I've done."

Maya gave her number, and Quinn sent her the picture. "Now you have my number as well."

"It was... lovely to see you again." Maya took a few deep breaths. "I can't wait to see what you come up with. I really love what you've done with the ones in the corridors. You're obviously very talented and good at what you do." Not that Maya was comparing Quinn to Tommy, but sometimes she wished her son had more of her artistic, frivolous qualities. Just like his father, Tommy had become an accountant—although, when in the mood, he could bust a mean move on the dance floor. At least, between her ex-husband and her son, Maya never had to worry about her money being mismanaged.

"Thank you." Quinn shot her another smile. "I meant what I said earlier. I don't have anywhere to be right now. Do you want to go for a coffee?"

"It would be nice to catch up." Maya was curious to know what Quinn had been up to. "There's a place I like to go just around the corner."

CHAPTER 12

Quinn caught Maya's gaze sliding down to her wrists. She held them up, even though, when sat opposite from her, Maya could only see the words in the wrong order. She crossed her wrists so Maya could properly read what her tattoo said.

"*Radical Acceptance*," Maya said, then looked up into Quinn's eyes again.

"It's not the only one I got since..." Quinn couldn't help but smile.

"So, you're a photographer now." Maya stared into her cup of coffee and expertly ignored Quinn's allusion to that night.

"And retouch artist," Quinn added.

"Wow." Maya looked suitably impressed.

"And *you* moved to New York City."

"I did," Maya said.

"How long have you lived here now?"

"About seven months." Maya half-smiled. "Your mom did give me your number. She told me to get in touch with you if I needed anything."

"I take it you didn't need anything then."

"I've been too busy settling in to need anything from you, Quinn." Maya painted on a full smile again. "Being a granny has really taken it out of me."

"How old is your grandchild?"

Maya pulled her phone from her purse and started scrolling. "Ethan's four and a half months now. And Tommy's an accountant, like his dad." She showed Quinn a picture of Tommy who looked much older than Quinn remembered him, an absolutely stunning black woman by his side, and a tiny baby in her arms.

"That's Tommy's wife?"

"Beth," Maya said. "You might have seen her on CNN."

"No way." Quinn remembered now, not that she watched CNN that often. "Tommy's married to Beth Robbins?"

"He sure is." Maya sat there beaming as if she were responsible for their match-made-in-heaven.

"What's the secret appeal of accountants that they get the hottest women?"

Maya burst into a chuckle. "I don't know."

"What a lovely family."

"Beth's really going for it in the career department and Tommy's quite busy as well."

"So you're the nanny?"

Maya shook her head. "I fill in when the nanny's not there or when one of them is alone and it's all a bit too much. I do still have a job." The grin on Maya's lips said that she didn't mind spending time with her grandson at all.

"What happened to your dance school in Milbury?"

"I sold it. The house too. I used the money to buy a condo in Manhattan, if you can believe it. Up until quite recently, the thought had never occurred to me. I always believed I'd grow old in Milbury. But when Beth got pregnant, something in me shifted and I knew I wouldn't be happy as a suburban granny who only sees her grandchild when his parents can find the time. Both Tommy and Beth are so driven and obsessed with work. I figured that if I didn't come to them, I'd hardly get to see little Ethan."

"It's a big move."

"It's not the only reason I wanted to move to the city." Maya sipped from her coffee. "It all just came together and so far, it's been really good. I get to see Ethan and Tommy as much as I like, which is almost every day. The city's been a thrill after all those years in quiet old Milbury."

"I'm glad you like it here." Quinn raked her gaze over Maya. She stood out in the coffee shop with her red dress and matching lipstick. "It's such a treat to see you."

"Tell me about you. Where do you live?"

"Greenpoint. Quite a trek from here."

"Brooklyn?"

Quinn nodded. "Still in the same place I moved to that summer, actually, but with a different roommate."

"Really?"

"You don't easily give up a rent-stabilized apartment in New York." At least Quinn could always make her share of the rent these days and no longer needed to rely on monthly checks from her parents.

"And your roommate is a friend or...?" Maya's eyes sparkled with curiosity.

"Griff's a friend."

"Griff?"

Quinn understood the possible confusion. "Her name's Rose Griffin. She's a great roommate *and* friend." Quinn could sense what Maya really wanted to ask. She figured she might as well get it out of the way. "I'm currently single, in case you were wondering."

Was that a flush of pink on Maya's neck? "Just curious

about you." Maya still managed a confident enough smile. "Clearly, you're doing well in your professional life. Not that I equate being in a relationship with having a successful personal life. How could I?"

"But you're happy for Tommy that he has a family?"

Maya nodded. "I am. I can't help it. I want to be open-minded, but on the other hand, it's such a joy to me that he's not alone."

"How about you, Maya? Are you still... alone?" Quinn couldn't picture it. Then again, anything was possible.

"Still single." Maya shrugged. "But, for now, that only means I have more time for Ethan."

"I bet Tommy's happy with that arrangement."

"He didn't ask me to move here, if that's what you're implying. I did it of my own volition. I'm quite mature enough to make my own decisions."

Zing. Maya hadn't lost any of her sass. "It's not what I meant to imply. I—"

"Tommy hasn't seen me with anyone else since his dad and I divorced. He's used to me being on my own. Not that he hasn't tried setting me up in the past. At least he's too busy being a dad for any of that foolishness now."

"Let me guess. He tried to hook you up with a fellow accountant?" If only he knew what his mother had been up to with her all those years ago.

Maya confirmed with a nod. "More than one, although not at the same time."

They both chuckled, and Quinn was glad that the earlier possible moment of contention between them had passed.

"Is that one of the other reasons you moved to New York? Because the pool of eligible bachelors is much larger here than in Milbury?"

"Yes and no."

Quinn leaned back in her chair. "What does that mean?"

"I—I'm not sure I feel comfortable talking about that with you right now."

"Fair enough."

"If you want to talk about someone's adventures in dating, why don't you regale me with some tales of yours?"

"Again, fair enough." Quinn ran a hand through her hair. If she'd known she'd be photographing Maya Mercer today, she'd have gone for a trim at the salon. She was overdue one. Her blond curls were sticking up at angles they shouldn't be. "I've just come out of a... thing. Well, more than a thing. We were seeing each other for almost four years, but..." In hindsight, a good few months after she and Morgan had broken up, Quinn could so easily see that she'd wasted four years of her life—four of the very best years of her life age-wise, many a women's magazine article would claim. "It didn't work out in the end."

"It seems to be a thing with us," Maya said. "To meet after you've had your heart broken."

"Morgan didn't break my heart," Quinn lied. "Or if she did, I'm over it. She's not worth it. She strung me along for years."

"Why? Was she afraid to commit? Four years is a long time to..." Maya left the sentence open for Quinn to complete.

"Please don't judge me for this, although I know it's hard, but Morgan was—*is*—married. We had an affair. She did, anyway. A long one. She kept promising she'd leave her husband, but she never did. Clearly. So there you go." Quinn couldn't keep the bitterness out of her voice. It still stung—mostly because she had been so willing, so fucking eager, to believe Morgan would choose her when it came down to it.

"I'm sorry, Quinn. I'm sorry that happened to you."

"Well, it didn't exactly happen to me. I was there. I knew she was married from the get-go. I can't be absolved of guilt when it comes to that. Nor can I be absolved of being stupid enough to believe her when she promised me we'd be together." Quinn expelled a sigh. "I should have known that a woman who can so easily lie to her own husband would have no trouble lying to her bit on the side."

"Are you all right?" Maya leaned over the table and examined Quinn's face.

Quinn shrugged. "It just sucks and it'll suck for a while longer. Until it won't." She held up her wrists to Maya. "Radical acceptance, right? Of the good and the bad things that happen."

"Is that what that means?"

"It can mean so many things. That's why I had it tattooed on my wrists. So I can be reminded of it all the time." She put her hands down. "I accept my own part in it but I also accept that the way Morgan treated me was not okay. Just as I accept that it's more than all right to be majorly upset about this all for a while."

"Hey." Maya put a hand on Quinn's. "It's her loss. I hope you know that."

Maya's touch felt instantly comforting. Quinn stared at their hands for a beat. "Thank you, Maya. You've always been so kind."

"Do you mind me asking..." Maya gave her hand a little squeeze, then removed her own. "How old was Morgan?"

"A gorgeous fifty-one." Quinn didn't know why, but she suddenly felt silly saying it like that.

"Was she at her most beautiful?" Maya asked.

"You remember." Quinn felt a touch less silly.

"Some things are impossible to forget." Maya leaned back in her chair as if she wasn't going anywhere soon.

"How about another coffee?" Quinn asked.

CHAPTER 13

Quinn's presence was as magnetic as Maya remembered. She might as well enjoy it for a little longer because she had no intention of seeing her old neighbor again after today—although she was curious as to how Quinn's pictures of her would turn out.

Maya watched Quinn make her way to the counter. She was wearing the kind of high-waisted jeans that had been all the rage a few decades ago and had, as if by magic, become trendy again. Maya hadn't made it to Brooklyn yet—she'd been far too infatuated with Ethan to tear herself away from him for too long—but she imagined Quinn fitted right in.

Flashes of their night together sparked in Maya's mind. Even though it had happened so long ago, Maya still felt guilty about it. It was the main reason why she had, slowly over the years, spent less and less time with Bill and Brooke. Being in their company made Maya so uncomfortable, she could no longer relax. Every time either one of them mentioned Quinn, Maya felt the weight of her secret, and she was convinced that her neighbors would somehow be able to read off her face what had happened between her and their daughter.

"Here you go." Quinn deposited a steaming mug in front of her.

After she sat, she said, "I didn't mean to go all emo on you earlier, by the way. Sorry about that."

"That's all right." Maya picked up her coffee and inhaled the fragrant steam rising up from the mug. "Whatever happened to..." She remembered a lot from that night, but the name of Quinn's previous ex escaped her.

"Do you mean Rachel?" Quinn asked.

Maya nodded.

"Hell if I know. I never saw her again. Something must have happened that summer that helped me move on." She glanced at Maya over the rim of her cup. A silence fell.

That night hung heavy in the air between them. It was what simultaneously kept Maya glued to her seat and made her want to run away.

Quinn broke the silence first. "I never told anyone. As you asked."

Maya arched up her eyebrows. "Really? Literally not one other person?"

Quinn gave a slow shake of the head. "I've always wanted to keep my promise to you. Maybe in honor of that night, which was... special."

Heat rose in Maya's cheeks and it wasn't because of the hot cup of coffee she was holding. "I really appreciate that," she managed to say.

"Did you tell anyone?"

"No." Who would Maya have told? Her friends in Milbury? "Not a living soul."

"It really has been our secret then." A sparkle danced in Quinn's eyes. "I wonder what will happen now that it's being talked about again, after all these years."

Maya chuckled. "It's a treat to see you as well, Quinn. It's good to know you're doing so well, minus the blip in your love life, of course."

"Fuck Morgan." Quinn rolled her eyes. "As if she's suddenly going to be happy with her massive bore of a husband." She waved her hand about. "But let's not go there again."

"No more bartending for you?" Maya was more than happy to move on from the subject.

"My bartending days are well and truly over, but I do still very much like a party. That's how I made my name as a photographer. I shot parties. Then I started messing around with the pictures in Photoshop. One thing led to another. And here I am today, photographing you." She wiggled her fingers about. "I can't wait to get started." She tilted her head. "You do realize I'll be looking at you with laser-like focus for a great many hours to come."

Maya didn't know what to say to that. She still felt a touch flustered.

"Perk of the job." Quinn's gaze on her softened. "You no longer own your dance school. That must have been a big change."

"I mainly teach kids now, which I love, actually," Maya said. "Considering that they've been put in dance class by their parents, most of them go at it with great enthusiasm, which is wonderful to work with. When it comes to certain dance steps, you can't teach them young enough."

"Acton's very posh, though. Is that the only school you teach at?"

Maya nodded. "I don't want to work full-time anymore. Nor do I want the responsibility of running my own business any longer. I've done that all my life."

"Time to focus on yourself?"

"In a way." Quinn had a way of asking questions that made

Maya want to tell her things she should really keep to herself. That's how trouble started. Maya knew that much from when she'd last spent time with Quinn. "I haven't made this huge change in my life only to be Ethan's granny."

Quinn nodded and kept silent. The Quinn from all those years ago—the one who so shamelessly seduced Maya—would have taken the opportunity to insert some flirty banter here. But today, they weren't flirting. In almost every respect, it felt like two old friends catching up. Almost, but not quite. Because they weren't friends. They'd been lovers, albeit for one night only.

"When I was being coy earlier," Maya started, because, apparently, when Quinn Hathaway was around, she couldn't quite help herself. "When I didn't want to say why else I decided to sell everything and move here..." Maya took a quick sip of coffee. "It's because I wanted to, uh, explore dating women." There. She'd said it. It wasn't the first time, but admitting this to Quinn, who for all Maya knew might have sparked the whole thing, was a big deal to her. "It's easier in the city."

"I bet." Quinn smiled warmly. "And? Have you had any luck on the NYC lesbian dating scene?"

"Well, I mean, it's all apps now these days, isn't it?" Maya mumbled.

"Yeah." Quinn scrunched her lips together. "Which ones are you on?" She nodded as though something had occurred to her. "I must have missed you because after Morgan I changed my search parameters to below the age of fifty only."

"Oh, Quinn. You do crack me up." Maya had to grin.

"I haven't really been looking, though," Quinn admitted. "But how funny would it have been if I had seen you on Tinder?" She shook her head. "I wouldn't have known what to do with myself, to be perfectly honest."

They both chuckled although not solely out of mirth. Maya had a lot of nervous tension to release.

"I don't search below the age of forty-five, for your information," Maya said.

"Pity." Quin fixed her gaze on Maya's briefly, then looked away. "Have you been on any dates?"

"One since I moved here." One date in seven months wasn't overly industrious. "But I do have one lined up for this weekend."

Quinn burst into a giggle. "Do you know what my first thought was when you just said that?"

Maya shook her head.

"Is it anyone I know or have dated myself?" Quinn clearly had no trouble joking about her own age-gap proclivities.

Maya laughed with her. Now that she'd mentioned her upcoming date, the nerves she felt at its prospect added themselves to the agitation Quinn inspired in her. Laughing eased the tension somewhat. "I really wouldn't know. Her name's Beverly and she's in her fifties like me. But that's all I know."

"Hot?" Quinn waggled her eyebrows.

"She looked pretty good in the pictures I've seen." Maya couldn't believe the conversation had taken this turn. All of a sudden, she was talking to Quinn as close friends did. How had that happened?

"Beverly won't know what hit her when she meets you." Quinn looked very sincere as she said that. "Why did the other date not work out, if you don't mind me asking?"

Maya had only found the courage to install the app—and the patience to find out how it worked—a couple of months ago. She'd kept herself to browsing only for the first few weeks, until she'd chanced upon Kim's profile. "I guess I just... didn't feel the spark. She was perfectly lovely. I just didn't really feel like seeing her again afterward. That I'd rather stay in and babysit my grandson, who, although utterly adorable, is just a baby who demands things by crying his little heart out, told me all I needed to know."

"Wow." Quinn sank her teeth into her bottom lip. "I'm sorry, Maya. I'm still processing that you're dating women now. How did Tommy react when you told him?"

"I haven't told him," Maya blurted out. "There hasn't really been anything to tell."

"Okay."

"If I get involved in something serious I will tell him, of course, but I see no reason to upset his image of me while I remain single."

"His image of you? What would that be?"

"That I'm straight, of course. I've never given him reason to think otherwise in all of his twenty-eight years."

"Maybe the fact that you haven't had a relationship with a man in more than ten—or is it fifteen years now?—might give something away. Tommy wasn't born yesterday, Maya. You should know."

"Look, I know my son. He just... doesn't think of me in that way. In a way that allows a lot of room for change. I can hardly blame him for that, seeing as I'm the one who raised him."

"He's not a homophobe, is he?"

"No, of course not. He's never had one bad word to say about you, Quinn, and he has plenty of friends who are gay and gender-fluid and all the other things people are these days."

"But they're not this mother."

Maya nodded. This was simply not something she could easily discuss with her son. She'd have a much easier time talking about it with her daughter-in-law. She'd even come close to telling Beth's mother, Belinda, who had become a friend since she'd moved to the city. But the truth was that she'd only told Angus, her neighbor from across the hall, because he was gay himself.

Maya would worry about Tommy later. She was only exploring. Nothing had even happened with another woman. She'd only kissed Kim on the cheek and while Maya had expected a rush of feel-good hormones to engulf her—the way she remembered it from her night with Quinn—her hormones seemed to have gone on strike.

"You should take all the time you need, of course," Quinn said.

"I will." Maya had taken a lot of time already, she realized now that she was sitting here with Quinn.

"The rest will work itself out," Quinn added.

Maya downed the last of her coffee. "I should probably get going now."

"Oh." Quinn looked disappointed. "Already?"

"I have things to do."

"You're not running away because of what we just talked about?" Quinn wasn't one to beat about the bush.

"No. I—" Maya took a deep breath and looked into Quinn's face. "I'm in this overwhelming new phase of my life and seeing you has... I'll be honest. It has thrown me a little, Quinn."

"Believe me, it has thrown me as well."

"I said it ten years ago and I will say it again now." Maya tried her best not to sound as though she was preaching. "You will find your way. You'll get over Morgan, like you got over Rachel. You have your art and your passion and you're still as wonderful to be around as ever." Maya almost gave Quinn a maternal pat on the knee.

"How about you, though? Will you find your way?" Quinn asked.

Maya looked squarely into Quinn's eyes. They were so

bright and blue. Not the icy kind of blue some eyes could be, but the warm, azure blue of the ocean on a sun-drenched day.

"I don't see why not." Maya injected as much hope into her voice as she could.

"Good luck with Beverly. You'll knock her socks right off." Clearly, Quinn couldn't help some mild flirting, although Maya wasn't sure she could even interpret it as that. Maybe she was just being encouraging in her own way.

"Thank you."

"I'll be in touch about the pictures." Quinn pushed herself out of her chair.

"I look forward to seeing your work." Maya rose as well.

"Some of it will be displayed in a gallery in Brooklyn next month. If you're interested, you should come. I'll send you an invite to the opening."

"Okay." Maya was fairly certain she wouldn't be crossing the Brooklyn Bridge for a gathering of hipsters half her age.

"Or you can follow me on Instagram. I post a lot of my stuff on there."

"Sure." Even though it didn't really have to be, especially because they both lived in the same city now, it felt like a sort of goodbye again.

"Remember what my mom told you. Call me if you need anything." Quinn opened her arms.

Maya stepped closer and with Quinn's hands lightly pressing against her shoulders, kissed her on the cheek.

Her hormones no longer appeared to be on strike.

CHAPTER 14

"Guess who just slid into my DM?" Griff asked as she walked into the living room of the two-bedroom apartment Quinn shared with her.

"Your question's too vague for me to properly answer." Quinn was lying on the couch, scrolling through her phone.

"Mrs. Morgan Graham."

"Oh god." Quinn sat up a little straighter. "What does she want?"

"I think she wants you back. Look at this." Griff showed Quinn her phone screen.

Quinn's freezing me out. Is she okay? Can you ask her to get it in touch, please?

"Oh, please." Quinn rolled her eyes, remembering the message Morgan had sent her earlier, which she had pretty successfully erased from her conscious mind. "She's probably bored again. Do feel free to block her at once."

"Have you blocked her?" Griff asked.

"No," Quinn had to admit. "It's hard. I don't know why I can't bring myself to do it."

"How about you give me your phone and I give you mine and we block her on each other's phone at the same time."

Quinn laughed, although it was more out of some strange feeling of guilt than anything else. "It seems needlessly harsh."

"What she did to you for almost four years is harsh, Quinn. You no longer giving her the time of day is the only logical consequence of how Morgan treated you."

Quinn nodded. "I know. You're totally right. But... aargh. It drives me nuts that I can't just do it. Get it over with. Be done with her."

"You loved her for a long time." Griff held out her hand for Quinn's phone. "Maybe you need to get back in the saddle and go on the rebound. Spend some sexy time with another woman and put some distance between yourself and all the memories you have of Morgan."

"I haven't come across anyone sexier than Morgan to help me with that," Quinn said.

"You haven't exactly been looking."

"Maybe not." Griff was right. Quinn hadn't been looking. And yet. Instead of handing over her phone, Quinn scrolled to the images she had downloaded from her camera earlier. "Or maybe I have." She showed Griff the screen.

"Uh-huh," Griff hummed. "Looks right up your alley, girl. Who is she? A client?"

Quinn nodded. "Not just any client. I know her from before. She was my next-door neighbor in Milbury."

"Aha. Red flag alert." Griff peered at the screen again. "As red as that dress this woman is wearing."

"Why a red flag?" Quinn mostly asked because she needed to be told out loud by someone she respected.

"Well, I don't know, Quinn. If she was your neighbor, I suspect she was your family's neighbor too. What would Brooke have to say about that? Remember how she railed against Morgan?"

"Mom would have a stroke on the spot, that's for sure. But you just said I needed to go on the rebound..."

"Are you serious? Are you really interested in your old neighbor in that way? Is she even gay or will you make her gay-for-Quinn?" Griff sat there batting her lashes ostentatiously.

Quinn put her phone to the side. "What if I told you that, a long time ago, this woman and I had quite the night together?" Apart from the first few months, when she'd been dying to share the mind-blowing encounter she'd had with Maya with someone else, it hadn't been that hard to stay silent. It had turned into a precious little secret she kept buried deep inside her, something entirely her own that only one other person in the world knew about. Seeing Maya again had changed everything.

"What do you mean?" Griff, who was a reporter, slipped into journalist mode.

"We slept together about ten years ago when I was home for the summer. My parents were away for the weekend. It felt like Maya and I were the only people left on earth. It was pretty magical, actually."

"Hold on." Griff set her jaw. "What happened? How old were you, for starters?"

"I was twenty-four. She was forty-five at the time."

Griff shook her head. "Of course," she said, her voice dripping with sarcasm.

"Oh my god, Griff. It was so amazing. Like the most heavenly dream you've ever had, but for real. Afterward, she made me promise not to tell anyone and I didn't. I kept my promise.

Then this afternoon, I find out she's the new Acton Academy teacher whose portrait I'm doing."

"No shit." Griff blew some air out from between her teeth. "And that's her." Griff looked at Maya's picture again. "Fuck, Quinn. You must be quite beside yourself right now."

"You could say that."

"And still you can't bring yourself to block Morgan."

"I should just do it now, but I'm not sure I'm in my right mind after seeing Maya again."

"What happened when you saw her?"

"It was... lovely but also weird. She's still as hot as she was back then and—" Quinn wasn't sure she was allowed to share this information with someone else, but telling Griff would have no bearing whatsoever on Maya's life. "One of the reasons she moved to New York is because she wants to date women."

"No. Fucking. Way!"

"I know." Quinn hadn't really allowed herself to give the whole thing too much thought—perhaps for exactly this reason. If she did start thinking about it in earnest, she was afraid of where her mind would go next. "We went for coffee and had a really great talk. Nothing flirty or anything like that. More like catching up. Her son's married to Beth Robbins, by the way. They just had a child."

"*The* Beth Robbins of CNN?" Unlike Quinn, Griff could be glued to the TV news for hours on end. "Quite the good-looking family then."

"At least the women are," Quinn joked.

"What else do we need?" Griff gave a hearty chuckle. "So, your possible rebound lady is a granny?"

"A very young grandmother," Quinn corrected her friend. "Tommy's not even thirty yet. Who has children at that age these days?"

"Beth Robbins must have felt her clock ticking. If I'm not mistaken, she's in her early thirties." Griff rarely got it wrong. "If they want more than one bambino, it makes sense not to wait too long."

"Tommy likes older women as well," Quinn mused.

"I don't think Beth being a few years older than him compares to your over-sized mommy complex." Griff fancied herself an armchair psychologist at times. After Quinn and Morgan had broken up, she'd given Quinn a long speech on why she believed Quinn liked older women so much.

"Down, girl." Quinn hadn't really listened to Griff's explanation at the time. She'd been too upset to analyze herself for too long because she already felt like such a loser after allowing Morgan to trample over her heart. Griff had warned her about that too; luckily, she wasn't the type for obnoxious I-told-you-so's.

"So..." Griff rubbed her palms on her jeans. "What's the plan? Do you have one?"

Quinn shook her head. "Maya's not interested in me in that way."

"How do you know?"

"She *very* specifically told me she wants to date women her own age."

"I'm not talking about dating, Quinn. You're looking for a rebound person, remember?"

"There wasn't that kind of vibe between us this time."

"Have you made plans to see each other again?"

"Not as such, although I did invite her to my show next month. And I'll need to be in touch with her once I'm done retouching her picture. There are options, I guess." Quinn couldn't believe she was having this conversation. Seeing Maya had shaken her, which was perfectly understandable, but did she really want to go down that route with her again?

On the other hand, there wasn't any harm in it. So far, Maya was the only woman Quinn could even consider looking at in that way after Morgan, who was by all Quinn's standards and definitions the hottest woman she'd ever laid eyes on—the cruelest too, as it turned out.

"Indeed, girl, let me lay out your options for you." Griff tapped her fingers together the way she did when a plan was coming together for her. "Either you listen to what Morgan has to say to you, which I would not recommend. She had her chance. She blew it. She's out." She huffed out a breath. "Or you impress the hell out of Maya with the art you'll make of her, which will also give you the perfect excuse to contact her. Seeing herself in one of your compositions can make a lady go a little weak at the knees, we know this." Griff winked at her. "Or, you do nothing. Which is also fine. Personally, I have no moral objections against the latter two options."

"Or we go to Marnie's tonight and see what the night has in store for us."

"Ugh, Quinn, don't drag me out to Marnie's tonight with your emotional blackmail." Griff pushed Quinn's knees out of the way and sank into the couch next to her. "I had a big night of staying in planned." She gave Quinn a look. "Besides, when have you ever found anything resembling love at Marnie's?"

"I won't ask you to go with me, but I might just go and have a look myself." Quinn knew Griff was probably right. The crowd at Marnie's was not usually her taste—too young, too post-woke, too Gen Z.

"You do what you got to do, girl." Griff patted Quinn's knee. "Hopefully, you'll be wiser tomorrow."

CHAPTER 15

Angus mixed a rum and diet Coke for himself and a vodka and soda for Maya—she needed something to take the edge off, even though it was only early afternoon and she was due at Tommy's in a few hours.

"So her name's Beverly." Angus offered her the drink, sat, and slung one leg over the other. "Are you going to show me her picture or do I need to beg to lay eyes on this hot piece of lesbian ass?"

Maya showed Angus Beverly's picture on her phone.

"Hm," he emitted a low groan from the back of his throat. "Is that what's got you so agitated? She looks fine, but in my very, *very* humble opinion, you can do so much better."

"You've only seen her picture." Maya had known Angus for a mere few months, since she'd moved into the apartment across from him, but she knew him well enough to not take his superficial judgements too seriously. "We've been chatting. She comes across as very sweet."

"Sweet? Is that really what you want?" He fixed his dark gaze on her. "Girl, you want someone to blow your mind." He huffed out some air. "Someone you're not likely to find on an app like that."

"Anyway." Maya put her phone away. She wasn't going to let Angus ruin her date before it had even happened. "That's not the reason why I might appear a little tense this afternoon."

"You should take her out dancing." It took a while before Angus could settle into listening mode—like many men, gay or straight, he was rather fond of the sound of his own voice. "See what she's made of."

As soon as Maya had told Angus she was a dance teacher, he had pushed his living room furniture to the side and demanded she take him for a spin around the floor. He turned out to have a fabulous sense of rhythm and excellent knowledge of ballroom steps. "Don't date her if she can't dance, Maya. It will kill your beautifully free spirit." Maya was quite taken with Angus' flair for exaggerated dramatics. He was most certainly a high-maintenance man, but he also made her laugh like no one else had in years.

Maya waited patiently for Angus to catch up on what she'd admitted a few seconds earlier. She took a sip of her drink, which he always made too strong. She didn't mind today.

"Do tell," he nodded, and fell silent.

"I've never told anyone what I'm about to tell you." She swallowed hard. What would it feel like to give voice to what she had experienced with Quinn ten years ago? There was only one way to find out. "I slept with another woman for the first time ten years ago. It was a one-night thing because that's all it could be." Maya took a breath. "Yesterday I saw her again. It was completely unexpected and since then I haven't known what to do with myself. It's like seeing her has... I don't know. Awoken something in me? I can't really express it in words yet."

"Back up a little, Maya." Angus' thoughtful voice was low and soft. "I was under the mistaken impression that loving the ladies was a new thing for you, but now you're telling me that your first time with a woman happened ten years ago." He pulled at his earlobe the way he did when considering something deeply.

"Correct."

"What happened in the ten years since?"

"Nothing."

"What do you mean, nothing? Ten years make for a lot of days and nights to fill. How can nothing have happened? I know for a fact that the 'burbs aren't half as uneventful as they're made out to be."

"After... Quinn." It felt so good and so bad at the same time to say Quinn's name out loud in this context. "I didn't know what to do with myself for a long time, so I did nothing. I worked, which has always been a great source of satisfaction for me. I saw my friends. I did all the things I usually do. I even went on a few dates." She rolled her eyes at herself. "With men only. Life just passed. The days and then the months and years just went by, as they do. Until they didn't, I guess. Until I saw Beth and Tommy's pregnancy as the perfect opportunity to make this big change in my life."

"Until you finally gave yourself permission to date women," Angus said.

"Yes." Maya paused to gather her thoughts. "I've been thinking about this a lot lately and what I think happened is that after that night with Quinn I felt so... guilty—perhaps even a little disgusted with myself—that I couldn't let myself be the kind of person who dates women. Not after Quinn, because..." Maya expelled some air.

"What was so awful about this Quinn?" Angus asked.

"Oh my god, Angus." Maya buried her face in her hands.

"Hey, this is me you're talking to. I'm unshockable. I've seen it all, darling."

From the tales Angus had told her, Maya knew he had seen much more of a certain side of life than she had.

"Quinn was my next-door neighbors' daughter." Maya peeked through her fingers. "She was only twenty-four at the time and... it shouldn't have happened, but it did. And the worst part is that it was absolutely divine. Like nothing I'd ever experienced before or since."

"For crying out loud." Angus brought his hand to his chest. "She was twenty-four!" he cried out. "So fucking what, Maya?"

"I knew her parents very well at the time. After it happened, I kept wondering how I would react if I found out Quinn's mother had spent a night of passion with Tommy. Or even Quinn's dad." Her hands still half-covering her face, Maya shook her head.

"That's a lot of useless guilt to carry around for all those years," Angus said, a sudden sharpness to his voice. "For something that happened between two consenting adults."

"I've tried to assuage my guilt by repeating to myself that she came on to me. She straight-on seduced me. But it's no excuse. I should have known better. I should have been stronger and I should have said no."

"Why?" Angus made a tsking sound with his lips. "If a horny twenty-four-year-old came knocking on my door, I wouldn't dream of saying no, Maya. I would throw that door wide open."

"Even after all these years, it still doesn't feel right. That's why I never told anyone, and I asked her to do the same."

"Big mistake, darling. By not talking about it and keeping it bottled inside of you all this time you've given that stupid guilt of yours a powerful set of wings and let it wreak havoc inside you for years on end."

Maya finally dropped her hands. "Maybe." She hoped so. She had long ago surrendered to never receiving absolution for what she did that night—no matter how amazing it had been—but maybe there was hope in that department yet.

"And now you've seen this Quinn again and you're all out of sorts." He tilted his chin. "No fucking wonder."

"The oddest thing about seeing her again was that…" Maya couldn't help but smile. "It was fun. Yes, that's exactly the right word for it. Quinn was a lot of fun ten years ago, making it impossible for me to resist her. And she's still fun now. She's just so vibrant and alive and confident. A real joy to be around."

"Uh-huh." Angus tapped his fingers on the tabletop. "I can tell. Your eyes are sparkling."

Maya waved off his comment. "She's a photographer now." As if she'd told her only yesterday, Maya remembered how torn up Quinn had been about the breakup with her former photography teacher. "She's all grown up." Oops. That probably came out wrong. But Angus truly was un-shockable. "I mean that she has made a life for herself here and she's doing well. All of that."

Maya wasn't so sure about Quinn's emotional well-being, what with her recent breakup, but she sure as hell looked good—and had been totally in command of the photo shoot. Even though Maya hadn't seen Quinn for ten years, she'd always figured Quinn Hathaway would turn out as someone who preferred giving orders rather than receiving them. What didn't make sense to Maya was how Quinn could have given four years of her life to a woman who was married to someone else—who didn't exclusively choose her.

"And yet, you're going on a date with what's-her-name—Beverly." Angus stroked the beard he kept at a perfect quarter-inch length.

"What?" Maya shook her head. "That's got nothing to do with Quinn."

"The hell it hasn't." Angus was very skilled at rolling his eyes—he'd had a lot of practice. It was his preferred way of letting you know he was seeing right through you. "If you were to ask me—"

"Which I'm not." Maya had an inkling of what Angus was about to say and she didn't want to hear it. She didn't want someone saying the words out loud. She herself had already said too much in this conversation.

"I'll say it anyway," Angus continued, as expected.

"Of course you will."

"Maybe instead of going on a date with Beverly, you should ask Quinn out." Angus stated it so matter-of-factly, it almost sounded plausible. Almost.

"I'm not going on a date with someone twenty years younger than me." Maya could sound very resolute as well—decades of teaching had made it easy.

"Why not?" Angus waggled his eyebrows.

"I didn't tell you about Quinn because I want to go out with her, Angus. I only wanted to share this with someone who wouldn't judge me."

"I'm not judging, darling. Nu-uh."

"I know you're not, but you are insinuating something."

"I just call it as I see it. Maybe that's why you chose to tell little old me."

Maya couldn't think of anyone else she might have told. She might let Tommy know that Quinn was the photographer for the Acton shoot, but that would be the full extent of the information she would share with her son.

But Angus had been right about one thing. Ten years was a very long time to hold on to all the guilt being with Quinn had instigated within her. Maybe, at the very least, it was time to let go of that. From the way Quinn had behaved the other day, Maya could only conclude that it hadn't affected her life in an obvious negative way. On the contrary, because Quinn had been the first one to refer to their long-ago night together.

"I'm going on a date with Beverly and that's that," Maya said.

"Do you have a picture of Quinn?" Angus fixed his eyes on her.

"Why would I have her picture?"

Angus shrugged. "What's her last name? I'll Google her."

"Hathaway," Maya said on a sigh, because even though she had lightened her emotional burden by sharing her secret with Angus, she knew it would be a very long time before she heard the last of this from him. It was the price she had to pay for telling him.

"Let's have a look." Angus picked up his phone and typed in Quinn's name—an action Maya had stopped herself from doing a few times over the years. It didn't take long before Angus showed her his screen. "Is this her?" In the picture he'd found, Quinn's blond hair was pulled back into a ponytail. Her blue eyes seemed to glitter with some secret delight. All of Quinn seemed to be utterly elated about something, judging from the sparkling smile on her full lips.

Maya nodded.

"In that case, Beverly's got her work cut out for her," Angus said drily.

CHAPTER 16

Retouching the image of a person was always an intimate act, but working on Maya Mercer's picture was a never-ending flashback.

It wasn't that Quinn hadn't thought about Maya over the years. Of course she had. Quinn had reminisced about their night together often, but while doing so, she had only relied on memories. If she wanted to, she could make Maya look exactly like the memory she had of how she was ten years ago, but Quinn didn't want to do that at all. She found herself staring into Maya's dark-brown eyes for long stretches of time, not getting any work done—mesmerized by how she looked now.

The concept for the final image she wanted to create had come to her much quicker than usual. Maybe because where any other subject was concerned, Quinn had to do some hard graft to make them part of a magical looking scene while with Maya, there was something naturally spellbinding about her. In the elongation of her arm and the curve of her fingers. In the stretch of her neck and the flow of her hair. The red dress she wore in the picture lent her the aura of a proper movie star from a long-gone era.

Fucking hell, Quinn thought, as the cursor moved over Maya's face without altering anything about it once again. Maybe Griff had a point. Maybe Maya was the key to unlock Quinn's romantic future. Not in the sense that she and Maya would fall in love and live happily ever after—nothing as ludicrous as that—but in the sense that Maya turning up in Quinn's life like that, now of all times, was a golden opportunity to get double closure—for two defining experiences in her life. To look Maya in the eye again and simply have a conversation about the night they'd shared would already be a win. While doing so, Quinn could remove herself—her heart and her soul—from Morgan a few inches farther. From previous bouts of heartbreak, although none as gut-wrenching as this one, she knew all too well that getting over someone was a slow process. To get over someone like Morgan, someone she had foolishly staked her future on and had given so much of herself to, would take a very long time. Unless Quinn could find a way to speed things up. A blast from the past might be just what she needed. Something so powerful it couldn't help but snap her out of her post-Morgan funk. Because that night with Maya had been quite something.

Quinn still had no idea how she had managed to keep it a secret from every single person she knew. She hadn't even told Morgan, with whom she'd shared so much. She had told absolutely no one, simply because Maya had asked her not to. There wasn't anything else she could ever do for Maya, except keep their secret. So she'd done just that. Until she'd told Griff last night. After seeing Maya again, it was no longer an option to keep it to herself. That's what being in the same room with Maya had done to her.

Granted, over time it had become much easier to keep the

secret. If she had never seen Maya again, Quinn might have taken the memory of that night to her grave. But she had most certainly *seen* Maya. She had photographed her. She was working on her picture now—she was supposed to be anyway, when daydreaming didn't keep her from doing any actual work.

She gazed at Maya's face again and asked, "What do you think, Maya? Should we do this? Should I ask you out?"

If a repeat of that night were ever on the table, Quinn would most certainly not turn down the opportunity. She had nothing but exquisite memories of her time with Maya. From the first dive into her pool, until the last time she'd looked into her eyes. Only their goodbye had been bittersweet although Quinn knew that it was the only realistic way for things to go between them at the time. The rest of her time at home that summer had been spent pining for Maya, trying to catch a glimpse of her, to no avail. If Quinn remembered correctly, Maya had gone away in the days following their time together. It had felt like a punch to the gut. Maya had made it abundantly clear that she had already swiftly moved on from their time together.

Quinn had returned to the city while Maya was still away. She had started the next chapter of her life, a life in which her night with Maya had only been a brief interlude, a precious one, but a mere interlude nonetheless, no matter how amazing.

The sooner she finished her work, the sooner Quinn would have the perfect excuse to contact Maya. Just a little bit of patience was required. And a lot of gazing at Maya's face and body in that red dress. By the time she was finished with this, Quinn figured she'd be well acquainted with every last inch of Maya.

She took a deep breath and tried to snap herself back into

focus. Just as she was getting into the groove again, her phone buzzed with a message. The first thought at hearing the alert was as fleeting as it was ridiculous: *Could it be Maya?*

She checked her phone. Of course, it wasn't Maya. It was Morgan—again. For some reason that she was probably too cowardly to admit to herself, Quinn still hadn't blocked Morgan. Quinn still wanted to hear from her. She didn't want to delete all lines of communication because she still had so many unresolved feelings for Morgan. She stared at Morgan's message:

Can we talk please, babe? M. xo

M. She imagined the M stood for Maya, but Quinn had no history with Maya. She had one night ten years ago. With Morgan, Quinn had years to look back on. Still, the thought of Maya calling Quinn 'babe' and ending a text message with 'xo' wasn't unappealing. It was also impossible. But taking the time to indulge in her imagination was harmless enough and it was a welcome relief from the post-breakup anguish Quinn had been victim to.

She put her phone to the side and resumed her work. For the sheer hell of it, and as a way to cosmically give Morgan the finger for bailing on them after all those years, while Quinn studied the details of Maya's face, she continued to pretend it was Maya who had messaged her. It had been her first thought, after all, whereas before, her mind had always automatically landed on Morgan first.

Despite working on Maya's picture, the power of faking it soon wore off, and Quinn started to consider a reply to Morgan's message. Morgan had been a bitch, no doubt, but she was also being very persistent. What did she have to say to Quinn that hadn't already been said? Could Griff be right? Did

Morgan want her back? And if so, would Quinn even consider it? She knew she shouldn't. The only thing that could possibly make her reconsider anything was if Morgan had left her husband.

Quinn's breath stalled in her throat. Could that be the reason for Morgan's recent increased attempts at trying to reach her? Had she finally done it? And if she had—if the impossible had finally happened—could it still really make a difference four months after they'd split? Or would even that be too little too late for them?

There was only one way to find out. Quinn walked away from her computer, picked up her phone and, heart slamming against her chest, called Morgan.

CHAPTER 17

Maya had to leave in the next five minutes if she wanted to be on time for her date.

"Are you sure you don't want to stay for dinner?" Beth asked. "Mom made enough casserole to feed a few large families."

"I have dinner plans." Maya didn't even know why she was here. She'd only dropped by because she hadn't known what to do with herself. She looked into Ethan's crib. He was sleeping in that cute way babies have, his tiny fists balled and his eyes scrunched so tightly shut he looked as though he was still furious about having been born.

"Hot date?" Beth asked.

A flush crept from Maya's neck to her cheeks so she kept her gaze firmly on her sleeping grandson. "Of course not," Maya lied. "Just a friend."

"Someone I know?" Beth was pottering around the kitchen, putting Ethan's bottles in the sterilizer.

"I wouldn't think so." Maya could have lied some more and said she was meeting with someone from Acton, but she didn't want the lie to become so big she lost herself in it later. If she'd been going on a date with a man, however, she would have just told Beth without giving it any further thought. She surely would have told Beth's mother, whom she'd met for coffee earlier. Instead, because her date was a woman, she felt she couldn't tell either of them. How backward was that? Being able to date women more easily was one of the reasons she'd moved to New York City in the first place.

"Are you going to Pino's?" Beth asked, as though that was the only restaurant in all of the five boroughs Maya could possibly go to on a Saturday night.

"No." Maya finally looked up from Ethan's crib. She had considered using her daughter-in-law's name to nab an exclusive Saturday night reservation to impress her date, but Tommy and Beth were regulars at Pino's so that wasn't a risk she'd wanted to take. Instead, she'd let Beverly pick the place. She'd lived in Manhattan her entire life. "Somewhere in Midtown I haven't been before."

Maya heard the front door open and Tommy rushed in. He said a quick hello to Maya and Beth, but made a beeline for Ethan's crib before greeting his wife and mother more thoroughly.

"Try not to wake him," Beth pleaded. "It took ages before he went down properly."

Maya loved watching her son with his son. His body language seemed to transform in the steps he took from the door to Ethan's crib, from man-about-town to devoted dad.

Tommy whispered something to Ethan that Maya couldn't make out but made her heart melt regardless. Becoming a grandmother had been one of the most overwhelming experiences of her life. Maybe that was why she had stopped by Tommy and Beth's. To remind herself of all she already had in her life. To take the edge off her nerves with a dose of familiarity. To be aware that it was just a date, and she shouldn't feel too much pressure. And, perhaps, also to feel the love that she always felt at Tommy's and Beth, the unconditional love she had for her family and theirs for her.

"Hi, Mom." Tommy finally walked over. "I wasn't expecting you." He kissed Maya on the cheek before heading over to his wife and curling his arms around her waist and holding her.

"I hadn't planned on coming over, but the lure of catching a glimpse of Ethan was too hard to resist." Maya straightened her posture. "I have to run, though."

"Your mom has a hot dinner date, but she won't tell me with whom." Beth winked at Maya. If only she knew.

"What? My mother?" Tommy grinned. "Even the notion."

"Stop teasing." Maya picked up her purse. "I'll see you on Monday. Have a lovely evening." She blew them both a kiss and headed to the front door.

"You were joking, right?" Maya heard Tommy ask Beth. "I would know if my mother was seeing anyone."

With a smile on her lips, Maya exited her son's apartment.

"When I first saw you on the app," Beverly said, "I couldn't believe it." She pulled her lips into a grin. "When we matched, I thought I was the luckiest woman in all of New York." She leaned over the table a fraction. "Now that I'm sitting here with you, I'm practically beside myself." Ever since they'd gotten the awkward niceties out of the way, Beverly had become more and more of a straightforward sweet-talker. Maya didn't mind one bit.

"You're not too bad yourself," she said. Beverly might not be a knockout, but she sure was good company. She talked a mile a minute, but her trains of thought were always well articulated and easy to follow. She had two grown children.

An ex-wife. A career as an environmental lobbyist with the UN she seemed very passionate about. And she was only two years younger than Maya—an increasingly important fact since seeing Quinn again and Maya's subsequent conversation with Angus.

"You must be inundated with dating possibilities." Beverly's eyes sparkled when she looked at Maya. "Why did you choose to go out with little old me?" When she referred to herself as 'little old me' it didn't sound self-deprecating in the least.

"First of all, I'm not inundated. Let's get that fiction out of the way." Maya tilted her head slightly. She was ready to shift into a higher gear of flirting because why the hell not? "And I chose you because you appealed to me very much."

"At the risk of repeating myself, I'm very glad you did." Beverly pulled her lips into what could only be described as a seductive smile.

"You can repeat yourself all you want." Unlike the previous —and only—date Maya had gone on with a woman, she felt something stir inside of her. She really liked Beverly. She wasn't entirely sure yet whether she was physically attracted to her, but she was old and wise enough to know that she needn't worry about that yet. Maya wasn't looking for a *coup de foudre*. She was looking for something real and meaningful with a woman she could admire and have a rewarding conversation with.

"I will." Beverly took a sip of wine before locking her gaze on Maya again. "Inquiring minds want to know." Another smile. "Until you moved to the city, you've been passing for straight?"

"I wouldn't call it passing." Maya gave a nervous chuckle. "As far as I knew, I was straight."

Beverly nodded as though she understood. "But something must have happened to make you take that final leap."

"I don't feel as though I've taken any leaps just yet. I moved from the suburbs to the city, that's about it."

"That *is* a big leap and, let me assure you, you're not the first woman in her fifties to do so."

"I'm not?" Maya wondered if a city like New York, where you could find anything imaginable under the sun, would have some sort of support group for middle-aged formerly straight women.

"Of course not." Beverly grinned again. "You have no idea how many women our age are sick of men after spending decades in their company." She shrugged casually. "Not every woman is as fortunate as me to grow up knowing they're gay."

"It can't have been easy, though."

Beverly shrugged again. "It wasn't exactly hard either. My family didn't make much of an issue out of it. Don't get me wrong. It wasn't like nowadays when parents actually ask their kids if they're gay and some kids don't even have to come out of the closet anymore—which is how it should be, by the way. I still very much had to come out and there was some minor drama and the usual bullshit of 'are you sure' and 'maybe you shouldn't give up on boys entirely just yet', but, in the end, they accepted it, because what else were they going to do?"

Maya tried to imagine how her parents would have reacted if she'd told them she liked women, but it was an exercise in futility since her parents were both gone. She didn't want to attribute unearned qualities to the dead, yet she liked to think her parents wouldn't have made a huge deal of it. But what would they say if she were able to tell them about this date—if they were still alive—though? "Sorry," she said. "I was just thinking about my own parents. They'll never know I've gone on this date with a very charming woman."

"This one?" Beverly pointed at herself.

Maya nodded, a smile blooming on her lips.

"Trust me, my mother will hear all about you first thing tomorrow."

They burst into a companionable chuckle and Maya enjoyed the warmth that blossomed in her chest. Why had she waited so long to give herself this gift of going out with women? What had she been so afraid of?

"Actually," she started. "I got the first inkling I might like women about ten years ago." Maya wasn't going to divulge her indiscretion with Quinn to Beverly on the first date, but she did want to give her something of a timeline, just so she knew that Maya wasn't here on some whim. "But I've only now started telling people and doing something concrete about it."

"Since you've moved to the city?"

"Yes."

"You must have needed the time it took." There was not a hint of judgement in Beverly's tone. "And now here you are."

"Here I am." Maya was starting to warm to Beverly even more. She couldn't exactly imagine kissing her yet, but maybe in a few minutes, hours, days, or weeks, she wouldn't be able to stop imagining it. As far as she was concerned, this date with Beverly was the most promising one she'd been on since she'd started seeing the man she'd married.

CHAPTER 18

Argh, Quinn thought, why does she have to look so insanely hot? Through the window, she watched Morgan walk toward her building. She anticipated the buzz of the doorbell, which was a new experience, because, for years, Morgan had possessed a key to Quinn's apartment. It was their secret hideout place, away from prying eyes.

She waited in the doorframe for Morgan to climb the three flights of stairs. She would be slightly out of breath and look all the sexier for it.

"Hey." With a flourish, Morgan took the last two steps. She beamed Quinn a wide smile. "Fuck, it's good to see you."

Quinn quickly ushered her inside. They might have broken up, but the air of secrecy remained.

"Thanks so much for seeing me, Quinn." Morgan zipped open her leather jacket. "It's been so difficult. I miss you so much, babe." She swallowed. "Before you say anything, I know I have no right to say that. It's my fault it's over between us. But that's why I've been so desperate to talk to you." She shook her head. "If breaking up with you has taught me one thing, it's that I want to be with you more than anything."

"You could have been with me all along."

"I know. I know." Morgan rubbed her palms on her jeans. "I blew it, but..."

"Do you want something to drink? Shall we sit?" Quinn needed some time to absorb the emotional energy of having Morgan inside her home again.

"Griff's not here, is she?" Morgan asked.

"She's at work." Quinn working mostly from home had helped manage the practicalities of their affair a lot. She'd even been able to hide it from her roommate much longer than she'd thought possible, and much to Griff's dismay.

"I'd love some water, please." Morgan's voice sounded sweeter than Quinn had ever heard it.

Quinn led them into the kitchen where they sat around the tiny table that only had room for two chairs placed too close together for comfort.

"I'm going to do it," Morgan said. "I'm going to leave Steve."

Quinn knew not to get her hopes up. After all, this was hardly the first time Morgan had spoken those very words—and words came cheap. But when she looked into Morgan's face, her lips drawn into a hopeful smile, her eyes glittering with all the prospects for their future life together, it was difficult to ignore the instant joyful pitter-patter of her heart. In fact, this moment, Morgan sitting in her kitchen, so close Quinn could inhale her familiar scent, saying those very words to Quinn, came scarily close to most of the fantasies she'd indulged in over the past few months.

"Why would I believe you now?" Quinn had to ask. After what had happened, her instinct was to protect herself, even though protecting her heart had never been something that came naturally to Quinn. Being with Morgan had changed that about her. "Have you done anything to make it happen? Have you talked to him?"

"Not yet, babe." Over the small surface of the table, Morgan inched her hand closer to Quinn's elbow. "I wanted to talk to you first."

It irked Quinn that Morgan still called her 'babe', as though they were still together and the past four months of heartbreak meant nothing. "Then talk." Part of Quinn wanted to pull her elbow away from Morgan's approaching hand, but she didn't. Just as during their affair, Quinn had wanted to pull away from the madness of it, the sheer impossibility of it, many a time, but she never had. Not until their final and fatal blowout.

"I love you more than I love Steve," Morgan said. "I love you so much. I choose you, Quinn." Her fingers touched Quinn's skin. "I know I should have done so years ago and I'm sorry that I didn't." When she half-whispered like that, her voice was the epitome of sexy. "I should have taken us much more seriously from the get-go."

Quinn wanted to believe Morgan with all her heart. She wanted to drown in this serenade, in all these wonderful words Morgan was treating her to—words that would have been like the most exquisite symphony to Quinn's ears if they'd been spoken a year ago, or two years ago. Now they sounded like a bunch of false notes strung together by an amateur.

"If I understand correctly." Quinn did pull her elbow away now. "You want to hedge your bets. You want to know if I still want to be with you before you actually leave your husband."

"Is that so wrong?" The thing about Morgan was that her smooth, sugary voice could make you believe anything.

"Yes, because it's too late, *babe*." Quinn tried to ignore the tears that stung behind her eyes. "We were together for four years, Morgan. I loved you. I gave you all my attention and energy and affection, while I always had to share yours with someone else. And even after I gave you all of that for all those years, it still takes you four months after you've dumped me to figure out that I'm the one you really want? Excuse me if I don't want to buy that off the bat."

"Four absolutely grueling months."

"What do you think they've been like for me? A walk in the park?" Quinn looked up and found Morgan's eyes. "It would be different if you'd already left him."

"Come on, Quinn. You know I'm not one for big dramatic statements like that." Morgan said it so matter-of-factly, but it was so far from the truth Quinn could see through it so easily now. "Don't act as if this was all on me. No one ever forced you to give me four years of your life, to give them to a woman already married to someone else. Maybe that small detail was a little bit more convenient for you than you care to admit."

"Don't start with that bullshit now. You lied to me when you promised me you would leave Steve. That's the crux of the matter. Now you come here and tell me, *again*, that you want to leave him for me, well, you know what? Don't bother. Just stay with him. I'm not doing this with you anymore. I'm done."

"Don't say that." Morgan tried to reach for Quinn's hand, but Quinn pulled away again. "Take some time to think about it."

"Can't you see this is how it's always been between us? You with your promises and your sweet words and—" *Your sweet, sweet kisses.* Looking at Morgan's lips without kissing them profusely had always been a challenge, but not today, when they were the conduit for more of her meaningless promises. "I'm not giving you my hope anymore. I can't spend any more of my energy on wishing for a life with you."

"I know I sprung this on you, but—"

"No." Quinn shook her head vigorously. "You don't get to come here and tell me you still love me while you're still with Steve. You simply don't get to do that anymore. If you really still loved me and you really believed in a future with me, you would no longer be with him. You had four years and four months to make that decision. You don't get to make it anymore now." She pushed her chair back to put some distance between them. "It's too fucking late. You already broke my heart. And you're not the one who's going to fix it. I'll do that myself by staying away from you." Quinn surprised herself, but she also knew that if she truly valued herself and respected her own feelings, this was the only way forward. What would giving Morgan yet another chance accomplish? In her heart of hearts, she knew she had to let her go for good. This was the end. Their chance at a future had come and gone—more than once.

Morgan sat completely still. Maybe this wasn't what she had expected. But surely she hadn't thought Quinn would just take her back like that? Jump into her arms and pretend all the things that had happened between them never had? Quinn might be seventeen years Morgan's junior, but she'd often felt like the wiser one. When Morgan finally looked up, her eyes were wet with tears.

"Oh, fuck." She pushed at the moisture under her eyes with the heels of her hands. "I had my chance." She nodded slowly as though it had taken a while to process the information. "I hurt you too badly too many times." The feet of her chair scraped against the floor as she pushed it away from the table. "Now I have to pay the ultimate price."

As well as a husky voice, brooding dark eyes, and a pair of very deft hands, Morgan also had a shameless flair for the dramatic. During one of their more memorable fights, Quinn had accused Morgan of craving the sheer drama that an extra-marital affair entailed. Morgan might have denied it in words, but she'd remained as addicted to drama as ever. Quinn wondered where she'd found the energy all those years to deal with it. And, right now, it was crystal clear that this was over. That despite her feelings for Morgan, and the hurt she felt because she was no longer in her life, she didn't want to do this any longer.

Morgan rose. "Bye, babe," she said. "I hope—" But she never finished her sentence and Quinn would never know what it was Morgan hoped for, because she turned around abruptly and exited the apartment.

CHAPTER 19

On Sunday afternoon, Maya was telling Angus how lovely her date with Beverly had been, when her phone buzzed.

"No doubt she's already missing you," Angus said. He seemed to have warmed to Beverly after Maya had told him about how kind and wonderful she'd been in real life.

"It's probably Tommy," Maya said with confidence because it usually was. Still, there was a slight chance it was Beverly. They had agreed to go on another date sooner rather than later, possibly next weekend. Maybe Beverly was texting because she couldn't wait to set it up.

But when Maya checked her phone, the message she'd just received was neither from Tommy nor Beverly. It was from Quinn.

I haven't finished work on your picture yet, but I was thinking about you. Do you have time for coffee sometime this week? Quinn

Maya had barely read the first message when a second one came in.

You can tell me all about your date. ;-)

"What's that all about?" Angus asked. "Judging by that grin you can barely hold back, it must be some exciting news."

"It's Quinn." Maya didn't know what to make of Quinn's message—nor about Angus' comment about that grin. As far as she knew, she'd kept her face perfectly expressionless.

"Ooh. What does hot girl want?" Angus had a naturally energetic voice but now he sounded as though he'd swallowed a bolt of lightning.

"To go for coffee and to ask how my date went."

"How very *sweet* of her." He all but slapped his thigh. "She probably wants to know what she's up against."

"What are you talking about?" Maya looked at the messages on her screen again.

"Don't play dumb with me, dear. We've had this conversation before, remember? I'm only reminding you because you seem to conveniently want to forget about it although I don't quite understand why."

"We seem to have drawn totally opposite conclusions from the conversation." Was Angus really insinuating Quinn wanted to date Maya—and vice versa?

"What are you going to reply?" Angus ignored Maya's admonishing completely. He was very skilled at only hearing what he wanted to hear.

"I don't know yet. I need to think about it."

"Aaah, come on, throw an old fellow a bone." He flashed her a wide smile. "You know I don't get out much anymore, and right now you're my window to the very exciting outside world."

Maya rolled her eyes in a way that could rival Angus' impressive eye-rolling expertise. "You're so theatrical.

Honestly. Thanks, by the way, for reducing me to your entertainment of the day."

"I don't mean it like that, Maya. Come on." He pursed his lips. "I'm not going to lie. Since you moved into the building, you've brightened up my life considerably. It's not every day a gorgeous lady like yourself moves in across the hall. I can't help it that I knew we would be great friends from the very first time you rounded the corner in those bright-red Louboutins."

Despite herself, Maya had to chuckle. She felt the same way about Angus—minus the shoes—and especially during her first few weeks in the city he'd been an equally bright spot in her day, always there to cheer her up with a hilarious observation that took her mind off the insecurities that came with such a big life change. Angus made her laugh and their banter acted as a reminder to not take herself too seriously.

She took a sip of coffee, which reminded her of Quinn's suggestion they go for coffee. At least she wasn't suggesting cocktails.

"How would *you* reply to Quinn's message?" Maya was throwing Angus a big juicy bone by asking him that.

He nodded as though he was giving it a great deal of thought. "It's just coffee," he said, after a while. "Maybe you can be friends."

Maya shook her head. "Bring back the real Angus, please."

Angus broke into a huge, toothy smile. "Don't overthink it, Maya. Just say yes already. You and I both know you want to."

When she was back in her own apartment, Maya sat with her phone in her hands. She still hadn't replied. She decided to follow Angus' advice and started typing.

Coffee sounds good. My date went very well, thanks for asking.

She erased the last sentence. It didn't feel right to give Quinn that information. Before she pressed 'Send', she added:

How about Tuesday?

Maya had barely had time to take a breath before the reply came in.

I'm doing a shoot in the afternoon, but I'm free in the evening. Shall we make it drinks or dinner instead?

Maya expelled a small sigh. The last text reminded her very much of the Quinn of ten years ago—of the person she'd spent that passionate night with. This was New York, where coffee houses were open twenty-four seven. It wasn't because Quinn was only free in the evening that coffee—which had a different connotation to it than drinks, and most certainly than dinner—had to be replaced with cocktails. On the other hand, Maya had already agreed to coffee, so why the hell not go for a drink later in the day instead? *Don't overthink it*, she repeated Angus' words in her head. Just do it. She agreed to drinks on Tuesday evening. As they were discussing a time and place, another text message came in.

I know I said it last night, but I just have to repeat myself (again): I had a lovely time with you. Are you free for dinner sometime this week? Beverly. xo

Maya let a smile curl up her lips. Wasn't this why she had moved here? To discover her true self, although she didn't think she had that much discovering left to do. The absence of female romantic interests in her life hadn't made her less aware of what it was she really wanted—on the contrary. But there had always been something holding Maya back. Until now. Maya ended the text conversation with Quinn and focused on Beverly.

While they exchanged messages, and she waited for a reply, Maya wondered what she would have been doing on an ordinary Sunday afternoon back in Milbury. She wouldn't have gone on a date to a glitzy restaurant with another woman the night before. She wouldn't have been texting with Quinn Hathaway because she'd never have run into her on a photo shoot for work. And it wasn't very likely that she would have been setting up a second date with another woman for next Friday. For the first time since she'd moved to the city, Maya felt more like a woman in her prime, a woman who turned heads, a woman desired by others, than she felt like a grandmother.

As she and Beverly texted some flirty niceties back and forth—Beverly much more forward than Maya—Maya's thoughts skipped back to her earlier text conversation with Quinn.

Did she have to tell Beverly about Quinn? Was there some sort of moral code of dating that she had to adhere to? She didn't think so because she and Quinn weren't going on an actual date. Or was she just fooling herself into thinking that? Maya guessed she would find out on Tuesday.

CHAPTER 20

The only reason Quinn had texted Maya on Sunday, long before she'd finished her project and thus before she had agreed with herself that she could, was that Morgan's visit had frustrated her so much. Quinn had wanted to take her mind off Morgan and the easiest and quickest way to do so at the time had been by texting Maya.

Maya had been on her mind. Not only because Quinn had been working on her portrait non-stop, but because of what she stood for and, even more so, because of how she'd once made Quinn feel. Quinn surely wouldn't mind feeling like that again, even though it seemed impossible with the cloud of Morgan hanging over her head.

When Maya had texted back and had agreed to go out with her—for drinks, not just coffee—Quinn had been slightly beside herself. She was meeting Maya at a swanky bar close to Acton Academy. Even though she'd had to travel all the way to the Upper East Side during rush hour, Quinn didn't mind one bit.

When she arrived at the bar, Maya was already there. She was dressed in a navy pants suit that made her look more like a business woman than a dance teacher. She slipped off her tall chair and greeted Quinn with the warmest of smiles and a friendly kiss on the cheek.

"Thanks for meeting me." Quinn sat opposite Maya. When she tried to look her in the eye, Quinn found it difficult, which puzzled her. She wasn't usually one to look away.

"It's my pleasure. That's one reason I moved to New York: to go for after-work drinks with, uh... old and new friends." She pushed the drinks menu in Quinn's direction.

Quinn was happy to direct her attention to the menu. What was going on with her? If she'd known she would feel like this, she might not have pushed for meeting Maya. She could hardly focus on the drinks list. "What are you having?" The lack of confidence in her tone of voice was another unexpected worry.

"Guess." Maya said.

Quinn looked up and her gaze stalled at the low opening of Maya's white blouse, exposing more than just her neck. "I honestly have no idea."

"Are you okay?" Maya sounded genuinely troubled. "You look a bit... I don't know. Not like yourself, I guess."

"I've had a weird couple of days." A server came by to take their order.

When Maya asked for a manhattan, Quinn ordered the same, even though she liked her cocktails much fruitier.

"How silly is it of me to get a thrill out of ordering a manhattan in Manhattan?" Unlike Quinn, Maya sounded much more casual than the last time they'd seen each other. Maybe because the shock of being confronted with a very particular night in her past had worn off and she could now see Quinn as a possible friend—an old and new one at the same time.

"Utterly adorable is what it is." Quinn's trepidation was ebbing away at the sight of Maya's easy demeanor.

"Why are you so out of sorts?" Maya cut to the chase.

Quinn could hardly admit to Maya that seeing her again, dressed up like that, made her feel all funny inside. "Just stuff with my ex." Surely, Maya hadn't dressed like that for Quinn's benefit? If she had, Quinn might start feeling even funnier.

"Ah," was all Maya said.

"I don't really want to get into it, even though in a weird roundabout way, she's the reason I texted you."

"How so?"

Oh, shit. Quinn hadn't meant to admit that either. She was seriously off her game tonight. She blamed Morgan for that as well. "It's kind of hard to explain but, well, I guess I just really felt like seeing you again."

"Here I am." Maya sounded as though, in the space of a week, she'd really found her feet in the city. Maybe it was the date she'd been on. Maybe she was smitten. Quinn didn't really want to consider how she felt about that.

"So your date went well?" Quinn might as well get that topic out of the way. It wasn't that she didn't wish Maya well. Of course, she did. But aside from feeling a little off, Quinn also detected a few pangs of jealousy running through her.

"Beverly and I had a lovely time."

Quinn perked up her ears for any change in Maya's tone when she spoke of Beverly. She couldn't immediately detect any, but she was hardly an expert on the inflections in Maya's voice. "That's wonderful."

"I feel a touch bad talking about my successful date when you're still so down in the dumps about Morgan."

Quinn waved off Maya's comment. "I asked you about it and I'm not that depressed. We had a frustrating altercation that mostly reminded me of all the reasons it's actually a good thing we broke up. So, please, feel free to tell me all about Beverly."

The server arrived with their drinks. Quinn could do with a quick sip or two.

"To old and new friends." Maya raised her glass and Quinn clinked hers against it.

"Griff almost went berserk when I told her Tommy's married to Beth Robbins." Quinn seized the opportunity to change the subject.

"Really?"

"She's kind of a news junkie. CNN is the preferred background noise at Casa Griffin-Hathaway."

"It's funny. To me, Beth's just Beth. Tommy met her in college, long before she started presenting the news."

"Tommy didn't do too badly for himself then."

"Whenever he didn't feel like it, I always assured him he would thank me for being such an accomplished dancer later and guess what? Mom was right."

Quinn was relieved they could share their first genuine laugh of the evening. She'd needed that much more than a sip of liquor. The stiffness in her spine gave way a little.

"Beth's lovely, in case you're wondering. She works long hours, though. Ethan was barely two months old when she went back to work." Maya shook her head. "But I realized years ago there's no point telling young people that they shouldn't work themselves into such a frenzy. Tommy and Beth don't listen to me when it comes to that. At least Ethan has two very doting grandmothers. Between Belinda and me, I think we might end up raising that boy."

"That should make for another excellent dancer in the Mercer family." Quinn loved how Maya lit up even more when she talked about her family.

"You should have seen their wedding dance." A radiant

smile burst onto Maya's face. "I couldn't believe it when Tommy came to me for help."

"How long have they been married?"

"It'll be three years soon."

"Three years? Tommy was only twenty-five when he married Beth?" Quinn had never before in her life felt old, let alone past her prime, but she did now. Compared to Tommy, who was married to Beth freaking Robbins, Quinn was a loser at all things romance, what with her four-year affair with a married woman just having ended.

"He was nineteen when they met. They hardly rushed into it."

"And you get the joys of being a super young grandmother." *And a super hot one.*

Maya nodded. "I should probably tell Tommy and Beth about, um, me dating women soon. It's like a reverse coming out."

"That's not what you said last week."

"I know, but... things can change quickly in this city." A soft smile bloomed on Maya's lips.

"Your date went *that* well?"

"It's not just how the date went or how lovely Beverly is." Maya peered into her cocktail glass. "I stopped by Tommy's before I met up with Beverly and I felt like a fraud keeping something like that from the people I love the most. It didn't sit right with me."

"Just tell them, Maya. What have you got to lose?"

"It's surprisingly difficult to defy your child's expectations of you like that. Tommy might never see me the same way again."

"I'm trying to imagine Mom or Dad telling me they're gay, but I can't really see it," Quinn said.

Maya chuckled. "Oh, god. Can you imagine Brooke

coming out to you?"

"It's not possible. My mom, she's..." Quinn could only shake her head.

"Did she know about you and Morgan?"

"She knew about her, but for obvious reasons Morgan never accompanied me to Thanksgiving or Christmas at home. She had her own family to be with."

"That must have been hard."

Only a permanent state of semi-broken-heartedness, Quinn thought. But she hadn't come here to wallow in self-pity so she kept that thought to herself. "It was my own choice also." She waggled her eyebrows. "According to Morgan, the situation was quite convenient for me as well. I still don't really get what she meant by that."

"She was probably just lashing out." Maya tilted her head. "Or do you think it was part of the attraction?"

"I don't know." Quinn shook her head. "I'll figure it out some time."

Maya shot her a soft smile. "I've always remembered something you told me ten years ago. I don't know why it has stuck with me, but it has." Maya paused. "You said you couldn't afford a therapist to figure out your mommy issues."

"Oh Christ." Quinn gave an embarrassed chuckle. "Did I really say that?"

Maya nodded.

"I must have said a lot of things that weekend."

"It wasn't really so much about what you said, but how you paraded around my garden in that skimpy bikini."

"I was young and reckless back then." Quinn could feel how the conversation was taking a turn—very much in the direction she wanted it to go. She hoped to be fully back on her game soon. "That being said, ten years down the line, given the chance, I'd do exactly the same."

Maya cast her a quick glance, then looked away. She took a sip, then cut her eyes back to Quinn. "Since seeing you, more memories have been coming back to me. Like that tattoo on your belly." Maya looked at the tattoos on Quinn's wrists.

"Even though I was still quite young when I got that one, I've never regretted it for one second."

"A great topic of conversation, I imagine."

"Not just conversation." Quinn circled a finger over the rim of her glass.

"Can I get you any more drinks, ladies?" The server had appeared out of nowhere at the worst possible moment.

Maya studied her empty glass, then looked at Quinn. Quinn waited for Maya's lead.

"Why not," Maya said and beamed the server a wide smile. "Quinn?"

"Same, please." Quinn didn't care about the fruitiness of her cocktail any longer. She just wanted to get back to their conversation. But when the server had gone, so had the intensity of what they'd been saying before. A short silence fell.

"You're dressed very formally tonight." Quinn took the opportunity to inspect Maya's perfectly tailored suit again.

"We had a parents thing at the academy earlier for which we were asked to dress 'businesslike'." Maya sat up a little straighter and pulled at the hem of her sleeve.

"Businesslike agrees with you."

"Thank you." For the first time, Maya looked her straight in the eye. It was a look Quinn could most certainly work with.

CHAPTER 21

Maya gazed into Quinn's blue eyes. What was it about her that obliterated every last one of Maya's boundaries as though they might as well not exist? And why-oh-why did it feel a million times more exciting to sit across from Quinn than it did from Beverly?

Maya couldn't answer any of these questions. Not now, not since the image of Quinn's lower belly tattoo had settled itself at the forefront of her mind again.

Quinn seemed a touch less forward than last week, and yet, Maya could hardly bear to look away from her. The fast-forward button had been pressed on her life since she'd run into Quinn again. She had taken her sweet time getting her bearings in New York, but now, it seemed, it was high time for some sort of action.

"Do you have any other new tattoos?" Maya heard herself ask Quinn. It wasn't that she didn't want to know the answer to that question—she did. But part of her still felt she shouldn't be asking questions like that.

Quinn nodded slowly. "I sure do."

"Not in any visible places?" Quinn was wearing a long-sleeved blouse of which the cuffs covered the tattoos on her wrists.

"Correct."

"Pity I no longer have a swimming pool." Had Maya's manhattan been spiked? What on earth was she saying? Quinn had only been flirting a little bit earlier, almost innocently, but referring to the pool Maya used to have was hardly innocent.

Quinn gave a low chuckle. "That's a damn shame, indeed." Her gaze drifted sideways and an instant later their new cocktails arrived.

After they'd clinked rims, Quinn asked, "After I left your house that morning, do you remember what was going through your head?"

Maya had to take a sip before she could reply. "My mind was all over the place. So much so I changed the date of my trip to Puerto Rico so I could leave earlier. I didn't know what to do with myself because a large part of me was disgusted by what I had allowed to happen, while the other part of me..." She huffed out some air. "The other part of me wanted to do it all over again."

"Disgusted?" Quinn sounded appalled. "Why would you be disgusted by it? What we did, what we so briefly had between us, was fucking beautiful, Maya."

"Maybe from your point of view. You were the carefree twenty-four-year-old who was home for the summer and managed to seduce her neighbor. I was the older woman who had ended up in bed with someone much too young for me *and* of the same gender."

"If you put it that way."

"How would you put it?" Maya had suffered through enough guilt to last her a lifetime. She was more than ready for a different perspective.

"I had the night of my life." Quinn sunk her front teeth into her bottom lip for an instant. "While I understood your reasons, I was pretty crushed when all of a sudden you were gone. Honestly, that night... even after all this time, it's still the stuff a lot of my dreams are made of."

That had been the thing about Quinn back then and it was still very much the thing about her now. She always knew exactly what to say. At least she did where Maya was concerned. There was something about Quinn that Maya couldn't help but react to, especially when she spoke to her like that—as though Maya really was the woman of her dreams.

"Surely you've had much more spectacular nights since."

"I can't say that I have," Quinn said. "Because that night was something special. The circumstances made it so. *You* made it so. God, Maya, you... just blew my mind. I don't just mean when we were in bed, but how you were with me in general. The way we talked and flirted and how you responded to the things I said and did. There was something about it, something special that I will always cherish."

Maya took her time sipping her drink. Despite all the guilt and shame it had caused her, she had also known that night had been exceptional, but Maya had always believed that to be because her circumstances had been so different than Quinn's, who still had so much of her life ahead of her, who still had so many women to meet. She wanted very badly to believe what Quinn had just said but took it with a pinch of salt nonetheless. Because, over time, memories get distorted and can turn into emotional events of which the accuracy fades and the associated feelings become amplified. Still, Maya was flattered by what Quinn had just confided in her.

"There *was* something special about it," Maya confirmed. "Something I forced myself to forget about."

"God, Maya. If I had one wish it's that you hadn't felt so badly about it afterward. Life's for living, not for the energy-consuming, useless activity of feeling guilty. Fuck guilt. Really." Quinn narrowed her eyes and something close to a grin appeared on her face. "I might have something along those lines tattooed in a..." She paused, injecting the air with suspense. "...rather intimate spot."

If it was Quinn's objective to have Maya longing to see that particular tattoo right there and then she was succeeding.

Maya drank again. What else was she going to do? This was why, she now knew, when saying goodbye to Quinn last week, she had made herself believe that they wouldn't see each other again. Paradoxically, it was the same reason Maya was sitting here with Quinn tonight, their conversation quickly descending into a deep flirt. Maya hadn't been able to resist her years ago and something told her that she wouldn't be able to resist now either.

Quinn slanted her body into Maya's direction. "But I want it on record that I'm not going to seduce you again, Maya. I'll happily take credit for doing so ten years ago, when I only cared about myself and my twenty-something urges, which were greatly satisfied." She inserted a smile that disappeared as quickly as it had come. "It's not that I don't want to, but it's just not something that I'm going to do again."

Quinn might as well have given Maya the sexiest of lingering kisses. She might as well have disrobed and shown Maya her latest tattoo. She might be claiming to not want to seduce Maya again but with those words, that was precisely what she was doing.

"Why not?" Maya had no choice but to play along.

"What if I cause you another ten years of guilt?" She sounded much more serious all of a sudden.

"What if you don't?" Maya quipped.

"That's not up to me, though."

Maya had a choice. She was still sane enough, still sober enough, to decide between taking a deep breath and walking away or, as Quinn would say it, to live her life. To live the life she wanted to live which, right now, could only mean one thing: bridge the distance between them and kiss Quinn on the lips.

"You're right," Maya said. "That's entirely up to me." She gazed into Quinn's eyes again, into those soft oceans of blue—the same color as the water in Maya's former pool. "And so is this." Maya closed her eyes then and, not caring one iota that they were in a bar close to her place of work, leaned toward Quinn, and kissed her.

The instant their lips touched, it felt like someone had flipped on the electricity in a long-vacated building. The kiss was soft and short, but powerful enough to leave Maya wanting so much more—to choose anything but the darkness she'd been plunged into for far too long.

Quinn flicked her tongue over her lower lip before she shot Maya a smile. She didn't say a word but her gaze was full of meaning.

"Do you want to come back to my place for some, um, dinner?" Maya asked, even though it wasn't food she was hungry for.

Quinn nodded. "I still owe you a dinner, by the way."

Maya took a few quick sips of her manhattan. "You don't owe me a single damn thing, Quinn."

CHAPTER 22

Quinn had wanted this more than anything, she realized as she stood in the elevator with Maya, but this was not her doing, which made it all the more enthralling. She had flirted and had initiated a first, very tentative move, but she certainly hadn't expected Maya to kiss her in the bar.

Upon arrival at Maya's, first the door of the cab had been opened for her, followed by the front door of the building. This was a swankiness Quinn wasn't used to. Her friends didn't live in buildings with doormen who pressed the elevator button for you. She and Griff lived in a fourth-floor walk-up that left them breathless every time they climbed the stairs.

"Are you hungry?" Maya flicked on the lights.

Quinn whistled through her teeth. "How much was that dance school of yours worth?" she blurted out at the sight of Maya's apartment.

"Enough," Maya said. "It's not as big as it looks and certainly a whole lot smaller than my house in Milbury."

"Remind me to never invite you to my place." Quinn followed Maya into the kitchen.

Maya opened the fridge. "I have leftover quiche from last night."

"Maya." Quinn could look at Maya, in her elegant suit, sauntering through her kitchen all night long, but there was something else she wanted more. "I'm not hungry."

"We had those cocktails. We should eat something." Maya kept staring into the fridge, as though she was afraid to turn around and face Quinn now that they were in the privacy of her home. Now that their options to do certain things had multiplied.

"Maya," Quinn repeated. "Will you look at me?"

Quinn watched Maya's shoulders go up and down as she took a deep breath. She closed the fridge and turned around.

"I don't know what it is about you." Maya put her hands on the edge of the kitchen island. "It was never my intention to kiss you. To invite you over."

"Do you want me to leave?" A knot formed in Quinn's stomach.

"Fuck no." Maya held out her hands. "I want you to come here."

Quinn walked over to her but kept a small distance between them. She pulled the side of her blouse out of her jeans and hiked it up. "Read this." She pointed at the tattoo that ran along the side of her torso.

"*Life is for living,*" Maya said as she read. "You actually have that tattooed on your body?"

"I do."

"Does it make a difference?" Maya reached out her hand and ran a finger over Quinn's side. "In your life?"

"I'm here with you now, so what do you think?" Goose bumps popped under Maya's finger.

"Fair enough." Maya chuckled. "Do you have any others?"

Quinn nodded. "I told you they were in a more intimate spot."

"You did." Maya pulled her finger away. "Look, Quinn... I don't really know what to say. Frankly, I'm not so sure how we ended up here, but—"

"We're here because we want to be." She took a step closer, leaving barely an inch of space between them. "Isn't that more than enough?"

"You..." Maya took hold of Quinn's hand. "What am I going to do about you?" She locked her gaze on Quinn's.

"I'm not an issue you have to deal with," Quinn whispered as she leaned in. "But you could start by kissing me again." She didn't wait for Maya to bridge the final gap this time, but pressed her lips against Maya's.

As soon as their lips touched, Maya placed her hands on Quinn's cheeks, pulling her closer.

As though she'd been starved of another woman's touch for much longer than the four months since Morgan had left her, Quinn latched on to Maya. She remembered how uncharacteristically nervous she'd been when she'd entered the bar and seen Maya sitting there all done up and glamorous with that air of unattainability to her that drove Quinn crazy. Quinn was no longer the girl who believed, without much doubt, that she could get anything or anyone she wanted. Life might be for living, but living taught you some harsh lessons along the way. That she stood here in Maya's kitchen, losing herself in kiss after scorching kiss, was nothing short of a miracle.

"Come," Maya whispered when they broke from their kiss, and took Quinn's hand. She pulled her into a short hallway, right into her bedroom. As though Quinn finally had full permission to let it all wash over her, memories from when she'd stood in Maya's bedroom ten years ago flooded her brain. She couldn't wait to see what Maya looked like now underneath that suit. She couldn't wait to see how she would respond to her touch. Quinn had still been so inexperienced back then, although, at the time, she'd been convinced she knew it all.

Maya shrugged out of her jacket and draped it over the back of a chair. She kicked off her shoes and sat at the foot of the bed, as though she needed to take a breather. Maybe she did.

Quinn kneeled next to her. "Are you all right?"

"I want you so badly, I can barely believe it, but that doesn't mean I'm not ambivalent about it."

"That's understandable." Quinn did understand because, unlike ten years ago, she now wondered if she had to protect her own fragile heart in this situation. Her heart that had just been broken into a thousand pieces. She, too, had to take a moment to question what this was.

Maybe they both wanted to relive the spark they'd shared between them all those years ago, for their own reasons. One thing Quinn knew for sure: that spark was still there and then some. Time and reason had not erased it. She'd known that from the second she'd laid eyes on Maya again. Whether they should act on it was another matter altogether. But they'd made that decision earlier in the bar. The biggest difference with ten years ago was that it could no longer be attributed to a moment of temporary madness, an almost innocent act, even, without consequences. They weren't the same people they'd been back then. Everything was different now.

"You really are doing your best not to seduce me." Maya smiled down at her and Quinn melted under her gaze.

Quinn shook her head, pushed herself up, and kissed

Maya again. Because when they kissed, all lingering doubts were instantly erased. When they touched, any remaining doubt evaporated, and Quinn knew exactly why she was here. To make love to Maya Mercer.

CHAPTER 23

Quinn's half-naked body pressed against Maya's side. Quinn's lips were all over her, kissing their way from Maya's neck to her breasts and then back up again.

"Before things get too heated," Quinn whispered in her ear.

"Before?" Maya asked, barely still able to catch her breath.

Quinn pushed herself up and looked at her, a wide grin on her lips. She nodded, as if to say that merely taking off a few items of clothing was nothing compared to what was to come. Maya had always remembered how confident Quinn had been that night. A lot of things about her might have changed in ten years, but Quinn still had that same air of bedroom confidence about her.

"Do you have any lube?" Quinn asked, as casually as if asking for a glass of water.

Maya's cheeks flushed but she guessed it would barely be visible because of the semi-darkness of her bedroom and because her skin had already been worked into a healthy blush. "In the bottom drawer of the nightstand." Maya might not have a flourishing sex life with other people, but she knew how to take care of herself and lube had become indispensable for that purpose.

"Okay. Good." Quinn's eyes sparkled. "Everything's better with lube."

Maya chuckled. She was still a little too bashful to openly acquiesce, although she figured she might wholeheartedly agree with Quinn later. "I have a question for you."

"Shoot."

Maya had caught a glimpse of them earlier when she'd taken Quinn's clothes off, but it had only left her wanting more. "Show me all of your tattoos," Maya whispered. "Before things get too heated."

"You have my full permission to discover them." Quinn fell onto her back. Maya pushed herself up so she could explore Quinn's body.

First, she had to see the tattoo on her lower belly again—the one that had haunted some of her more feverish dreams over the years. She pushed the waistband of Quinn's panties down a fraction and there it was. *Your secret's safe with me.* Maya's secret had most certainly been safe with Quinn all these years. She ran her finger over it the way she had done ten years ago and, for an instant, it was as if time folded in on itself and she was back in her old bedroom on that hot summer night. She was that woman she'd been back then, stealing a night of passion with the neighbors' daughter. Back then, she'd never have believed she'd one day see that particular tattoo again, yet here she was, running a finger over it. Quinn's belly tensed under her touch—a sensation even more divine than seeing the tattoo again.

Next, Maya focused her attention on the side of Quinn's torso, on the tattoo that said: *Life is for living.* It was far less cryptic than her other one. Maybe because she had acquired it later in her life, when she was older. Still, Maya was much older than Quinn and she could definitely do with a daily reminder to just live her life. How had Quinn figured this out at such a young age?

Maya wasn't in the mood to answer philosophical questions like that. What she wanted more than anything was to discover Quinn's other tattoo. She figured she'd need to shuffle downward a bit. She ran her hand from Quinn's side to her lower belly again, then along her hip to her inner thigh. Maya had noticed something there earlier when Quinn had taken off her jeans.

Quinn spread her legs and propped herself up on her elbows. She probably wanted to witness Maya's charting of all her body art.

Maya had to bend over a little to read what the small, curly text said on Quinn's right inner thigh.

You take me to, Maya made out. Her gaze continued along Quinn's panties. She had to turn her body so she could read the text that continued on Quinn's left inner thigh.

A breathless place.

Maya didn't know what to make of it intellectually but on a baser, much more primal level, seeing those words inked into Quinn's flesh ignited something in her. The desire to trace her lips over those particular patches of Quinn's skin, definitely, but Quinn's tattoos seemed like such an elemental part of her, seemed to contribute to the person she was, made her special —then and now—and it made something unfurl deep inside of Maya.

She looked up at Quinn's face. There was something almost triumphant in her gaze, as if having those tattoos, having chosen the words and the part of her skin where they would be etched forever, gave her an edge. As if she knew they made her more desirable to Maya. Or maybe that was just what Maya was reading into it.

"Come here," Quinn beckoned her.

She scooped up Quinn's wrist—the one that had *Acceptance* tattooed on it—and pressed her lips against the dark letters before moving closer to Quinn.

Of course, Maya wanted to ask what all her tattoos meant and why she had gotten them, but that could wait. Unlike last time, she didn't know if there would be a morning after—because, this time, the possibility was there. Maya didn't know anything, except for one thing: she wanted Quinn. Being with Quinn, or a woman like Quinn, hadn't been the reason she'd moved to the city, but here she was, in her new home, with Quinn in all her glory in her bed. Sometimes, life threw you a curveball like that.

Quinn pulled Maya closer and kissed her again and again, soon making Maya forget where she was at all.

Quinn came to lie on top of her again, her skin hot against Maya's. Her hands danced from her hair to her breasts to all the spots on Maya's skin that mirrored the locations of Quinn's tattoos—all very sensitive spots, as it turned out. Surely that was no coincidence. Unlike all those years ago, Maya burned to know more about Quinn, to find out who she really was, who life had turned her into. She didn't just want Quinn's hands all over her; she wanted to talk to her, get to know her, laugh with her and, more than anything, dance with her.

"You're so fucking hot, Maya," Quinn whispered in her ear just as her hand drifted between Maya's legs.

Maya spread for her. Her skin had felt on fire for a long time, but now her clit was throbbing hard, aching for Quinn's touch as well. Maya let her own hands roam freely over Quinn's body, caressing her gorgeous breasts, her voluptuous ass. She couldn't get enough of the feel of Quinn against her hands, of her soft skin against her own—making Maya wonder why she had felt so guilty for so long about something as beautiful as this.

"I'm going to get the lube out," Quinn whispered in Maya's ear. Before she did, she kissed Maya slow and long on the lips. Tonight, it felt as though they had the luxury of time.

When Quinn leaned away from her to open the nightstand drawer, Maya took a deep breath. When Quinn took a little too long for her liking, she found herself clawing for her, pulling her on top of her again.

"Got it." Quinn flipped the lid and put the tube on Maya's other side. She kissed Maya again, while her hand meandered down between Maya's legs again, her fingers featherlight against Maya's nether lips, carefully avoiding the ticking time bomb of her aching clit.

Maya got so lost in Quinn's touch and even more so in her long, lingering, heavenly kisses, that she missed the moment Quinn squirted lube onto her hand. All she knew was that, all of a sudden, Quinn's fingers against her were wet and slippery and ready for something more than the divine caresses she'd been bestowing onto Maya.

The addition of the lube heightened Maya's senses. Her skin tingled. The heat in her belly intensified. Quinn broke their kiss and looked her in the eyes as her fingers dipped lower and deeper, until those same fingers were inside Maya.

Maya gasped for air. Quinn held her fingers completely still as she kept staring into Maya's eyes.

Maya thought she might melt under Quinn's gaze.

Then Quinn moved her fingers. Gently at first, until there was nothing gentle about it anymore. As if Quinn had known much more than Maya knew about her body and what she wanted in that moment. Quinn fucked her until all Maya saw on the backs of her closed eyelids were bright shooting stars.

Maya had no idea what acrobatics Quinn was performing

with her hand, but while moving deeply and satisfyingly inside her, she also managed to stimulate Maya's clit in a way that made her arousal skyrocket. Maybe this was ten years of pent-up lust. Ten years of hankering for another woman's touch—or maybe just Quinn's touch. Maya had no way of knowing in that moment. All she knew, as Quinn touched her so deftly, so tantalizingly, as though her fingers had found their exquisite final destination, was that she was coming at the hands of Quinn Hathaway once again, and she wouldn't be getting enough of that explosive sensation any time soon.

CHAPTER 24

How an evening could turn. How it could impact your thoughts, your actions, and possibly, ultimately, the course of your life. Quinn could hardly wrap her head around how, just moments ago, her fingers had been deep inside of Maya, and Maya had cried out her name as she clamped onto Quinn, and her fingers, for what seemed like dear life.

One thing was for sure. Morgan could not be further from her mind, because Quinn's brain was suffused with all things Maya, who was still as gorgeous and elegant as ever. And as willing to play along.

"Jesus," Maya said, as she pulled Quinn against her. "I can't believe you just did that to me again."

Just maybe, Quinn thought, as she nuzzled her lips against the warm skin of Maya's neck, there had been more between them that night than they had allowed themselves to admit. If the passage of ten years, ten years of life lived to the fullest—at least for Quinn—hadn't been enough to erase that spark between them, then what ever could?

"I did clearly state earlier that I wasn't going to seduce you," Quinn said. "So this is all your doing."

Maya wrapped her arms around Quinn. "Believe what you want to," she said. "I'll always know the truth."

"Which is?" Quinn asked.

"That you still have the hots for your neighbor, even after all these years."

Quinn chuckled as she felt Maya's body convulse with laughter against hers. "I plead guilty to the hundredth degree." Quinn ran a finger over Maya's belly. "Are you going to kick me out again in the morning?" *Oops.* Surely that was the wrong question at the wrong time. Quinn found Maya's ear. "Forget I asked. It doesn't matter right now."

"It's a fair enough question." Maya pushed herself away from Quinn a little. She looked her in the eye. "You will have to leave at some point."

"But not to go back to my parents' house this time around."

"You do know I never meant to hurt you, Quinn." Maya took her hand and pressed a soft kiss to her knuckle. "There was just no other way."

"I know." Of course, Quinn knew. "I shouldn't have brought that up just now. I'm sorry."

"It must be on your mind. It's on mine too." Maya's voice was soft, unthreatening, and very sexy. "For now, though, why don't we just let this be what it is."

"And what is it to you?"

"Two old friends having a gay old time." Maya's eyes narrowed as she lifted Quinn's wrist to her lips and kissed the inside of it.

While it was impossible to ignore the history they had together, Quinn was more than happy to just let things run their course, because her skin was flushing with excitement, and Maya's kisses weren't helping to subdue her desire. She pulled Maya close again, her hands getting lost in her luscious mane of hair, as she kissed Maya's lips. As she pressed her body against Maya's, against the heat of her skin, Quinn's knee pushed in between Maya's legs again, because she couldn't help herself. Maya drove her a little wild in a way that rarely happened to her. Maybe because part of her felt like she needed to make the most of it—that this, once again, could be over before it had well and truly begun.

Maya pushed until Quinn toppled onto her back so she could let her hands roam across Quinn's skin. Her fingertips caressed the outside of Quinn's breast.

Quinn's nipple hardened with need. She gazed down, at the trajectory of Maya's hand. She loved watching Maya's hand, that nimble extension to her ever-graceful arms. Her fingertips circled Quinn's nipple and Quinn let out a groan. She didn't know how much more of this she could stand even though Maya had just begun. But that wasn't entirely correct. They might only have been lying in Maya's bed for a short while, but the flirting had started last week, and a whole lot of that flirting was rooted in something that had happened years ago.

At times, over the years, Quinn had indulged herself and allowed her mind to wander to thoughts of Maya. She imagined her walking barefoot by the side of the pool. She envisioned her dancing and, while doing so, looking deep into Quinn's eyes, an inviting smile on her lips. She had even pictured Maya's hands doing the very thing they were doing now: playing with Quinn, arousing her. Elevating her need for Maya with every flick of her wrist. Though potent enough for Quinn's goals at the time, those fantasies had been just that. This was the real deal. It was all so unbelievable that Quinn buried her hands in Maya's hair, dug her own fingertips into the flesh of Maya's back, to ascertain her realness. But there was no question this was real. Quinn didn't reach such sharp levels of arousal when she was on her own. She only burned like this under Maya's touch—and burn she did.

Maya ran her hand over the tattoo on Quinn's side.

It was always hard to predict how someone would react to the phrases Quinn had chosen to immortalize on her skin, but Maya seemed quite taken with them. When she'd gone on a little discovery tour of her body earlier, and had traced her fingertips over Quinn's inner thighs, Quinn imagined it wasn't just her blood pulsing with desire.

Maya's fingertips meandered to the waistband of Quinn's panties which, for some reason she couldn't begin to fathom, she was still wearing. She pushed them down a fraction the way she had done earlier and exposed Quinn's original tattoo—the one that had enthralled Maya ten years ago. How could ten years pass and not a smidgen of the attraction between them have diminished? At first thought, back then Quinn believed they'd ended up in bed because she'd been audacious enough to flirt with Maya and Maya had been in the right frame of mind to be receptive to it. Tommy had just left home. Quinn had instinctively known how to say the right things. All those years, she had believed that she and Maya sleeping together, the two of them sharing the most incredible night, had been mostly her doing. But, as Maya's fingers disappeared inside her panties, she felt like she needed to reassess. It had been more than that. In fact, it was quite arrogant for Quinn to believe that the stars had aligned that night merely because she'd taken a fancy to seducing her neighbor. She knew better now. Both of them had played an equal part because both of them felt what had been growing between them over the course of that divine, sun-drenched weekend. Many outcomes had been possible but there had only been one that they'd both wanted equally that night.

The exact same thing could be said for this night. Quinn

had met Maya with the possibility of something like this in mind. It had even made her much more nervous than she would usually have been, because it was Maya, and Quinn attached a different kind of importance to it—because it really mattered to her what Maya thought of her. This wasn't some first date with a random person she had picked to help get her over Morgan. This was Maya Mercer, of whom the idea and the memory had had years to grow into something otherworldly in her subconscious.

"Ooh," Quinn groaned as Maya's fingertip skirted along the edge of her clit.

Maya craned her neck and looked back at her. In her eyes, Quinn believed she saw all her own desire reflected back at her. Then again, maybe what they had between them was just the very simple notion of two people madly, desperately wanting each other.

Maya hooked her finger underneath Quinn's waistband and started pulling her panties down. Quinn gave her a hand and a few seconds of fumbling later, lay naked in front of Maya, her skin hot with need, her clit throbbing as though utterly beside itself.

Maya looked at her again, as though she couldn't quite believe this was happening—again. Then, she leaned over Quinn's belly, and kissed a sizzling hot path along Quinn's tattoo.

Maya's lips on her there made every hair on Quinn's body rise up in anticipation. Ever so slowly, Maya's lips moved downward, until she was kissing the skin around Quinn's other tattoos—the ones on her inner thighs. The ones Quinn had decided to get on a whim to break the predictable yet frustrating mold her life as Morgan's mistress had become. And now, Maya was dragging the tip of her divine tongue along the words *You take me to* Quinn had tattooed there, up to the apex of her thighs and then, a delicious pause, before Maya's tongue meandered down the other thigh, over *A breathless place.*

Morgan could go to hell and never return. Because Quinn was done with her. Her focus was on Maya now. She wouldn't throw her heart into the game so foolishly anymore—and she most definitely would never be anyone's dirty secret ever again. For all those reasons, Maya giving her this pleasure was at the same time safe and enthralling.

"Ah," Quinn moaned as Maya's tongue flicked against her clit. Oh, it was definitely enthralling and exquisite and utterly beguiling, because Maya was all of those things. She was excellent company, a treat to feast your eyes on, and she had some game. And she sure knew how to use her tongue in a most satisfying way.

Quinn gazed down at the mane of dark hair between her legs, and while teetering on the cusp of climax, an insuppressible smile broke on her face.

CHAPTER 25

Maya woke with Quinn's body glued to her back. She'd only slept in fits and starts because she wasn't used to another person in her bed, although that was far from the only thing keeping her awake. As soon as Quinn had fallen asleep, the old guilt had come for Maya again. It wasn't exactly the same as back then because their situations were very different now, but sleeping with Quinn Hathaway had most decidedly not been part of any of Maya's plans.

She had a date with Beverly on Friday.

She had intended to tell Tommy and Beth about wanting to date women.

And now, after one night with Quinn, everything was up in the air again.

Still, Maya grabbed hold of Quinn's arm that was draped across her. It was getting light outside and Maya could make out the word *Radical* on her wrist. It was all well and good to have *Radical Acceptance* tattooed on your wrists, but no amount of radically accepting anything could resign Maya to the fact that she had done this again. Exquisite as it may have been—

and it had been—she loathed herself for her weakness when it came to Quinn.

What was it about her that made Maya lose her mind? What was it about her that had made Maya kiss her in the middle of that bar? She hadn't had the slightest inclination to do so with Beverly last Saturday, whereas kissing Beverly was much more acceptable on every level. Beverly, or someone like her, was the perfect kind of woman to introduce her family to in the process of coming out. Quinn was the opposite of that. Maya imagined the look of horror on Tommy's face, the disapproval in his glance.

"Hm," Quinn groaned behind her. She pressed her warm body against Maya's, her breasts soft against Maya's back. Next, she gently kissed Maya's shoulder and the action was so tender and so foreign to Maya that, despite its smallness, it overwhelmed her.

She interlaced her fingers with Quinn's and lingered in her warm embrace. She knew how she should react when she turned around and looked Quinn in the eye, yet her actual reaction was impossible to predict. Last night had proved that Maya could not be trusted around Quinn.

Quinn kissed her shoulder again but with more boldness this time. Next thing Maya knew, Quinn playfully sank her teeth into her flesh.

"Ouch," Maya said, even though it didn't hurt one bit. It did something else to her, however. It awoke her arousal again and it also showed her what it was like to wake up with someone else in her bed. Quinn's early morning affection more than made up for any lack of sleep. Besides, it wasn't as though many hours last night had been spent trying to rest. They'd been far too busy doing other things.

"Morning." Quinn's mouth had reached Maya's ear. She kissed her on the cheek.

Maya turned around in Quinn's embrace and faced her. She was met by a gently smiling Quinn with a surprisingly tender look in her eyes. "Hey." Maya was even more surprised by the mellowness in her own voice.

"Hey, yourself." Quinn briefly touched the tip of her nose against Maya's. Then she brought her hand to her stomach which made a gurgling sound. "I'm starving."

"I did offer you dinner last night, but you stubbornly refused."

Quinn shook her head. "Not stubbornly. I'd even dare call it wisely."

Maya couldn't help but smile. "I'll make us some eggs."

Quinn brazenly brought her hand to Maya's backside and pulled her close. "I'm not *that* hungry." She kissed Maya on the cheek again.

"Do you have to go to work?" What day was it again? Maya mostly taught after-school afternoon classes and was used to leisurely mornings, although her mornings had become much less leisurely since Ethan had arrived into the world.

"That's the beauty of being freelance." Quinn squeezed Maya's ass again. "I set my own hours, which makes me free as a bird this morning. You?"

Maya could easily make up a reason to get out of bed instantly—or to ask Quinn to leave—but no part of her wanted to do that. "My first class is at three," she said truthfully.

Quinn chuckled. "And you don't want to throw me out yet?"

"To be perfectly honest, I have no idea what to do with you, Quinn." Maya made sure to at least grin while she said that.

"You seemed to know very well throughout the night." Quinn sucked her lower lip between her teeth.

It was Maya's turn to chuckle—she also figured her cheeks had just turned a shade pinker. "We should probably talk. How about you take a shower while I make us some breakfast?"

"Am I hearing that right? You're offering me a shower *and* breakfast? What kind of alternate universe have I landed in?"

"Keep that up and I'll boot you right out." Because Maya didn't mean that in the slightest. Instead of kicking Quinn out, she pulled her as close as she could. She inhaled her scent and luxuriated in the warm softness of Quinn's skin against her own.

"You're right," Quinn whispered in her ear. "We should probably talk."

"I'm supposed to go on a date on Friday." Maya wrapped her hands around her mug of steaming coffee. "Needless to say, this kind of situation is quite new to me."

"You did move to the city to sow your wild oats." Quinn sat on the other side of the kitchen island. She'd wolfed down her eggs earlier.

Maya had done the same because, as it turned out, a night of hot sex did leave one rather famished. "Sow my wild oats?" she repeated.

"Play the field. See what's out there. Get your lez on."

"Now you're just making fun of me." Maybe Maya needed to be mocked a little bit.

"I'm sorry." Quinn sounded sincere. "I don't really know what to do with this either. All I know is that last night was spectacular. Even more so than my memory of our previous night together."

Maya nodded. She could hardly deny that they'd had an amazing time together.

"Ordinarily," Quinn said, "if it were only up to me, the chemistry we have is not something I would walk away from."

"What does that mean?"

"It means that maybe *we* should go on a date. Have a night out on the town. See where it leads..."

"If you put it like that," Maya replied. *You make it sound so easy, so plausible.* She didn't say that last bit out loud because she wasn't sure she should be putting ideas into Quinn's head —or her own.

"Just for the record, I would never ask you to cancel your date with Beverly. I know you like her. That's not what I'm after here."

"I—I just don't see how I can go out with her now. After last night, it wouldn't feel right."

"I can't help you decide that, Maya. That's your own thing."

Maya would need to sleep on it. It wasn't as though she and Quinn were dating now. "You're right."

"Will you go out with me, though? We can make a night of it in Brooklyn. Have you even crossed the bridge since you moved here?"

"If I say yes to that, you have to promise that you won't take me somewhere that'll make me feel much older than I actually am. You know, one of those hipster millennial places where all the guys have their hair up in a bun and the girls..." Maya didn't really know how to describe millennial girls, even though she had one sitting right in front of her.

"Don't worry, Maya. I know exactly where to take you and it will make you feel like a million bucks, I promise you."

"Oh, yeah? Where would you take me?" Maya's interest was already much too piqued.

"You will only ever know if you agree to go."

"Wow. Such manipulation." Maya put her mug down.

"You're right." Quinn smiled at her as though she didn't agree with that at all. "It's up to you, Maya. I've put my cards on the table. I would love to take you out and while I can't guarantee you will have the time of your life, chances are you might have the most fun you've had since moving here." There was the grin Maya remembered from ten years ago. "You think about it and let me know."

Maya shook her head. "Is this the NYC way of asking someone out?"

"I don't know, but it sure is *my* way after I've had the most amazing night with someone."

"But, Quinn..." Maya took a deep breath. "We have to be realistic. Sure, we might have a great time, and then what?"

"Then we will have had a great time. We will have made a memory worth keeping." She shrugged. "Isn't that enough?"

"More than enough, and that's the problem. Say we go out and we..." Heat bubbled up from Maya's core. "We sleep together again and we want to do it again and again."

"Say we start dating and it gets serious," Quinn stated matter-of-factly, saying what Maya had trouble articulating because it sounded so ludicrous.

Maya nodded. "What if that happens?"

Quinn chuckled. "I don't know, Maya, because this has never been an issue for me."

"It hasn't?" Maya could be just as straightforward as Quinn, especially if she really wanted to get to the bottom of something.

Quinn tapped a finger against her chin as though she was lost in thought. "My thing with Morgan turned into a big mess in the end, but that was because she lied to me about wanting to leave her husband."

"But in the beginning, when you just started seeing her, you must have had some issues with that?"

Quinn expelled some air, her cheeks puffing up. "I didn't have a conversation like this with Morgan when it all started. That's the thing. It started and then it continued and before I knew it, I was in love with a married woman."

"Which makes a good case for having this discussion right now."

"As far as I know, you're not married, Maya." Quinn started shuffling in her chair, a nervous twitchiness to her movements.

"You know what I mean." Maya leaned over the kitchen island. She stopped herself from grabbing Quinn's hand. "Last time we talked, you advised me to just tell Tommy that I wanted to date women. I can hardly do that when I'm going on a date with you."

"You don't have to tell him you're dating *me*." Quinn sounded a touch exasperated.

"But what if, at one point, I do?"

"Would that really be the end of the world?" Quinn asked.

Maya had to give that question some serious thought, although her gut reaction was that, yes, it could very much signify the end of what was most precious to her in this world—her relationship with her family.

"I don't know, but it sure wouldn't be easy." Maya didn't even want to begin picturing telling Tommy about Quinn right now. It was a bridge too far. They were only discussing going on a date hypothetically.

"Think about it." Quinn slid off her chair and walked over to Maya. She slipped her arms around her waist and looked her in the eye. "But try not to think it to death beforehand, because that would be a real shame." She planted a gentle kiss on Maya's lips. "Also because I can't wait to see you again. No strings attached. It's just some fun." She leaned in again and Maya was expecting Quinn to kiss her again but, instead, she pulled back, let go of Maya, and started gathering her things.

CHAPTER 26

"Look what the cat dragged in." Griff was sitting on the couch, watching CNN.

"We don't have a cat." The conversation she'd had with Maya this morning had been on repeat in Quinn's mind all the way home. "We're bad lesbians like that."

"I thought you were just going out for drinks last night?"

"I thought you had to work today."

"I am. Following the news is part of my work." Griff nodded at the screen. "Look who's on."

Quinn looked at Beth Robbins' face. Good for her that she never changed her name to Mercer, she thought. It was kind of funny to see Maya's daughter-in-law on TV after the conversation they'd just had. But Beth was hardly presenting Fox News. She was a news anchor of color at a left-leaning news station. Even if Tommy was a bit square—although how square could he really be if he was married to Beth?—surely she had the power to set him straight.

"If it isn't my future daughter-in-law," Quinn joked.

"Beth and I would be honored to be your bridesmaids," Griff quipped.

Quinn fell onto the couch. "Drinks turned into something... more," she said, a flicker of the warmth she'd felt last night still burning brightly inside her.

"Wow, Quinn. Just when I think you can't surprise me any more than you already have, you go and do it again."

"Believe me, I'm the one who's more surprised." Quinn was distracted by Beth's face on TV. "Can we switch that off for a second?"

"Sure. I'm suddenly much more interested in your news." Griff pressed the power button on the remote and turned to Quinn. "Tell me."

"Things turned flirty as soon as we sat. So much so that it made me nervous, because, well, this is Maya Mercer. I have this memory of her that's been kind of sacred to me all these years and then we were having drinks together and she was looking more gorgeous than ever, and she was just as kind and engaging and interesting as she was then and there was still something between us." Quinn came up for air. "It was just there, like that night we had together didn't happen ten years ago but ten days ago instead. And I swear to you, Griff, she came on to me. She kissed me in the bar. Can you believe that?" Quinn could hardly believe it herself, although she could still feel the imprint of every last one of Maya's kisses on her lips—and various other body parts.

"No fucking way." Griff slapped Quinn on the knee with excitement.

"After that, it seemed almost natural that we would end up at her apartment." A flash of heat coursed through Quinn's body. "I'm still so attracted to her." She let her head fall onto the backrest of the couch. "It was fucking amazing, Griff. I can't really explain why. Maybe it was part nostalgia. Maybe even part unfinished business. Or maybe, over the years, in my subconscious, Maya has developed into the archetype of the one woman I can't have and then to finally be with her... It blew my mind. And she... She seemed to be having the time of her life as well."

"Did she ask you to keep it a secret again?" Griff asked.

"No. I even asked her to go out with me on a proper date this time."

"And?" Griff was bouncing up and down with excitement, personifying how Quinn felt on the inside but was trying to keep a lid on.

"She didn't say yes, but she didn't exactly say no, either. I told her to think about it because she has all kinds of misgivings, of course. So do I, if I'm being completely honest. I want her, yes, no doubt, but I'm not so sure she's someone I should actually go out with. Not after Morgan. One night of passion." Quinn nodded. "Yes. Definitely. It did put some distance between Morgan and me. But... At the same time, I want more." She blew out some air. "Maybe I shouldn't have asked her out, but it just tripped off my tongue. I didn't even think about it. I just looked at her, got this glow inside me, and blurted it out."

"Maybe she won't get back to you," Griff said. She could be much more of a realist than Quinn. "Maybe it will just fizzle out before it has the chance to go anywhere."

"Maybe." That would certainly make Quinn very sad, but perhaps it would be for the best. "I still have to finish her portrait."

"How many more hours of work?"

"A day or two, if I can focus." Quinn forced herself to smile. She'd just had an amazing night and she refused to be down about it one minute longer.

"Get it over with then. So you can move on. I'll even go to Marnie's with you this weekend, if you want."

Quinn feigned utter surprise, letting her mouth fall open theatrically. "No. Fucking. Way!"

"Only if you need a wingwoman."

"Wouldn't it be great to meet Beth Robbins in the flesh one day, though? She's a real workaholic, apparently. She'd barely given birth before she went back to work."

"You don't have to tell me how cutthroat the news business is," Griff mused.

"That's why you're sitting on your ass in the middle of the day, drooling over hot news anchors."

"It's important to be informed, Quinn," Griff stated drily.

"It sure is." Quinn leaned her head in the direction of her friend. Thank goodness for Griff. She had always tried to talk some sense into Quinn, although she rarely succeeded. When it came to all things love, Quinn was very tunnel-visioned. And once she had her sights set on someone, it was hard to have her even glance in a different direction.

But Quinn was also burned out by a long-term relationship that had gone nowhere, in which she'd had very little agency, and that had wounded her with all its hard-edged broken promises. Maybe she should just take things easy for a while. Stay home and follow the news with Griff. They'd have to change the channel, though.

CHAPTER 27

Maya had managed to avoid Angus since Quinn had left on Wednesday. She wanted to talk to him about her. He was still the only person she could confide in about something like that, but she wasn't ready for the myriad of questions he would undoubtedly fire at her. He might well try to convince her that she should go on a date with Quinn, whereas Maya was putting all her energy into telling herself it was the worst idea ever.

"Have some fun," Angus would say. And Maya wasn't opposed to fun, especially not the kind of fun she and Quinn had had all of Tuesday night, but to what end? And at what cost? Fun like that didn't come cheap to a woman like Maya. She was fifty-five years old. She hadn't moved to the city to 'sow her wild oats' the way Quinn had put it. She had come here to date women like Beverly with the ultimate goal of finding someone to spend the rest of her life with.

Even though her attraction to Beverly wasn't comparable to how Maya felt when Quinn even so much as glanced at her, she knew she had to give Beverly another chance. She knew, deep down, that if she wanted to ever reach that goal of finding love, she should keep her date with Beverly and say no to Quinn's proposal of a night out on the town, although Maya was dying to know what Quinn had in store for her. But this was the time for reason, not for emotional foolishness. Therefore this was also the time to avoid Angus at all costs. Because Maya also knew that it wouldn't take much convincing to choose going out with Quinn over Beverly. That's why it was important to keep herself out of every situation where she could be convinced to let her emotions overrule her rationality.

She would snap out of the haze of bliss Quinn had left her in soon enough. All it would take, most likely, was spending some time with her family. That should plant her feet firmly back on sensible ground.

Tomorrow, she would be ready to see Beverly again. Her night with Quinn would have started to fade into the background, and Maya would be sitting opposite a woman who was, at the very least, appropriate for her. At her age, those things were increasingly important.

Maya reached for her phone and texted Beverly, telling her how much she was looking forward to their upcoming date. Then she invited herself to dinner at her son and daughter-in-law's so she could be reminded of what was most important in her life. Five seconds with Ethan in her arms would surely be enough to do the trick—and to banish those pangs of heat that coursed through her at the most inopportune times whenever she let her mind wander and it, inevitably, presented her with an image of Quinn in all her naked glory.

"Maya?" Beverly asked. "Do you want white or red wine?"

"Oh." Maya had been lost in thought again, foolishly cataloging all the traits that made Beverly objectively attractive. As though that was an exercise that could ever yield a result. "White, please. Sorry. I was distracted."

"I'd like to think your mind was already venturing past dinner." Beverly was laying on the innuendo much thicker compared to their previous date. Maya figured it was their texts that had created a sense of familiarity for Beverly that Maya didn't yet feel.

Maya offered a smile that she tried very hard to let come across as more than polite, but it was a difficult task because as soon as she had greeted sweet, lovely Beverly, and they'd kissed each other lightly on the cheek, Maya had known that this was not what she wanted. Beverly was not who she wanted to spend her evening with. They weren't even an hour into their date and while it wasn't exactly painful for Maya—Beverly was still good company—Maya wasn't attracted to her. She had hoped to be able to write off her attraction to Quinn as something in a category of its own, something that didn't count because it wasn't rooted in reality, but she realized now that she'd been wrong. Because, even as she sat opposite Beverly, who truly had some genuinely interesting tales to tell, and from whom Maya could surely learn a thing or two about life, and life in New York City specifically, all Maya could think of was Quinn.

But she was here and she was going to make the most of it. She was still adamant to give this a chance. Maybe she couldn't stop thinking of Quinn because she forbade herself to do so. Many a scientific study had shown how hard it was not to think of an elephant when you were explicitly told not to think of an elephant. Let alone a gorgeous woman who had given Maya a night that she would never forget—a night that only made the memory of their previous night together even more spectacular.

"I'm so sorry," Maya said. "Ethan's been colicky and he's been crying a lot and it's been driving us all nuts." This was only partly true. Maybe Ethan had cried a bit more than usual when she'd spent time with him last, but that's just what babies did. They cried. It hadn't worried Maya all that much. But she couldn't tell Beverly about what was really preoccupying her mind.

Beverly nodded as though she understood. She had three children and five grandchildren, after all. But she was the type of woman, Maya believed, who couldn't be fooled for too long. She actually liked that about Beverly. If she really put her mind to it, Maya could probably have a wonderful time with her. They could strike up a long, meandering, satisfying conversation, if only Maya's brain would give her some space to do so. But it felt so crowded up there, with all these images of Quinn screaming for attention.

Half an hour later, Maya was so appalled by her own thoughts that she escaped to the washroom so she could talk some much-needed sense into herself.

She looked in the mirror and shook her head. Whenever she tried to listen intently to something Beverly said, something she'd had no issue with last weekend—*before*—a little voice in the back of Maya's head started telling her that she could be doing god knows what with Quinn right now and it wouldn't be an effort and she certainly wouldn't have to force herself to enjoy it. Because that was what Maya had been doing throughout the date and she knew it was ridiculous but not half as ridiculous as going on a date with Quinn.

And that was the real issue. Maya felt caught between a rock and a hard place. She already knew that things wouldn't work out between her and Beverly, albeit through no fault of Beverly whatsoever. Although, as she stood there, admonishing herself in her head, Maya didn't think it was really her fault either. It was Quinn's. She was too irresistible. Too delicious. Too easy to be around. Too much fun. Her lips were too soft. Her fingers too nimble. Her tongue too.... Maya had to stop herself. She took a deep breath. "Get a grip," she told her reflection. She no longer had the luxury of prancing around like a hormonal teenager. This was temporary, she told herself. It would pass. It had done so before. She squared her shoulders and returned to Beverly.

"What's her name?" Beverly asked after Maya had sat again. "Or *his*, for that matter."

"What do you mean?"

Beverly chuckled. "I'll show you my driver's license if I have to, Maya, and it will confirm I wasn't born yesterday." She shrugged. "A woman like you was always a long shot for me."

"I'm sorry." Maya looked into Beverly's eyes, but she had to look away swiftly. "I really am. I had the best intentions, I promise you, but..."

"You're besotted with someone else."

Besotted? Maya wouldn't put it like that. She had some work to do to get past this whole Quinn thing, yes, but she was hardly besotted. She still had her wits about her. She still knew what needed to be done. That was one of the reasons she was here tonight—not that it was working. "There's someone else. She's like a blast from the past that I don't really know what to do with."

"That's a damn shame for me, because I really like you." Beverly drummed her fingertips on the tabletop. "So much so that I'm feeling a little sting of rejection." She sucked her lips into her mouth and released them with a smacking sound. "Although I do want to be the bigger person here and not end this date in an overly dramatic fashion."

"Maybe we can be friends," Maya tried.

Beverly scoffed. "I have plenty of those already. I had zero intentions of ever putting you in the friend zone." She leaned over the table. "You are absolutely smoking hot, and I sincerely hope that this woman you're so obviously infatuated with treats you right." With that, she pushed herself up, and left.

Maya settled the check, took a deep breath and another generous glug of wine, before reaching for her phone to take Quinn up on her offer of taking Maya out.

CHAPTER 28

The smile on Maya's face was the exact reason Quinn had brought her to Noches.

The club was in Queens and hardly around the corner from where Quinn lived, but Quinn could—hopefully—show Maya around her neck of the woods some other time. If she wanted that smile, and it really was all she wanted, this was the best place to bring Maya on a Saturday night.

It was dark and sweaty and, granted, most people were probably a few, if not many, years younger than Maya, but the music and the way they danced was worlds away from most of the clubs Quinn frequented. As soon as they walked in and their ears were treated to the enticing salsa beat, Maya responded the way Quinn had pictured in her best-case scenario.

"It's like I'm in Puerto Rico," Maya said.

"That's the beauty of New York. If you know where to go, you can find yourself anywhere you want."

"Sounds like another one of your tattoos," Maya joked as she cast her gaze about the dance floor. "This place is amazing, but…" She leaned closer to Quinn and half-whispered. "Is it, um, LGBT-friendly? I mean, can we dance together?"

"The only obstacle to us dancing together tonight is that you are a pro and I'm anything but." Quinn threaded her fingers through Maya's. "I'll do my very best not to step on your toes."

Maya shook her head. "You stepping on my toes is the very least of my worries."

Quinn nodded at a pair of men on the dance floor. "Check them out."

"Is it a gay club?" Maya asked.

"It's a club in New York, which means it doesn't matter what or who you are." She tugged at Maya's hand and they headed to the bar. "I used to tend bar with one of the owners before he started this place. That's how I first heard of it. They mix a mean mojito. Can I get you one?"

"I see what you're doing." Maya was already strutting around as if she owned the place. "Plying me with drinks so you can have your wicked way with me later." She pulled Quinn close. "For the record, dancing the salsa makes me very, *very* frisky."

As she chuckled, Quinn noticed, from the corner of her eye, a man making his way toward them. She hadn't expected any trouble coming here, but it had been years since she'd been to this club—Morgan wasn't much of a dancer, nor was she one for going out much. Quinn waited to place their drinks order until she figured out what was going on.

"Excuse me," the man addressed Maya. "But are you four times US and two times World Professional Latin Dance Champion, Maya Dixon?" he asked, his eyes so wide Quinn feared his eyeballs might topple right out of his head.

"I am." Maya brought a hand to her chest, as though she was bashful about this.

Quinn suspected the opposite was true.

The man—a fan, Quinn guessed—pointed at a picture on the wall left of the bar. It was the second in a series of about a dozen frames. In the picture, Maya smiled broadly, looking a few decades younger than she was today.

"Oh my god. Is that me?" Maya exclaimed.

The man nodded feverishly. "When you won your first world championship." He didn't look nearly old enough to have been alive when this happened. He brought his hands together in a praying position. "Please, please, please, may I have a dance with you? It would be the greatest honor of my life."

Maya looked at Quinn.

"Go," Quinn said. "Show them what you've got." Of course, Quinn wanted to dance with Maya, but she certainly didn't mind just watching her either.

"It would be a pleasure," Maya said. "What's your name?"

"Ernesto," he said. "But call me Ernie." He held out his hand to Maya, as though they were at some Victorian ball. The way Ernie wiggled his hips as he led Maya to the dance floor, Quinn could only conclude he'd danced a few salsas in his life—or he just really liked to swing his ass about. Maybe both.

"On the house," someone said behind her. She turned around and saw two mojitos she hadn't yet ordered in front of her. The bartender shot her a wide smile. "For you and Miss Dixon. Enjoy!"

Quinn thanked him and took one of the drinks in her hand. When she turned around her eyes were drawn like magnets to Maya on the dance floor. Whether Ernie was a capable dancer or not had become completely irrelevant. All she, and anyone else in the club, Quinn guessed, could see was Maya. She was wearing an emerald dress and even though it was dark in the club, as Maya danced the fabric seemed to flow around the floor.

They twirled around so quickly, Quinn could hardly keep up with their movements, yet Maya and Ernie seemed in utter control of their bodies.

Quinn took a sip of her mojito, which was strong and tart and, she thought, even if this was all she did all night, sip from this drink while watching Maya in her element, it would still be the kind of night to always remember.

Even though, for days that seemed to last for weeks, it looked like this night would never happen. Maya had only texted her the day before, when Quinn had started to give up hope. But here they were. There Maya was, being the queen of the dance floor. Quinn had never even noticed the pictures on the wall before, let alone that there was one of Maya. Maybe in this alternate Latin dance universe that wasn't really hers—until today—it made sense. Just like it seemed to make perfect sense to Ernie to invite Maya to dance. It wasn't the done thing in the clubs Quinn went to. But this club was different.

The skirt of Maya's dress ruffled up as she danced, and Quinn's gaze was drawn to her toned, gorgeous legs. Philosophically, Quinn was opposed to women wearing high heels. She never wore them because they were uncomfortable and painful and just another means for the patriarchy to keep her down—of course—but, admittedly, when she watched Maya dance in her three-inch heels it did not stir up any protest inside her. On the contrary.

The dance ended and as soon as the next song started Quinn lost sight of Maya because she was surrounded by a group of people, probably more contenders for a dance with her. A few moments later, Maya emerged from the group and, gingerly wiping the sweat from her brow with one outstretched finger, walked toward Quinn.

"Ernie knows his moves," she said.

Quinn gave her the cocktail. "Here. Rehydrate. I have a feeling you won't get a lot of time to rest tonight."

"Nor will you." Maya locked her gaze on Quinn. "I'm out with *you* tonight. I want to dance with *you*." She grabbed hold of Quinn's blouse. "Come on." She put her glass back on the bar and, without even considering no for an answer, dragged Quinn onto the dance floor.

Even though the club was packed, they were automatically given space, as if in reverence to the great Maya Dixon. Quinn felt self-conscious because she didn't have moves like Maya—or Ernie. Admittedly, after asking Maya out, and knowing where she would be taking her if she said yes, Quinn had looked up a few salsa videos on YouTube and she'd practiced the steps in the living room when Griff had been out.

"Just follow my lead," Maya said into her ear. "Trust me," she said. "You've got this."

Of course, Quinn stepped onto Maya's toes and her hips swayed in the wrong direction while sweat trickled down her spine, pooling at the small of her back. Of course, she made mistakes and her feet didn't feel like they wanted to cooperate, but, in the end, it didn't matter. Because when she got it right and they were in sync for half a minute here and ten seconds there, it felt like the most exhilarating taste of freedom Quinn had ever experienced. Even in those too-brief moments of unison she could feel why people became addicted to dancing with someone else in this way. The rhythm, the fusion of bodies, the steady hand of your partner on your arm. In this case, that partner was Maya, whom, Quinn concluded as they reached the end of their first dance, it was going to be impossible not to fall completely in love with.

CHAPTER 29

Maya's legs wobbled like jelly when she got out of the cab. She hadn't danced this long and this hard for years. She'd searched on the internet for clubs like the one Quinn had taken her to but she hadn't had any luck finding a place like that herself.

"The elevator in your building better be working," Maya said on a sigh. She was tired but her fatigue didn't match the euphoria that coursed through her. To dance the night away like that was like a delicious dream.

"This," Quinn pointed at a rather decrepit-looking building across the street, "is what they call a Greenpoint walk-up. We're on the fourth floor. I hope you have some juice left in those sublime legs of yours."

"You've got to be kidding me." Maya eyed the building. It reminded her of Tommy's first apartment after college.

"I'd carry you up but you all but exhausted me." Quinn unlocked the front door. A too-bright light flickered on, illuminating a stairwell that had seen better days. Quinn led the way and Maya didn't have much choice but to follow, although the post-dancing euphoria was quickly leaving her.

"Jesus," Maya panted when she made it up the stairs. "You could have warned me to save some of my energy."

Quinn held a finger against her lips. "It's late, and Griff will be asleep."

Oh yes, the roommate. Add that to the walk-up, and going home with Quinn was beginning to feel more like a cold shower—especially after the hot, scintillating bath Maya had just stepped out of. She didn't much feel like a harsh dose of reality this late at night. Truth be told, she just wanted to collapse into a soft bed.

Quinn showed Maya into the apartment. Maya tried to stop herself from casting her gaze about—she didn't want to judge how Quinn lived any more than she'd already done—but her gaze seemed to have a mind of its own. The apartment was so small it felt like there was no room to move.

Quinn fetched two glasses from a cabinet and filled them with water from the faucet. She handed one to Maya. "Welcome to Casa Hathaway-Griffin." She stood there grinning, and it made Maya forget where she was for a moment—Quinn's smile had that effect on her.

"Thank you for taking me dancing." Maya drank some water. "What a night. I felt like royalty."

Quinn set her glass down and bridged the small distance between them. "There was only one queen of salsa in that club tonight and that was you." She took Maya's glass and put it in the sink. Then she grabbed Maya's hand and stroked her palm. "You were phenomenal out there. Not to mention fucking hot." She put Maya's hand against her lower belly, fingers pointing downward. "Care to find out how wet I am for you right now?"

Maya was quickly forgetting about her surroundings even more. Quinn had a real knack for setting a mood with her smooth words and small actions, like guiding Maya's hand down her pants. Maya nodded, because of course she wanted to find out. Quinn had not only given her one of the best nights she'd had since moving to the city, but they had danced together most of the night, their hips glued together, their gaze connected, their arousal growing as time passed.

Quinn flipped her jeans button open and Maya let her hand slide down. Quinn took a step back until she was against the fridge door. Maya's hand slid lower as she followed.

"Not a word of a lie out of your mouth," Maya whispered when she encountered Quinn's wetness.

"I want you so much," Quinn groaned. "It should be illegal."

Maya slid her finger a little deeper between Quinn's legs. "What about your roommate?" she asked.

"I'll be quiet," Quinn murmured. "Just fuck me please, Maya. It was torture to be so close to you all night."

"Torture, huh?" Maya slid two fingers all the way inside. "You youngsters with your hyperbole."

Quinn probably didn't register what she was saying any longer. She let her head fall back, exposing her neck, as she let out a half-suppressed groan.

Seeing Quinn like that, and having her fingers deep inside her, quickened Maya's pulse. Fatigue made way for something else—even more feelings of infatuation for Quinn, Maya guessed. She kissed Quinn's sweat-salty neck. Because Maya, too, had dreamed of a moment like this while they were out there on the floor.

She hadn't only felt like royalty, she'd felt like Quinn's one and only princess.

A bead of sweat pearled on Maya's forehead. She wanted to take some space from Quinn, but the bed was so small, there was nowhere to go. Maya didn't much feel like pressing herself against the wall either. She didn't actually believe the apartment Quinn lived in was dirty, but it gave a too-lived-in impression and Maya might as well be honest with herself, she was used to a different standard of living. She had swanky wallpaper on her bedroom walls that was soft to the touch. Her kitchen had marble countertops instead of cheap plywood, and in the unlikely case one elevator broke down in her building, there was always the second one.

Maya understood that people in their thirties lived like this, although Tommy wasn't even thirty yet and he most certainly didn't live in a 'Greenpoint walk-up' as Quinn had put it. But Tommy was married to a TV news anchor and people who were on TV got paid a hell of a lot more than people who weren't. Rationally, she knew it was perfectly normal for Quinn to live in a place like this in a city like New York with astronomical rents, but it did drive home a point to Maya as she lay squeezed against Quinn, who seemed totally out of it. If Maya listened closely, she could detect a soft purr coming from Quinn's mouth at regular intervals.

Even though her body was exhausted, Maya's mind refused to quiet down. When she heard a noise outside the closed bedroom door, she gently extricated herself from Quinn's bed, found a robe that was hanging off the foot of the bed, and got up. Maya guessed she was about to make the acquaintance of Griff.

The apartment was so small, it wasn't hard for Maya to find her way back to the kitchen in the dark. A woman of about Quinn's age with short, tousled hair and dressed in a tank top and shorts sat at the tiny kitchen table, drinking a glass of water.

"Hey," she said. "You must be Maya."

"And you must be Griff." Maya thought it a bit silly to offer her hand for a formal handshake in the middle of the night.

"The one and only. Do you want some water?"

"Sure." Maya sat on the other chair and once Griff had rejoined her, found herself almost touching elbows with Quinn's roommate.

"I hope we didn't wake you," Maya said.

"Nah. Sometimes I just wake up in the middle of the night for no reason. I suspect it's hormonal." She beamed Maya a warm smile. "How was your night out? Did you like the club?"

"I loved it. Have you been there?"

"It's been a while." Griff took a sip of water. "Couldn't sleep?"

"Hm." Maya chuckled. "Must be my hormones as well." Maya couldn't very well tell Griff the truth. For all she knew, Griff's bed was even smaller than Quinn's.

"New surroundings and all that, probably," Griff said.

Maya nodded. "You didn't go out last night?" Maya figured she might as well make some conversation, if only to take her mind off the issues that were keeping her awake.

Griff shook her head. "I'm keeping a low profile this year."

"This *year*?"

Maya could see Griff hesitate, but then she nodded, and said, "I'm doing a 'year of no'. It's an experiment I'm doing for a book I'm writing."

"How does it work? You say no to everything?"

"Nothing as drastic as that." Griff laughed. "One full year of no flirting, no sex, and no relationships."

"Seriously?"

"Oh yes."

"Where did that idea come from?" Maya was intrigued. Quinn hadn't told her that much about Griff.

"I've always been interested in how much of what we do and how we act is influenced by what we've internalized just by living in society, in this world that we've created. Being romantically involved with other people has been the norm for so long now, I wanted to experience what it would be like to actively go against the grain."

"And? What does it feel like?" Maya had been single long enough to know exactly what it felt like. "For the record, I've had multiple years of no."

"Until Quinn came along?" Griff asked.

"Kind of." It wasn't entirely true, although it felt like it had some truth to it.

Griff smiled at her again. "To answer your question, now that I'm a few months in, I had truly believed that it was going to be a lot harder. But maybe you should ask me again after spring. Or at the height of summer when everyone's strutting around frisky as hell."

Maya chuckled. "I can't wait to read that book."

"Quinn's totally nuts about you, by the way," Griff said.

Warmth bloomed inside Maya's belly. "She's, um... Well, I'm quite fond of her as well," Maya half-said, half-stuttered.

"I'm just happy to see her like this again after Morgan did such a number on her." Griff sounded concerned for Quinn. Either she was a really good friend or she had more than a friendly interest in her roommate.

Maya didn't know what to say to that. She didn't know what to think of any of this, which was why she was sitting at this kitchen table instead of lying in bed next to Quinn, soundly asleep. "We had a lot of fun tonight, but..."

"It's complicated?" Griff emptied her glass while keeping her gaze on Maya.

"Her parents were my friends. That's not something I can just ignore. She's only six years older than my son." Maya huffed out some air. "So, yes, complicated is surely the right word for it."

"Yeah. My dad's new wife's barely older than me. She's supposed to be my stepmother now. I'm not going to lie. It's weird."

Maya's ears perked up. "Do you and your dad get along well?"

"Let's just say I prefer to spend Thanksgiving at my mom's." Griff slapped her hand over her mouth. "Sorry. I didn't mean it like that. I've always got along better with my mom, even before my dad married Brittany."

"His new wife isn't the main reason you don't see him very often?"

"She contributes to it, but it's more of a personality thing than an age thing. She's just... insufferable half the time. Quinn's like the opposite of Brittany. I didn't mean to imply anything."

"It's like fifty/fifty in here." Maya pressed her hand to her chest. "I have such a good time when I'm with Quinn. It's magical. But I can't picture it going any further than what we have now because of our age difference and our families. I just can't see it."

"Give it some time." Griff twirled her empty glass between her fingers. "Enjoy yourselves together and see where it goes. No life-changing decisions need to be made right off the bat."

"True." Maya let her gaze wander around the kitchen. If she was going to enjoy herself with Quinn more, it wouldn't be in this dingy walk-up—although she wouldn't mind going to that club again.

"I've known Quinn for a long time and she's good people," Griff said. "She can be a little cocky but she has a kind heart and that's important, you know?"

Maya enjoyed Quinn's cockiness. It was what had brought

her to this point. It was also easy to tell that Quinn was a good person. But that didn't solve any of Maya's issues—on the contrary.

CHAPTER 30

When Quinn woke up she figured she was still in the exact same position she'd fallen asleep in, so deeply had she slept. The only thing missing from last night's picture was Maya. For a second, panic overtook her. Had Maya left without saying goodbye? And if so, why? They'd had an amazing time at the club—and afterward.

Quinn hopped out of bed, threw on a T-shirt and a pair of boxers, and went in search of Maya. She found her drinking coffee with Griff in the living room.

"You've met. Great." She hesitated a fraction before walking over to Maya resolutely and giving her a quick kiss on the cheek. "Morning."

"I'm going to take a shower," Griff announced.

"You don't have to go because of us," Maya said, surprising Quinn. How long had she and Griff been sitting here? And more importantly, what had they been talking about? Quinn couldn't put her finger on it, and maybe she was still tired from last night and brain fog was playing tricks on her mind, but she sensed something was off.

Griff waved off her comment and disappeared into the hallway.

Quinn took her place in the couch. She offered Maya her widest smile. "Did you sleep well?"

Maya shook her head.

"Oh." Quinn shuffled a little closer. "Are you a little grouchy this morning because you didn't get your beauty sleep?" She put a hand on Maya's knee. She was fully dressed already. When had all this happened? Quinn must have really been out of it.

"Quinn." Maya shook her head. "I didn't sleep a wink. I—" She puffed up her cheeks and slowly let out the air. "I'm really tired."

"We can go back to bed. Get some more sleep. It's Sunday."

Maya shook her head. "I just want to go home."

"Hey." Quinn gently rubbed Maya's knee. "I get that you're tired. Do you want me to take you home? We can hang out at your place, if you prefer." Quinn was getting the impression that was the very last thing Maya wanted.

"I don't 'hang out', Quinn." She sighed again and it sounded much more exasperated this time. "This is not who I am. This—" She gestured her hand about. "It's not how I live. It's not me."

"Last night you were you." Quinn found Maya's tone a touch too accusatory.

"Yes. I very much was." Maya put her hand on Quinn's. "And thank you so very much for that. I mean it."

"But?" Quinn asked.

"Maybe we should cool things off for a while. Take a breath."

"Cool things off? What do you mean? We went dancing. We had a great time. We can do it again whenever you want to.

That's it. I'm not asking you to marry me here, Maya. Nor am I asking you to tell Tommy that we're seeing each other."

"But can't you see what's happening?" Maya shuffled away from Quinn. "I'm falling for you and I think it's a really bad idea."

Such a fine line between elation and desperation, Quinn thought. "You're tired. Last night was amazing and now you're sitting here in the cold light of day, looking at me and wondering what the hell to do with me. I get it. It's confusing. It might all seem like a bad idea right now, but you should sleep on it. Properly sleep, I mean."

"I really should." Maya held out her hand. Quinn took it in hers. "I know I'm being impossible."

"It's only because you're feeling your age," Quinn quipped but regretted it immediately.

Luckily, Maya could just about manage a chuckle.

"We'll get you an Uber. Go home and rest. Call me tomorrow. Or later today. Whenever you feel like it. Okay?"

"Come here." Maya pulled her close. "Why are you the reasonable-sounding one right now?"

"I've had a lot of experience dealing with... ladies like yourself." Relief coursed through Quinn because she'd managed to defuse the situation.

"Oh fuck, Quinn, what am I going to do with you?" Maya cupped Quinn's cheeks in her palms and kissed her softly but quickly on the lips.

"So, I hear you're falling for me." Before Maya left, Quinn would really like to hear her say that again.

"Turns out you're very easy to fall for."

Quinn batted her lashes. "That's the first time I've heard that."

"Sure." Finally, Maya smiled, before leaning in and kissing Quinn properly.

"I'm pretty crazy about you as well," Quinn whispered when they broke from their kiss.

"I know," Maya said. "Griff told me."

"Griff?"

"What a gem of a roommate."

"Griff's the best." Quinn tried to peer deep into Maya's eyes. "What else has she told you?"

"She told me about her 'year of no'."

"About me, I mean." Quinn was well aware of how self-centered she sounded, but she was curious. If Maya didn't tell her, she would grill Griff as soon as Maya left.

"It's not very considerate of you to bring me to this apartment you share with her while she's abstaining."

"Griff and I discussed all of that beforehand. I didn't do anything we didn't agree to."

"I'm just teasing." Maya tilted her head. "It's not easy to get you flustered like that." Maya rose. "I'm really beat, Quinn."

Quinn stood as well. She curved her arms around Maya's waist.

"Thank you so much again for last night. I had such an amazing time," Maya said.

"I'm sorry you didn't get any sleep."

"I'll get over it," Maya said, "I'm not that old."

"How is Maya?" Quinn's dad smiled at her fondly across the dinner table. "That's a big move she made, from living in Milbury to a place like Manhattan."

"She has a grandson she adores." Quinn grinned at her dad. It was always good to meet up with him on his infrequent visits to New York. "But don't let that put any ideas in your head. I'm not feeling broody in the least."

"I remember when Tommy married that hotshot news anchor. What's her name again?"

"Beth Robbins."

"That's right." Her dad nodded. "There used to be a time when we were close enough with Maya that it felt like a given to invite each other to our children's weddings, but something changed over the years. I've never really known what." He shrugged. "But it's good to hear she's doing well. She's a lovely woman."

Quinn could only agree, but not too vehemently.

"Tell me about you, sweetheart," he said. "Are you getting over that nasty business with Morgan?"

Her dad had always been so much easier to talk to than her mom. He asked as though it had never bothered him one bit that Morgan was 'emotionally unavailable'—which was how Quinn had described Morgan's marital status to her family. Quinn figured they were more than smart enough to know what she really meant.

"We met up, but nothing's changed. I think I am actually getting over it." Quinn couldn't help a smile from bursting all over her face at the thought of Maya and how she'd been helping Quinn put Morgan behind her in an extremely efficient manner.

"That's wonderful." Her dad narrowed his eyes and examined her face. Sometimes Quinn forgot that he could read her like an open book. "Someone new in the picture perhaps?"

"Maybe." Quinn could omit things, but she couldn't flat-out lie to her father. "It's early days and she'll probably turn out to be more like a transitional person, but, yeah..."

"Tell me more." He nodded in encouragement.

"No, Dad. I really shouldn't."

"You can tell me her name, at least." He laughed. "Don't tell me how old she is, though."

"I'm not telling you anything. Let's pretend the conversation never took this turn and talk about something else pronto."

"Why? Judging by that grin on your face, you obviously like this new woman quite a bit."

"Trust me, Daddy, you don't want to know."

"I do very much want to know, especially now that you've said that I don't." He arched up his eyebrows. "I'm your old man. You can tell me anything."

"Not this." Or could she? Quinn's mother would break out in hives, but telling her father could be a good test for telling other people.

"Who is this woman? Is she a high-profile Republican or something along those lines?" He huffed out some air. "We can turn this into a guessing game, if that's what you want."

"She's not a politician."

"Okay." He tapped a finger against his chin ostentatiously. "I'm trying to think of plausible reasons for you not wanting to tell me. Is she famous? Is it Oprah? Or Ellen?"

Quinn burst out laughing. "Neither one of them lives in New York and no, she's not famous."

"So what's the catch? I don't get it." He jutted out his bottom lip. "This is me, Pumpkin. Whoever it is, I won't tell your mother. You have my word."

"That would certainly make your life easier as well," Quinn said.

"Come on." He drummed his fingers on the table impatiently. "Out with it. You've tortured me long enough."

Quinn looked at her father. Maybe he'd never see her in the same light again after she told him. But something inside her wanted to tell him. Not only because he was her father and she'd always felt safe with him and understood by him, but also because it would lend a certain legitimacy to whatever she and Maya were doing. And he was one of the most non-judgmental people she knew. "It's Maya, Dad. Maya Mercer."

His forehead wrinkled into a deep frown. "Maya Mercer? Whose portrait you took? Our old neighbor?"

"Yes." Quinn's palms started sweating. Maybe she'd finally pushed too hard against her father's boundaries of understanding. "We've been seeing each other."

"But Maya... She's, um.... not, you know."

"A lesbian?"

"Well, yes."

"She might be bi, Dad."

"Nice try, kiddo," her dad said. "You almost had your old man there." He shot her a big grin. "Well played." Quinn hoped he wasn't going to give her a thumbs-up next.

"It's not a joke," Quinn said.

"Of course, it's a joke. Not even you would pull something like that."

"What's that supposed to mean?"

"Nothing. I'm sorry. Let's move on."

"Do you really not believe me or you don't want to believe me?"

"Quinn, sweetheart. Listen to yourself." He leaned over the table. "Are you all right?"

"Dad. It's true."

He took a deep breath and looked away.

Quinn realized she might have made an error in judgment. She shouldn't have told him. There wasn't even that much to tell. She could hardly confide in her father that she and Maya were madly in love. They'd only seen each other a few times and all of those times Maya had expressed great doubt about what they'd been doing—although that doubt had clearly never been powerful enough to stop her from doing it.

"Okay. Fine," Quinn said. "Let's move on. Let's pretend I didn't tell you. Erase it from your memory forever, please."

"Are you… in love with her?" Her dad swirled what was left of his wine around in his glass.

"I don't know. As I said, it might just be a rebound thing and Maya, well, she doesn't know what it is either, nor does she know what to do with it. With us. It's all very unclear. But… I do have feelings for her. We have a great time together. We went dancing at this salsa club on Saturday night and it was the most fun I've had in months."

"But it's definitely romance?" he asked. "Not just friendship?"

Quinn could hardly say they were more like friends with benefits at the moment. Her relationship with her father didn't extend to being able to share comments like that. "Yes," she said, even though she could hardly be certain. "Much more romance than friendship."

"Also from Maya's side?" He scrunched his lips together. "I never knew that about her. She was single for a long time after she and Drew divorced, but she never said anything about being interested in women."

"You were never really close enough that you would know that about her," Quinn said. She had zero intention of letting her father in on the secret she and Maya had shared for years. "Besides, I think it's quite a new development in her life." Quinn was beginning to see Maya's side of the argument. Their families might complicate matters between them too much—and to Maya, family was everything.

He blew out some air. "Jesus, Quinn. I'm going to need some time to process this. It's no reflection on you. Or Maya. But I wasn't expecting this. I didn't mean to be harsh or to judge you in any way, but you must understand that this is quite out of the ordinary."

"I know, Dad. I know."

"Your mother," he said on a sigh, then fell silent.

"Don't tell her. She won't be able to cope."

"I won't, but... what's going to happen? Are you going to keep seeing each other? Surely, this isn't easy for Maya either."

"I'm not sure. When it's just us, we're fine. But as soon as we start thinking about family, it's not so fine. Maya hasn't even told Tommy that she's dating women. Imagine the shock when she tells him I'm the woman she's dating."

"I wish I could help make this easier for you somehow."

This conversation was turning into a big downer. "I'll probably need to face the music sooner rather than later. Realistically, I know we don't really stand a chance."

"Love has conquered much greater challenges," her dad said.

Quinn scoffed, although it felt great to have her father on her side.

"Maya Mercer." He slowly shook his head. "Let me know if it will be dinner for three next time I come to town." He sent her a soft dad-smile.

"It's hardly likely."

He put his hand on the table, palm upward. "You know that all your old dad really wants is for you to be happy. That's all."

"Unfortunately, the world doesn't only consist of people who are my father." Quinn put her hand in his and relished the short-lived yet familiar comfort it brought her.

CHAPTER 31

Maya couldn't avoid Angus forever. She hadn't spoken to him in almost a week when they usually didn't go more than a day or two without a chat, even if it was just some quick banter in the hallway.

When a knock came on her door on Tuesday evening, she knew it could only be him. She opened the door.

Angus stood in the doorway with the biggest pout on his lips, and his hands on his hips as if to say, "What's it going to be, dear?"

Maya waved him in and without asking mixed him a rum and diet Coke.

"I won't claim to have eyes everywhere," Angus said. "But I have seen things I can't un-see."

Maya burst into a chuckle she sorely needed. Ever since leaving Quinn's on Sunday, she'd had a heaviness in her chest. An unpleasant sensation she could only explain as anticipatory heartache.

"Do enlighten me. What is so impossible to un-see?" Maya looked into Angus' friendly face.

"A woman arriving on Tuesday evening and only leaving the premises the next morning. I didn't get too good a look at her, but she quite resembled a woman I've seen a picture of. Might she go by the name of Quinn?"

"Correct." Maya had zero need or desire to be coy about Quinn with Angus any longer. "Quinn spent the night. I went out with Beverly on Friday and it was a big dud because all I could think of when I was with her was how much I wanted to be with Quinn instead. Then Quinn took me to the most fabulous club on Saturday and we had an amazing time and now, ironically, I find myself wishing we hadn't had such a good time, because..." None of the reasons had changed. Maya lay awake at night thinking of ways to tell Tommy so he wouldn't be too shocked but she could only ever imagine him so disgusted with his own mother that he refused to ever let her see Ethan again. "It's doomed. Maybe that's why we have so much fun, because time started running out for us before it even started."

"Oh, please." Angus performed one of his more impressive eye-rolls. "So that's why you've been avoiding me? Because I refuse to be the harbinger of doom like that voice inside your head?"

Maya shrugged. "I don't know what to do. I want to see Quinn again, but I really shouldn't."

"Of course, you should see her again." The ice cubes in his cocktail glass rattled. "Because why wouldn't you be entitled to the kind of joy Quinn brings you? Because you are a mother and a grandmother? Let me tell you something, darling, you are much more than that and you deserve to live your life as much more than those motherly roles you cast yourself in."

"Oh, Angus... I just can't." Maya sighed. "I had a chat with Quinn's roommate whose father married a woman not much older than her, and she and her dad barely speak."

"Do you honestly think Tommy would stop speaking to you just because you fell in love with someone he doesn't immediately approve of? He's your only son and you are his only mother."

"He has his father and his mother-in-law."

"So." Angus pursed his lips. "They're not you." He cut his gaze to her and looked into her eyes. "I know you're afraid and it's normal that you are. Quinn represents this big upheaval in your life. A life you've only just started rebuilding for yourself. But the very definition of life is that unexpected things like this happen and, trust me, much uglier events can occur in this life of ours than falling in love with someone who might not be the most appropriate. Who cares if she makes you feel the way she does? Do you know how many people would give up everything they had for a love like that?"

"A love like that?" Maya chuckled. "You're getting a little carried away there, Angus."

He waved off her comment. "That may be so, but that's my nature. It's how I get my point across." He drew up his eyebrows. "Is it working?"

"I haven't been in touch with Quinn since Sunday. I said I needed some rest as well as some time to think."

"You've had forty-eight hours. Either you're going nuts with desire for her or you've wrapped yourself in a shroud of gloom." He narrowed his eyes. "I suspect the latter."

"Both," Maya admitted. "I could so easily fall for her, but... only if I let myself."

"Sure, as if you can will feelings like that to just stop existing."

"Haven't you ever had feelings for the wrong person?"

"Darling, that's the story of my life. It will be the title of my memoir." He pulled up his shoulders. "And look at me. As single as they come."

"From what you've told me, one doesn't really have anything to do with the other."

"Maybe not directly, but back to your point." Angus cleared his throat. Maybe he needed a reset after all his theatrics. "If I could do it all over again, I'd pay more attention to love. To how I really feel inside." He tapped his chest. "I'd find a way to not care about all the things that don't really matter and that only stand in the way of true happiness. In your case, I mean the opinion of others. In my case, I mean the relentless chase of new lovers, all the men I was never able to resist. In the end, it never gave me what I really wanted." He sighed. "You see, there's always a parallel to be drawn, darling."

Maya appreciated Angus' ability to see through his own drama. If only she could see through hers with such sharpness.

"Imagine yourself ten years from now," Angus said. "You might have more grandchildren and a great relationship with your son, but what else will you have if you walk away from Quinn?"

"Surely, I'll get over her." Maya tilted her head. "I may very well meet someone else."

"Someone like Beverly who doesn't thrill you in the least?"

"Would that be so bad?"

Angus slammed his palm onto the armrest of his chair. "Damn right. It would be horrible and inexcusable. You can compromise on everything else in your life, but not on love, Maya. That, you will always regret."

"I've been single for a long time. It really isn't as awful as it's made out to be."

"Sure, but remember why you moved to New York."

"To spend time with my family. That came first when I made the decision and it always will."

"Things change," Angus said laconically. "Priorities change."

"If push comes to shove." Maya took her time to formulate the thought that was the crux of her current predicament. "Say I continue seeing Quinn and we develop deeper feelings for each other. Say I tell Tommy and my worst-case scenario comes true and he asks me to choose between Quinn and my family. What then?"

"Then your son would be a terrible person and I don't believe he is, Maya, because you raised him. He's your flesh and blood. How could he ever make you choose like that?" Angus shook his head. "Tommy's not a moron."

"I'd like to think he isn't." Still, Tommy's disapproval was the most persistent thought in Maya's head, just because he was her son. Because she had raised him. If he rejected her for falling in love with Quinn, did it mean that Maya's upbringing had failed? Or was there only so much a mother could do when it came to raising her child?

"Please don't tell me you're not going to see Quinn again because you're afraid of something that might never happen." Angus didn't sound as though he would be taking no for an answer.

"It's not just my family. It's hers as well. And it's not only the age difference, it's the difference of where we are in our lives." Maya huffed out some air. "When I arrived at Quinn's apartment, I couldn't believe that was how she lived. I'm in my fifties and used to a certain standard. Because I worked for it and I earned it." She paused. "Before I sound too much like a princess, it's not so much about Quinn's bed not being comfortable enough or her kitchen being too dingy, it's about us belonging to different generations. She's of Tommy's generation. I'm of her parents' generation. It doesn't make things any easier."

"But still," Angus mused. "If you really love her, what does it even matter?"

CHAPTER 32

Quinn put what she believed to be the final touch to Maya's portrait. She would miss looking at that face, but it was time to wrap things up. It was Wednesday and Quinn still hadn't heard from Maya. Quinn had wanted to text her, call her, or even go to her apartment and force Maya to tell her to her face that it was all over. But she had some sense left. Pushing Maya was probably not the best idea right now. And the picture she'd made for Maya might say more than all the words Quinn had ready in her head.

Quinn had made two versions of Maya's portrait. One for the hallways at Acton, the second as a personal gift. She'd finished the official one earlier that week. She was looking at the unofficial one now. At Maya's outstretched arm. At her smooth leg protruding from the red dress she'd been wearing that day. In the picture, it was now the green of the dress Maya had worn last Saturday, when she'd shone on the dance floor, when she'd had all eyes on her, when she and Quinn had danced the night away in utter bliss.

Quinn peered at the picture, at the glossy patch of skin just above Maya's left knee. Maybe this work wasn't finished just yet. She took a deep breath and added one last element.

Quinn heard Griff rummage around in the kitchen and pondered asking for her opinion before sending both portraits to Maya—one for official approval, the other for very different reasons—but Quinn didn't want to wait any longer. She downloaded the pictures to her phone and texted them to Maya. Then, all she could do was wait. Quinn did go into the kitchen because from the instant she'd pressed 'Send', time had slowed down and seconds had begun to feel like long minutes.

"You forgot," Griff said when Quinn walked in.

"What?" The fact that she didn't know what she might have forgotten proved Griff's point.

"I'm interviewing you for the Greenpoint Calendar. For your upcoming show, remember? This thing at the Flashpoint gallery where a bunch of your pictures will be on display and local hipsters as well as art connoisseurs from all five boroughs will marvel at your brilliance." Griff narrowed her eyes. "I believe even Brooke and Bill Hathaway will make an appearance. As well as all your exes, although let's hope Morgan doesn't hear about it." She shrugged. "But with how she's all over your Insta, I wouldn't count on that. Unless she has decided to really move on after your most recent blowout."

"Good grief, Griff. What are you on?"

"A very potent cold brew from that new coffee shop across the street." Griff sighed deeply. "The new barista is cute as fucking hell. Her name's Roxanne." She pulled the corners of her mouth all the way down.

"Oh, I see. This isn't about me at all."

"She had the audacity to flirt with me," Griff said.

"You weren't wearing your T-shirt?" As a joke, Quinn had

given Griff a custom-made T-shirt that said 'No flirting, please' as a Christmas gift last year.

"I know. Silly me."

"Are you feeling frisky?" Quinn couldn't help but grin.

"Must have been all the noises I was subjected to over the weekend. My subconscious must have absorbed them and now, a few days later, I'm paying the price."

"I'm sorry." Quinn felt for her phone in the back pocket of her jeans. It hadn't buzzed yet. "I can pretty much guarantee it won't happen again."

"Your guarantee means nothing to me right now."

"You were bound to feel attracted to another human being at some point. Isn't your reaction to that going to form part of the book's premise?"

Griff nodded. "The worst part was that, according to my own rules, I wasn't allowed to flirt back."

"You could just tell her what you're doing."

Griff shook her head. "I think that would defeat the purpose."

"Next time you want a fancy coffee, I'll get it for you. Because that's what friends do."

"You've been glued to your computer," Griff said. "I take it that means you haven't heard from Maya."

Quinn had a tendency to obsess about work when her love life, or whatever passed for it, wasn't going how she wanted it to. It was one of the reasons she'd already selected all the photos for the exhibition, although, since about fifteen minutes ago, there was one she very much wanted to add. "Nope," Quinn said on a dramatic sigh. "I just texted her my work though, so I'm hoping she'll get in touch. She has to say something, doesn't she?"

"She will. She just needs some time," Griff said, as though

she knew all about what Maya was thinking just because they'd had a brief night-time chat over the weekend.

"Let's hope so." Quinn finally sat. "Shall we do this in the living room, perhaps?" she asked, alluding to the interview.

"Why?" Griff said matter-of-factly. "It's so cozy in our kitchen. Perfect for an intimate interview with Brooklyn's up-and-coming."

"I don't see why you need to ask me any more questions." Quinn leaned back in her chair. "You already know everything there is to know about me and my work."

"It's not because I volunteer my time for the Greenpoint Calendar that I don't take the work seriously," Griff said in a mock-serious tone. "Now, Quinn." She pressed the record button on her phone. "I've had an exclusive preview of the pictures that will be on display. Can you explain why three quarters of the human subjects are women over the age of fifty?"

CHAPTER 33

After her last class of the day, Maya checked her phone. Two text messages from Quinn awaited her, each containing a picture and no words. At least, Maya thought, if she ever had the opportunity to introduce Quinn to Angus, they would have their flair for the dramatic in common.

She looked at the first picture in which she was wearing the red dress of the photo shoot—that day she'd seen Quinn again after ten years of living with their secret.

Quinn had placed Maya on a background photo of Acton Academy, floating on a cloud above the building. Her arms were shoulder height in a perfect Viennese waltz hold, her head turned so she was looking down at the school over her shoulder. Her face was a picture of perfect concentration, but her lips were pulled into a tentative smile. Quinn had perfectly captured the marriage of effort and pleasure involved in executing the dance. The work was beautiful and would fit right in on the walls of Acton Academy.

When she looked at the second version Quinn had made, Maya's first thought was that it would never be allowed to grace the Acton hallways, nor should it be.

In this image, Maya was floating above the skyscrapers of New York City. Quinn had changed the color of Maya's dress into emerald green and had made it look like the dress was being blown upward by a gust of wind, revealing much more of Maya's legs than was appropriate for displaying in a school. Her right arm was extended to the side while she had her left hand on her jutting out hip. Her head was thrown back and she was laughing as if she'd been caught in a moment of pure ecstasy.

Maya didn't know what kind of material had come out of the photo shoot and Quinn might well have captured her in a bolder stance or in the middle of a move she hadn't been able to—or wanted to—stop. If she remembered correctly, which was hard because so much had happened since, Maya had been trying to impress Quinn. She'd been trying to show her that the passing of time hadn't had that much of an effect on her or her dance technique.

In this image, it seemed like the tables were turned, and Quinn was the one trying to impress Maya with her photographic eye and her editing technique. It was working. Maya could not imagine looking as stunning in real life as she did in the photo. Was this how Quinn saw her?

Maya's gaze was drawn to a black mark just above her knee. She expanded the picture and zoomed in. She burst into a chuckle. In the picture, Quinn had given her a tattoo. *Life is for living*, it said, in the same font as Quinn's own tattoo.

Quinn Hathaway was always ready to surprise her. She'd done so last weekend when she'd taken her dancing and she'd done it again now. She'd also very much managed to surprise Maya ten years ago, on that hot summer weekend.

Quinn was smoking hot, talented, full of surprises, and very clever. And she liked older women—Maya in particular. The only thing stopping Maya from calling Quinn right there and then was her own fear. But, as Quinn had just expertly reminded her, life was for living. Not for abandoning your dreams because of too much trepidation.

For that reason, instead of walking straight home after work, Maya visited her son. Maya often stopped by unannounced and Tommy always looked relieved when she arrived.

"Ethan's having one of those days," Tommy said. "Surely he can't be teething yet."

Maya took the baby from him so he could take a break. "It's a little early for that." Her gaze was drawn to the TV. "Look, Ethan, it's mommy," Maya said, as though Ethan could already see that it was his mother presenting the news.

"I've tried that, but it's not working. I'll see if a bottle will calm him down." Tommy headed to the kitchen. Maya followed him with a crying Ethan on her arm. She rocked him back and forth while gently rubbing his back. Even though he was crying, it was lovely to feel him in her arms. As though his grandmother's arms were made of different, more soothing material, Ethan soon fell silent. His breathing slowed and he fell asleep with his face pressed against Maya's shoulder.

"You were like this with your father," Maya whispered. "You'd cry all afternoon, until your dad came home from work and I'd hand you to him and you'd abruptly stop."

"I'm so glad you're here, Mom." Tommy stepped closer. He lay his hand on Ethan's head gently while he kissed Maya on the cheek. "Do you want to put him in his crib?"

"It's okay. I'll hold him for a while. Make sure he's fast asleep. How's work?" Maya asked while she slowly walked around the kitchen with Ethan.

"Working from home with a small baby isn't all it's cracked up to be."

They talked about work, Ethan, and his part-time nanny

while they settled into the living room couch and watched the rest of the news.

"I was just telling Ethan that he's lucky that he can see his mom on TV when she's at work." Tommy sounded exhausted.

"He's a very lucky boy." Even though Maya's arm was getting tired, she couldn't bring herself to put Ethan in his crib.

"How are you, Mom?" Tommy sent her a smile. "I feel like I haven't asked you that in such a long time."

"I don't expect you to worry about my well-being at all until Ethan's first birthday."

"I'm not worried. Just curious as to how my mother's doing." Tommy seemed to relax a little.

"I'm doing fine." Now that Ethan had settled down, Maya remembered her primary reason for stopping by. "I haven't had a chance to tell you, but guess who I ran into a few weeks ago when I had my portrait taken for Acton?"

Tommy huffed out some air. "Can you narrow it down? It could be anyone."

"She used to live next door to us in Milbury."

Tommy narrowed his eyes. "Quinn Hathaway?"

"The one and only." A shiver ran up Maya's spine. It felt inappropriate while holding her grandson. "She just texted me the picture she shot for Acton." Maya pushed herself up from the couch. "I'll show you. Let me put him in his crib first."

Nerves tingled in her fingertips as Maya dug her phone out of her purse and navigated to the pictures Quinn had sent her earlier. Maya made sure to only show Tommy the picture that Quinn had made for Acton.

"Wow," Tommy said. "It looks like you're flying over the floor." He stared at it for a while longer. "Do you think you can get a high-res version of this?"

"Um, sure. I can ask. Why?"

"I can picture that on the wall right over there." Tommy pointed at the wall opposite him. "It's really well done. Quinn's clearly good at what she does. How is she?"

"Well. I think." Maya's only intention was to tell Tommy that she'd seen Quinn. Nothing more. And to see how he reacted to hearing about the girl he grew up next door to.

"Married? Kids?" He grinned broadly. "Something tells me none of that is for Quinn. She never struck me as the settling-down type." He ran his hand through his hair. "I always imagined her traveling the world with her camera, taking pictures of all the places she visited. Being a digital nomad or something like that."

"She lives in Brooklyn." Maya put her phone away. "But she's not married and she doesn't have kids. She's, um, single, I think. She's gone through a bad break-up recently." Maya was skating on very thin ice, yet talking about Quinn set something alight inside her. "We had coffee after the photo shoot," Maya clarified, as though she had to explain why she had all this information about their former neighbor.

"She's a professional photographer?" Tommy asked.

"And retouch artist," Maya said, as though she'd known what that meant all her life instead of first hearing about it a few weeks ago. "I think she said she has an exhibition coming up soon." Now it felt like Maya was defending Quinn somehow.

"And that break-up she went through, that was with another woman?"

"Yes."

"She never really paid me much attention when we were kids. Do you remember?"

"You were a bit too far apart in age to play together, I guess." And thank goodness for that, Maya thought. If Quinn and Tommy had been actual friends everything would be different.

"I guess." Tommy rubbed his face with his hands. "Good to know she's doing well." He let his head fall back. "God, I'm tired."

"Take a nap, sweetheart. I'll look after Ethan for a while."

"Really?" Tommy looked at Maya as though he couldn't believe his luck. "Because he kept us up half the night." He nodded at the TV screen. "CNN must have a spectacular makeup department because Beth did not look like that when she left for work earlier."

Maya chuckled. "Yes, really. You know I don't mind."

"Thanks, Mom. You're a lifesaver." He pushed himself up.

"Tommy, um, Quinn and I." Maya's heart was beating in her throat. "We've met up a couple of times. It's been good seeing her again."

Tommy nodded. "It's great that you're making friends, Mom." Tommy sounded more condescending than surprised about Maya's small admission. Or perhaps his brain was too tired to process anything but rudimentary information.

"Have a good nap."

"I'll just be half an hour or so." Tommy didn't bother suppressing his yawns any longer.

"Sure." Maya remembered how easily a short nap could turn into a long sleep when you had a small baby.

She waited until he had disappeared from view to reach for her phone. She navigated to the picture with the green dress, and was again amazed by how Quinn had portrayed her. Maya felt like she had lived her life a little more intentionally by telling Tommy she'd seen Quinn. Although she hadn't really told him anything, and she had no inclination to tell him anything more any time soon, she had left the door ajar. She had let some light in. Quinn was now someone who actually existed in her life and Tommy was aware of that. It was a small step but it was a first one.

Maya took a deep breath and texted Quinn back. She thanked her for the pictures and asked if she'd like to go dancing again on Saturday.

CHAPTER 34

"Sometimes," Maya breathed into Quinn's ear, "it's better to dance than to talk."

The song was about to end, and Quinn needed a break but ever since they'd arrived at the club, Maya had politely rebuffed the advances of anyone else who invited her to dance. Apparently, tonight, she only wanted to dance with Quinn.

Then again, Quinn didn't much feel like rehashing all the reasons they shouldn't be together. Her feet might be tired, but it was still easier to try and keep up with Maya on the dance floor than to start another conversation about their differences and what they stood in the way of. As long as they danced, everything had infinite potential. So that was what Quinn did. She clung to Maya's body for dear life and moved her feet across the floor as elegantly as she could.

After two more songs, Quinn had no choice but to take a breather and get a drink. She didn't know how or when Maya had gotten so well acquainted with the bartender, but she got him to procure them a table in a corner of the club, away from most of the action. Maybe, Quinn thought, as she plopped down in a chair, there was another dimension to the language of dance that she wasn't privy to. Or some sort of secret hierarchy that was valid everywhere when dance royalty like Maya turned up.

"God, I love this place," Maya said. "I could come here every weekend."

"What's stopping you?" Quinn asked.

Maya stretched her arm out over the table, her palm open to Quinn. Quinn responded by putting her hand in Maya's. "Nothing, I guess." She grinned. "Hey, look, um, later, when we leave, I'd like to go back to mine instead of your place."

"Okay." Quinn studied their joined hands. Talk about mixed messages.

"You're welcome to join me," Maya said.

Quinn nodded. "All right. Let me think about it. See how I feel later."

Maya held Quinn's hand a little tighter. "Quinn, I *want* you to join me."

Quinn wanted to leave for Maya's place there and then, but she suspected Maya was far from danced out. "Okay. I'll go with you."

"Thank you." Maya sipped from her cocktail. "I'm sorry it took me so long to get in touch."

"I get it." This was starting to feel a lot like the beginning of Quinn's affair with Morgan, when Quinn had never known whether they'd still be on the next day because Morgan always had something more important in her life to focus on. Maybe Quinn should remind Maya of what she'd missed the entire week they hadn't seen each other.

"Maybe we can talk tomorrow." Maya squeezed her hand again. "Let's just enjoy the hell out of tonight." When Maya smiled like that, her face all lit up and her eyes sparkling like the brightest diamonds, Quinn would agree to anything. She had to make sure that didn't turn into an issue—she had to make sure to stand her ground. But not tonight. Maya was right. They'd come all the way to Queens to dance the night away.

"In that case, Mrs. Former National and World Champion, may I have the profound honor of the next dance with you?" Reinvigorated, Quinn rose from her chair.

"I thought you'd never ask." Maya was still holding Quinn's hand and pulled her close. "And in case you were wondering, you have all my dances tonight," she whispered in Quinn's ear.

After a few more rounds on the dance floor, Quinn said, "Come with me." She made sure to look Maya straight in the eye. "Don't worry, we're not leaving yet. I want to show you something."

"Okay." Maya sunk her teeth into her bottom lip and followed Quinn. "The bathroom? You're not showing me anything new."

"Come on." Quinn pulled Maya into a cubicle and locked the door behind them.

"Really?" Maya asked, her tone of voice more excited than questioning.

"This is what happens in club bathrooms all around the world. Surely you remember?" Quinn ran her hands alongside Maya's chest.

"Maybe you don't want to play the age game with me right now." Maya leaned in to kiss Quinn, but Quinn pulled back.

Quinn grabbed hold of Maya's hand and put it over the tattoo on her lower belly.

Maya tilted her head as if to ask, again, "Really?"

In response, Quinn flipped open the button of her jeans. She hiked up the hem of Maya's dress. "Dancing with you is the best foreplay I've ever experienced." Quinn inched closer so that Maya's hand slipped down her jeans with the movement. Quinn was too aroused to experience much doubt about this rather juvenile move of whisking Maya away to the bathroom. She could hardly use the defense of acting her age because, quite frankly, she felt a little too old for shenanigans like this as well, but a much more dominant part of her wanted Maya with a force strong enough to obliterate any rational objections.

Quinn edged her finger along the waistline of Maya's panties. "I want you, Maya. So fucking much," she breathed into the heavy air between them. Then, she finally kissed Maya. As Quinn's tongue dipped into Maya's mouth, she let her finger slip along the panel of Maya's panties.

Maya responded by lowering her hand farther inside Quinn's underwear.

"Jesus," Maya said on a groan. "You weren't lying about being aroused."

Quinn shook her head. She cupped one hand behind Maya's neck for support. Maya's fingers lingering inside her panties, exploring her wetness, made her knees buckle. Quinn tried to focus on her fingers between Maya's legs but it was no use trying to delicately circle her clit when she was amped up like this. She needed skin-on-skin contact. She slipped her hand inside Maya's panties.

"I can't believe we're doing this," Maya whispered. "What if someone hears us?" It must have been a rhetorical question because, as she spoke, she drove a finger high inside of Quinn.

Quinn tried to bite her lip to stop herself from crying out in pleasure but she only half succeeded.

"Shhh," Maya said, while she only made Quinn want to groan louder.

"Oh, fuck, Maya," Quinn said on a stifled sigh. "You drive me so fucking crazy."

Maya moved her fingers inside Quinn in such a way that Quinn forgot all about her own hand in Maya's panties. Maya's palm touched against her clit and Quinn soon forgot where she was altogether. All she felt, all she saw and smelled, was Maya, who was all over her and inside her, and who wanted to dance with only her tonight. As Maya had instructed earlier, they were enjoying the hell out of their evening. But if Maya still believed that their nights—and days—together were numbered, she hadn't been thoroughly introduced to Quinn's tenacity yet. There was simply no way Quinn was letting go of this, of what she had with Maya, for the sake of so-called decency.

She abandoned her mission between Maya's legs and focused on her own pleasure—she'd make sure Maya was properly pleasured later. On the soaring heat between her legs and on the woman who had created it.

All week long, Quinn hadn't been able to stop thinking about Maya. And then, she'd finally texted. For Quinn, that was the moment the foreplay leading to this had started. When Maya had asked her to go dancing again. Because Quinn knew Maya wasn't only asking to dance. She was asking for so much more. She was asking for this, and for Quinn to go home with her, and for them to explore the next step in this as yet undefined thing between them. There was something there and it wasn't something that was easy to walk away from, for neither of them.

Otherwise, Maya wouldn't have her fingers high inside Quinn right now. She wouldn't have followed her into the bathroom, and she wouldn't have responded to Quinn's advances. Ever since they'd arrived, despite ample attention from others, Maya had only had eyes for Quinn, making her feel like she was the one and only queen of this club. This wasn't rooted in any reality, but it was how Maya made Quinn feel. At least when she allowed herself to. When she set aside her apprehensions and made time for them to be together. When she allowed space in her mind to let the idea of them grow.

Quinn was about to climax in the club's bathroom cubicle. All the week's tension flooded from her body until she felt drained but much more like herself again. Until she collapsed against Maya's gorgeous body and asked, "Is there anything you're not down for?"

"Many things," Maya said. "But not tonight."

CHAPTER 35

"I told Tommy I ran into you," Maya said. Despite coming home to her own bed, she hadn't slept nearly enough. Not because the bed was too small, but because of the irresistible woman lying next to her.

"What did he say?" Quinn was scrolling through Instagram on her phone and barely looked up.

"I told him we've been sleeping together and I've been having the time of my life."

That got Quinn's full attention. She put her phone away and looked at Maya wide-eyed.

"I was led to believe you'd missed me terribly all week long." Maya did her best to sound as faux-petulant as possible even though it wasn't really her style.

"Sorry. Griff's write-up on my exhibition went online and I got a ton of new Insta followers." Quinn looked into Maya's eyes. "But none of that means anything to me if I can't be with you." She batted her lashes ostentatiously.

"Obviously, I didn't tell Tommy about, um, us like that, but I did tell him about the photo shoot. I showed him the portrait you did for Acton. He asked if he could get a high-res version to have printed and framed for his living room wall."

"My work in Beth Robbins' house. Griff will be green with envy."

"I just wanted him to be aware of you, if that makes sense." Maya sipped her coffee. She needed all the caffeine she could get. Fun as it was, dancing the night away might not be something she could do every single week any longer. Not if she wanted to have energy left for being an involved grandmother and teacher. And lover.

"It makes perfect sense." Quinn sucked her lips into her mouth and looked away. "My dad came to the city earlier this week. We had dinner."

"How's Bill?" Maya asked.

"Dad's fine, but..." Quinn rubbed her palm with her opposite thumb. "I might have told him about us. About... everything."

Maya was glad she had two hands wrapped around her mug otherwise she would have dropped it to the floor.

"He kept prodding, and in the end I relented. I just told him."

Maya swallowed hard. "How did he react?"

"He was quite shocked, as you can imagine." Quinn chuckled nervously. "He promised not to tell Mom."

Maya put her coffee down because she feared she might still drop it. "Jesus. I'm not sure how I feel about Bill knowing." She rested her gaze on Quinn. "How do you feel?"

"I feel like..." Quinn looked as though she was carefully weighing what to say next. "Telling my dad was not the end of the world. It wasn't easy and it didn't exactly make him jump for joy, but he's my father and he said that all he really wants is for me to be happy."

"He *would* say that." It sounded like something a responsible and understanding parent might say. Maya knew how much Bill worshipped his daughter. As a parent, she suspected that the words he had spoken to his child might not have conveyed how he truly felt about Quinn and Maya.

"What's the difference? Even if he only said it to not upset me at the time, isn't it his actual reaction that counts?" Quinn sighed. "I don't exist to fulfill my parents' dreams and aspirations. My mom might not entirely agree with that, but that's what my dad has always told me."

Maya huffed out some air. "God, I don't know, Quinn."

"He even said that next time he came to the city, I should invite you to come to dinner with us."

Maya burst into a chuckle. "That'll be the day."

"Why not?" Quinn drummed her fingertips on the countertop. "If we... keep going out, it's bound to happen at some point."

Before Maya had moved to the city, but after she'd already made the decision to do so, she'd often envisioned what her coming out would be like. She imagined falling in love with a suave New Yorker who could charm the pants off her son whether he wanted her to or not. Maya had been convinced that a woman her son could easily accept was the only kind of woman she could really fall for. Unfortunately, reality had different plans in store for her. "I can't believe Bill knows." She glanced at her phone as if Bill would call demanding to know what the hell Maya was doing with his daughter. "Truth be told, I have no idea how to deal with this part," she admitted. "With the whole telling-the-family thing while keeping my dignity intact."

"I gathered." Quinn slid off the stool she'd been perched on and walked around the kitchen island. "I wish you'd leave your dignity out of it, though." She curled her arms around

Maya's waist and hugged her from behind. "It has nothing to do with it."

"It's different for me." Maya folded her hands over Quinn's. "I'm the older woman in this affair. Not only should I be the wiser one, which I'm clearly not. I also look like the biggest perv, what with you being so much younger."

Maya could feel Quinn shaking her head against her back. "Do you know how many men in their fifties and sixties strike up relationships with women a lot younger than me? They don't think about it twice. In fact, it's what they want. It's what they actively search for. Do you consider them pervs?"

"I consider them clichés more than anything," Maya said. She pushed herself backward in order to get the most out of Quinn's hug.

"You are nothing like them." Quinn kissed Maya's neck. "In case you need reassurance, I'm not a gold digger, although I am very fond of your apartment and your doorman and your marble countertops and the heated floors." Quinn slid a hand upward from Maya's belly to her chest. "I'm really only after your body." She kissed Maya's neck again.

"You say that now." Maya closed her eyes. "My body's exhausted after last night." She turned around in Quinn's embrace so she could look her in the eye. "In the future, you're going to have to choose: either dancing all night long or making love. I'm too old for both in one night."

"I won't make any demands on your body for a few hours. I promise." Quinn's phone, which had been buzzing with notifications throughout their conversation, lit up again.

"Sounds like you're too busy for any of that, anyway."

"My show opens in ten days. It's going to be like that until then."

"I take it Bill and Brooke will be there?"

"They'd better be," Quinn said.

"You know what that means?" Maya looked into Quinn's eyes. "Assuming that you want me there?"

"I'd call the whole thing off if I knew you couldn't make it." Quinn shot her a seductive smile. "But, seriously, Maya, no pressure. You don't have to be there as... my girlfriend. If that would make you uncomfortable, with my parents being there."

"In what capacity would I be there then?"

"As my friend. My old neighbor." Quinn's eyes narrowed. "I've also been meaning to ask if I could include your portrait in my show."

"Which one?"

"Good question," Quinn said.

"The Acton one, surely." The other work Quinn had made would have to remain strictly between them forever. "Don't you have to check with Indira about that?"

"I own the images I create, it's in my agreement with Acton, so I can display them wherever I want. But I would need your approval."

"I can't possibly imagine a picture of me in a trendy Brooklyn art gallery."

"That's what happens when you date people so much younger than yourself."

"Are you saying it keeps me youthful?"

"It's hardly going to have the opposite effect," Quinn said. "Come to think of it, if there's a portrait of you in my show it would be the perfect excuse for you to be there without making my mom suspicious."

Maya felt sorry for Brooke now because she was deliberately being kept in the dark about her daughter's personal life. "Isn't she going to be even more furious later if she finds out that Bill knew all along?"

"There's a good chance of that, but it's too soon to tell her, don't you think?"

"She's *your* mom, Quinn."

"I can always be vague with the timing."

"You'd be surprised what mothers can intuit about their children."

"Not mine."

"Trust me on this," Maya said. "Half the things you think she has no clue about, she knows. She might just choose not to bring them up to avoid conflict." Maya had used this particular parenting skill since Tommy had become a teenager. Sometimes, it was simply better not to have the conversation and let whatever it was pass.

"My mom and I." Quinn loosened her grip on Maya. "It's complicated."

"Of course."

"She's not like my dad. She can't just let things go and simply be proud of me. Dad and I used to joke about it and call it Stepford syndrome."

"That's not very nice." They broke from their hug. "I'm sure all Brooke has ever tried to do is her very best. But mothers, like all humans, are deeply flawed."

"I bet Tommy doesn't feel that way about you."

Maya rolled her eyes. "Try divorcing your son's father when he's thirteen years old."

"Surely Tommy knew that wasn't only down to you."

"It's water under the bridge now." The last thing Maya wanted to do right now with Quinn was analyze her divorce, which happened fifteen years ago. "I just wish you weren't so harsh on your mom. I'm not claiming to know Brooke the way you do, but there was a time when we were fairly close. Just as your dad said to you, she has only ever wanted you to be happy. And let's be honest, you haven't always made it easy on yourself, at least in the relationship department. Brooke is much more of a realist than Bill. That's all."

"I'm very happy *now,*" Quinn said, sounding like she'd regressed into being a moody teenager. "But if I were to tell Mom that, she wouldn't be able to accept it without some sort of drama. She doesn't trust me to make the right decisions for myself. She never has. And of course I've made wrong decisions. Who hasn't? But Mom's always there with an I-told-you-so and I can't stand it."

"You have gone from a relationship with a married woman to one with her former neighbor." Maya hoped Quinn would be able to see the humor in what she was saying. "Cut the woman some slack."

"Can we stop talking about my mom, please? I'll deal with it when I have to."

"Have you ever had something serious with someone your own age?" Maya was suddenly curious.

"Sure," Quinn said. "In high school."

Maya nodded. Maybe Quinn really did have some mommy issues to deal with, but Maya wasn't going to get into that now either. She had other plans for the day.

"How about I draw us a bath?" she asked.

"I thought you'd never ask." Quinn took Maya's hand and dragged her into the hallway. "Have I told you how much I adore your bathroom?"

CHAPTER 36

The following Wednesday, after she'd spent the morning in Manhattan taking pictures of a glitzy new Mexican-Chinese fusion restaurant, Quinn headed to Maya's. She could get used to having a pad on the other side of the East River. She wasn't sure she could live outside of Brooklyn—she never had since she'd moved to the city—but she sure could get used to the luxuries Maya's condo offered.

When she arrived the doorman was already holding the door for an older man in a very colorful, debonair suit.

Before Quinn could say she was here for Maya Mercer, the doorman held up a finger and said, "Fifth floor. You and Mr. Levison are getting off at the same floor. I'll ring up to Mrs. Mercer while you're in the elevator." *So much for doorman discretion.*

The elevator doors had barely closed when the man said, "You must be Quinn."

Maya had mentioned the flamboyant gay living across the hall from her, but Quinn couldn't remember his name. "And you are?"

"Angus from-across-the-hall." He held out his hand.

"Maya's friend and... neighbor." He put a strange kind of emphasis on the word 'neighbor'—as if he was very much in the know of who Quinn was.

Quinn gave his hand a quick shake. The elevator stopped and Angus let her get out first.

"Maya, dear," Angus said when he noticed Maya waiting in the front door. "Quinn and I have finally made each other's acquaintance. About time."

"Wonderful." Maya sounded a little different when she spoke to her neighbor, making Quinn wonder again what the old man knew.

Angus didn't get his keys out. He was clearly waiting to be invited inside Maya's apartment.

Maya cast her gaze to Quinn. Maybe she'd had other plans for them this afternoon but she gave Angus a nod and apparently it was enough for him to understand that he was in. Again, he let Quinn go first.

"It's lovely to meet you, Quinn," Angus said formally. "To be able to put a face to the person Maya can't shut up about."

Maya shot him a look. "Coffee?" she asked.

Angus drew his lips into a pout. "I guess it's a bit early for cocktails."

Maya went into the kitchen and Angus walked into the living room as though he owned the place. Quinn dropped her equipment in the hallway and followed Angus, who had already taken a seat in the armchair by the window.

"So, Maya can't shut up about me?" Quinn asked. She sensed that Angus was the type who welcomed a direct question.

"Girl." He rolled his eyes. "Any fool can see how nuts she is about you. Any fool, but her."

"I can hear you," Maya shouted from the kitchen.

"I only ever tell the truth, my dear," Angus yelled back. "And you can't hear enough of that!"

Quinn believed she was in for an unexpected afternoon of gaiety. She might learn a thing or two about Maya along the way.

"I'm probably the only person on earth, apart from you two, who knows the full story." Angus kept his voice low. "The whole *shebang* from ten years ago included." He obviously believed this to be very witty because he leaned back, his gaze glued to Quinn, waiting for her reaction.

Quinn took an instant liking to the man and happily gave him an enthusiastic chuckle.

"How about you, Angus?" Quinn asked. "Anyone special in your life?"

Maya walked in with a tray of coffee cups. "Angus much prefers to stick his nose in other people's business than to reveal his own," she said.

Angus shook his head. "I'm well and truly over the hill," contrary to what he'd just said, he sounded rather spritely. "But a lady never gives her age away." He clasped a hand to his chest dramatically. "Let's just say that, at my age, it takes a lot of effort to look twenty years younger than you actually are." He sighed. "If I were to put that kind of effort into finding a man, I might very well succeed, but what would I have to offer him but this old and wrinkled face?"

"In case you hadn't noticed"—Maya distributed cups—"Angus used to be in theater. Hence the flair for the dramatic."

Quinn made a mental note to ask Maya if she knew how old Angus actually was. He looked late-sixties, early-seventies perhaps, which, in Quinn's eyes, would hardly put him over the hill.

"Well," Angus said, apparently taking Maya's remark as a point of pride instead of a jibe, "I daresay that if it weren't for me, you and Quinn might not be sitting here this afternoon having coffee with little old me." He gave the kind of sharp nod that insinuated, "Just try to contradict me on that."

"It's true," Maya said. "Angus saved me from myself and my many thoughts of doom."

Quinn couldn't tell if Maya was being serious or just putting on some sort of elaborate play of quips and banter with her neighbor. Either way, it was amusing. Quinn had never seen Maya interact with any of her friends—the times she'd been over at her parents' house back in the day notwithstanding.

"I'm glad we're on the same page about that." Angus sipped delicately from his coffee. "I hear you have a fancy exhibition coming up next week," Angus said to Quinn. "Might one invite oneself to such a glamorous occasion?"

"Of course," Quinn said. "The more, the merrier. The opening's next Thursday." A flash of nerves coursed through her. Quinn had been sharing her work on social media for ages, but seeing people react to it in the flesh would be a very different experience. She'd gotten plenty of negative comments over the years, but, after the harsh sting of the first few, it had gotten easier to shrug them off. She suspected that a bad review of a real-life exhibition might be harder to shake.

"In that case, I'll be there with bells and whistles on," Angus said. "I've seen your work online. It's nothing short of spectacular."

"Despite being over the hill, Angus is all over Instagram," Maya said.

"The things you see on there." Angus sounded genuinely in awe. "It's hard to believe half the time."

"Better than Grindr," Maya said, surprising Quinn with her knowledge of the app.

Angus waved her off. "I'm all for making it easy for men to

get their rocks off, but I'm way too old school for a virtual meat market like that." He shrugged. "Or maybe just too old in general." He shot Quinn an unexpected wink. He downed his coffee and put his cup down. "Now, I'll leave you ladies to it. I'm sure you have *things* to get on with." He pushed himself out of his chair energetically. "I'll see you both very soon."

CHAPTER 37

Quinn had been in the tub for almost an hour—she did seem extremely fond of Maya's bathroom. Maya suspected she was scrolling through Instagram again. Whatever she was doing was distracting enough for her not to notice that the water was getting cold. Maya decided to go and have a look. Upbeat pop music blasted from Quinn's phone and she was humming along as her thumb scrolled and scrolled. She hadn't heard Maya walk up to the open door.

Before Maya could make her presence known, the doorbell rang. It was the middle of the afternoon on a Wednesday. Maya wasn't expecting anyone. She hurried to the intercom.

"Mrs. Mercer," the doorman said, "your daughter-in-law is on her way up with your grandson." He sounded very jolly. Usually, an announcement like that would make his jolliness infectious, but today it was hard for Maya to get excited about having an impromptu visit from Ethan and Beth.

Maya quickly thanked the doorman, even though she wasn't pleased with how he'd handled this. Of course, it wasn't the poor guy's fault that Quinn was lounging in her bathtub in the middle of the day and that Beth was about to ring her bell. *Damn.* There it was already.

The super-fast elevators in her building were mostly a blessing but today Maya wished she'd had more time. Not that her brain was functioning the way it should. She was already walking toward the front door when she thought about asking Quinn to stay sequestered in the bathroom until Beth left—what difference would half an hour extra in the bath make to her, anyway? Maybe Quinn had heard the bell and would be wise enough to hide herself. Maya hoped she could count on Quinn's common sense, because there was no time to run to the bathroom. She heard Ethan crying outside the door already. She quickly opened the door, trying to look cool.

"Beth? What a surprise!"

"I'm so sorry, Maya." Beth looked flustered. "I was out walking with him and we were having a great time." She pushed Ethan's pram into the living room. "Until we weren't. I think he urgently needs his diaper changed. I was two blocks away from here so I thought I'd check if you were home. Thank goodness, you are." She picked up Ethan and started for the bathroom. "Can I quickly change him?"

"Sure, but, um..." Before she could finish her sentence, or come up with a viable reason for Beth not to use the bathroom other than her secret lover was soaking in the tub, Quinn appeared in the hallway, dressed in nothing but a towel, her hair dripping wet.

"Oh, I'm sorry," Beth said. "I didn't know you had company." Meanwhile, Ethan was crying as if, in his own tiny universe, the third world war had just broken out.

"Oh my god." Quinn clasped her hands to her mouth, making the towel almost slip off her. She quickly reached for it. "Beth Robbins!"

"Nice to meet you..." Beth said.

"Quinn," Quinn said. "Bathroom's free."

"Thanks." Beth hurried inside with Ethan.

Quinn looked at Maya wide-eyed. "Beth Robbins," she mouthed.

"Quinn," Maya whispered. "Please."

"I'll put some clothes on."

Maya followed Quinn into the bedroom because she didn't know what else to do with herself.

"Damn it," she muttered under her breath. "What am I going to tell Beth?"

"Tell her my shower broke down." Quinn toweled off her hair.

"And you came all the way from Brooklyn to use mine?"

"I was in the neighborhood for a shoot. That's not even a lie. And compared to your bathroom, mine might as well not work, that's how inferior it is."

"This isn't a joke, Quinn." Maya pointed at the wall beyond which Beth was busy with Ethan.

"It's not the end of the world either." Quinn rummaged through her bag for clean underwear. She'd come prepared for a sleepover.

Ethan had stopped crying. Beth would come out of the bathroom soon. For a split second, Maya considered telling Beth who Quinn really was, but it was inconceivable.

"Maya?" Beth had exited the bathroom.

"Yes." Maya hurried out of the bedroom and closed the door behind her.

"Do you want to say hello now that he's all cleaned up?" She thrust Ethan into Maya's direction.

Maya held her grandson in her arms and his plump weight against her shoulder calmed her down. She walked him into the living room.

"I don't mean to stick my nose where it doesn't belong, but, um, who's that woman using your bathroom?" Beth's job was to ask direct questions and she didn't shy away from doing the same in personal situations.

"That's Quinn." Maya tried to sound matter-of-fact. "Our old neighbor from Milbury. We're, um, friends, and she... her shower broke down."

"Okay." Beth sounded as though she had no reason to doubt that explanation—or maybe Maya was just doing some hard-core wishful thinking.

Maya didn't know if Tommy had told Beth about Quinn. He'd been so tired when Maya had mentioned running into their former girl next door again, he might well have forgotten. But Beth would certainly tell him about the young woman dressed in nothing but a towel she'd come across at her mother-in-law's apartment. How would Tommy react to that? Maya had to get ahead of this but she didn't know how. If she asked Beth not to mention Quinn to Tommy, it would only raise more suspicion.

Then again, neither of them knew that Maya liked women, so there was a good chance they wouldn't put two and two together. But then what would it look like when Maya did eventually tell them? Long-term, Maya couldn't win. She could spin a short-term lie to keep some sort of peace, although peace of mind would be impossible for her to find as of now.

This was her family. The people most precious to her. She didn't want to lie to them. But she didn't want to tell them the truth either.

Maya focused her attention on Ethan. She cradled him in her arms so she could get a good look at his adorable face. "How's the little guy been?"

"Pretty good. But that baby does not like a full diaper."

"Which baby does?" Maya asked Ethan, as though he

could reply. "You little cutie pie. You little prince of Manhattan." She allowed herself to be wrapped up in the magic of her grandson for a moment. Until Quinn joined them—fully dressed this time.

Maya gave Ethan back to Beth, hoping they would leave soon.

"I don't mean to go all fangirl on you, but at our house, you enjoy goddess-like status," Quinn said. "My roommate is totally gaga for you."

Did Quinn really have to start with that stuff right now? Couldn't she read the situation a little better and let Maya handle this—let her subtly urge Beth out of the door?

"Thanks." Beth smiled sheepishly. She was used to this, of course, although not in her mother-in-law's home.

Maya could only hope Quinn wouldn't start with the selfies next.

"Tommy is one lucky guy." Quinn offered a wide smile but Maya could tell the corners of her mouth were a little twitchy, betraying how uncomfortable she really was.

"That's what I tell him every single day." Beth painted on her TV smile.

"Your baby's hella cute as well," Quinn said.

"Thanks." Beth put Ethan back into his stroller. "It was lovely to meet you, um, Quinn. I need to get home because this little mister here will be hungry soon."

Maya walked Beth to the door. She bent over the stroller and said, "I'll see you tomorrow, baby boy." She kissed her daughter-in-law on the cheek. "See you soon, dear."

"Thanks for you-know-what," Beth said.

"Any time. Give my love to Tommy." Maya held the door open until Beth and Ethan had disappeared into the elevator. As soon as they were out of sight, she banged the door shut, the harsh sound an apt translation of the frustration that raged inside her.

"Hey." Quinn walked up to her. "It's okay. This doesn't mean anything. Beth Robbins is a working young mother, no doubt with so much on her mind there's no space to even consider what you and I are up to. I'm totally sure of it."

"That might be so, but it doesn't change how I feel in here." Maya put a hand on her stomach. "I hate lying to them."

"You didn't lie."

"I didn't exactly tell the truth either."

"It wasn't the right time to tell the truth." Quinn shrugged. "You could hardly bombard her with the news of what we've been doing."

"I'm just shaken that she arrived like that totally out of the blue."

"Does your family often drop by unannounced?" Quinn asked.

"Not really. This week's a school holiday. Any other week I would have been teaching in the afternoon."

"Look." Quinn took her hand. "It's normal to feel shaken by this, but I'm pretty sure Beth will have forgotten all about it by the time she gets home. She's probably thinking about the news or trying to interpret Ethan's latest smile or something like that."

"Or I'll get a phone call from Tommy later, quizzing me about you."

"Then just tell him what you told Beth."

"The real issue," Maya said, "is that I feel like I should tell them something."

"You don't have to, though. It's too soon." Quinn caressed Maya's knuckles. "This is coming from someone who has been another woman's dirty little secret for years. Someone who has zero desire to exist only in the shadows of love ever again.

Just so we're clear on that. I'm never doing that again, but this is not that. You have to give yourself time to get used to this first. Only then can you tell your family a clear story and only then will you be ready to answer all their questions. Just let this slide for now. Let it go."

"I don't want you to be my secret." Maya pulled Quinn close to her. "I'm not ashamed of you, Quinn."

"But you're ashamed of *us*." Quinn might as well have given Maya a punch to the gut.

Maya couldn't say that she wasn't.

"It's okay. I know it's not the same as being ashamed of me. I know it's a challenge for you to accept that you're..." Quinn looked up at her. "Falling in love with me?"

Maya couldn't help but smile at her. "I'm crazy about you."

Quinn's lips curled into a smile. She extricated herself from their hug and pulled up the side of her sweater. "Then remember this." She pointed at her tattoo. "Life's not for feeling ashamed, not even for one single fucking second."

"That's what I love about you most of all," Maya blurted out. "Your spirit. Your attitude that nothing can touch you or when it does, you'll find a way to rise above it. That you can get over anything." Maya touched her hand against Quinn's exposed belly. "How did you get to be so strong at your age?"

"You're making it sound as though I'm still twenty-four. I'm almost thirty-five, Maya. I'm a lot younger than you and I always will be but that doesn't mean I haven't learned certain things about life." She turned so her tattoo was visible again. "And that's what it's all about in the end. It's only for living. Not for any of the bullshit we always manage to saddle ourselves with."

"You're right on many levels," Maya started to say, but was interrupted when Quinn's phone rang.

"It's my dad," she said without looking at the screen. Even

Maya recognized Bill's special ringtone on Quinn's phone by now. "I'll call him back later."

"No, please, take it." Maya could do with a breather. And perhaps also with a reminder that Quinn had told her father about them and he still called his daughter every day as though it was all just so very normal. "Talk to your dad."

"Okay." Quinn took the call and walked to the window.

It was soothing to hear her talk to her father. Maybe he had really meant it when he'd told Quinn he wanted her to be happy, no matter who with. Because the evidence of him being a great parent was standing right in front of Maya. Quinn was remarkable in every way, although Maya did see her through rose-tinted lenses on account of her growing feelings for her. But still. Quinn was kind, considerate, wise beyond her years, talented and utterly gorgeous. She'd also managed to speak to Beth in a disarming enough way.

Quinn turned around, her phone still glued to her ear. She mouthed something that Maya couldn't make out. She covered her phone with her other hand, and said, "Dad wants to talk to you."

"What?" A shot of nerves exploded in Maya's stomach. "No. I can't talk to Bill right now."

"He just wants to say hi. To be polite. You know what he's like."

"For crying out loud. How's it going to come across if I refuse now?" Maya asked.

"Just speak to him for a minute, Maya. It's not as big a deal as you think it is." Quinn thrust her phone in Maya's direction.

Heart pounding in her throat, Maya put the phone to her ear. She tried to sound upbeat. "Hi Bill. How are you?"

"God, Maya, it's been so long. I hear New York is treating you well? How's Tommy and his growing family?"

That was the thing about Bill. He'd always been easy to

talk to. He was the king of small talk and very skilled at making you feel at ease—something Quinn must have gotten from her dad.

Maya engaged in some innocent chitchat about Tommy and Beth and how adorable Ethan was. Bill told her about his new neighbors and that he was having them over for a barbecue the coming weekend. When the natural flow of small talk dried up, he said, "Can I ask you something serious, Maya? Something concerning my daughter?"

"Of course." Maya braced herself for what was to come.

"Quinn is very good at acting tough. She always has been. Like nothing could ever hurt her. But I know how much damage Morgan did and I don't think Quinn can take much more. Either way, I don't want her to get hurt like that again. So if this is just some game to you, some... way for you to discover yourself after which you will just dispose of Quinn and thank her for services rendered ... If that is the case, Maya, then please walk away now before it gets too serious. I don't want her to suffer like that again."

Maya didn't know what to say. Maybe Bill's fatherly concern was a bit over-developed. Or maybe this was his way of driving them apart. "It's not the case, Bill," she said after she'd gotten over the initial shock of being spoken to like that. "You take care. Bye, now."

Maya ended the call and stared at the phone in her hand.

"What did he say?" Quinn eyed her intently.

Maya wasn't sure she should repeat Bill's words. Quinn worshipped her dad as much as he worshipped her. But she had to be honest. She was in a relationship with Quinn, not with her family.

"I think he's a little concerned about my intentions toward you."

"How so?" Quinn's eyes narrowed.

"He basically told me to end it now if I wasn't serious about being with you."

"Oh, fuck." Quinn expelled a deep sigh. "That bastard."

"Quinn, he's still your dad."

"That's right. He's *my* dad, not yours. He has no right to speak to you in such a condescending manner. I truly believed he just wanted to have a chat with you, to hear your voice and get a feel for things, you know? Nothing more than that." Quinn was pacing back and forth in anger.

"Maybe he's just genuinely worried about you. He said that Morgan hurt you much more than you let on. He doesn't want that for you again. In a way, it's understandable."

"That doesn't give him the right to go all Tony Soprano on you." Quinn stopped her pacing. "What's he going to do if I do get my heart broken again? Chop off your legs?"

Maya burst into laughter. "I really can't see Bill doing that."

Quinn gave a slow shake of the head. "I wouldn't put it past my mom, though."

They shared a moment of much-needed lightness, which seemed to calm Quinn down somewhat, after which Maya had to ask. "Did Morgan really hurt you that badly?"

Quinn shook her head. "Morgan's history." She kissed Maya's cheek. "It's all about you now."

CHAPTER 38

Because she wanted the element of surprise on her side, Quinn had rented a car instead of taking the train. She also hoped the drive would calm her down. Since her dad had warned Maya off on Wednesday, she hadn't taken any of his calls, which was something she only did when she was very angry him, which had only happened once or twice before in her life, way back in her teens. This time, she was more disappointed than angry.

Even though Maya had tried to hammer it home that he was only looking out for her and that she should try to see things from a parental perspective, Quinn could only see her side of things. She wasn't a parent and she thought it was her right to only see her own view. This included her take on Maya's fear that Tommy would find out about them. What was it with parents and their offspring? Why couldn't they just let things go and see what happened? As if micro-managing a child ever worked better than a relaxed, hands-off approach?

Quinn was disappointed in her father because he didn't trust her, and it was inappropriate for him to talk to Maya the way he had. The things she wanted to say to him, she didn't want to say over the phone. That her mother would find out about her and Maya would be collateral damage. And she had to find out some day. She might as well start processing now. The sooner she started, the better, because she would probably take her sweet time.

Quinn was still drumming her fingers on the steering wheel when she zipped up the driveway. It was almost noon on Saturday. They should be home although Quinn was no longer that familiar with their routines.

She let herself in through the front door and dropped her overnight bag in the hall. She wasn't sure whether she'd be staying. That would all depend on how the day went, but she hadn't wanted to rule it out, even though it meant she and Maya couldn't go dancing tonight. Maya hadn't seemed to mind that all too much—she had a babysitting date with Ethan tonight.

"Hello?" Quinn said. The house was silent. She went into the kitchen, which was empty. Maybe they were out shopping. But the door to the back garden was open. Quinn walked out and stopped dead in her tracks. Her parents were lost in an intimate embrace, their lips locked and their eyes closed. Her first instinct was to recoil and retreat back into the house, but she made herself linger and watch. In a way, it was lovely to see that they still had so much affection for each other.

After a few moments, Quinn'd had enough and she cleared her throat noisily.

Her mother jerked out of her father's embrace as though she'd been caught red-handed carrying out the most vicious crime.

"Darling! What a surprise." She straightened her shirt and walked over. "We weren't expecting you this weekend. Or did I get the dates wrong?" She curled an arm around Quinn's shoulders. "Not that it isn't a delight to see you." She pecked

Quinn on the cheek. Her father must not have told her about talking to Maya on the phone. If he had, Quinn would have received a much frostier welcome from her mother.

"Hi, sweetheart." Her dad had come over and put his hand lightly on her shoulder. "Great to see you."

"Did you drive? I would have picked you up, you know." Her mother went into the house.

"I'll make us some lunch," her dad said, but remained outside. "I have a feeling I'm the reason you're here," he whispered.

"That's right, Dad," Quinn said. She was glad that he was the first to acknowledge it.

"I'm sorry about speaking to Maya like that. I don't know what came over me. I just... got this vision of you in tears and I dealt with it poorly."

"A vision? Are you clairvoyant now?"

"Whether you like it or not, Quinn, I'm always going to worry about you. I know you're still fragile about what happened with Morgan."

"I don't understand why you keep bringing up Morgan. That's been over for months. I'm with Maya now."

Her father walked deeper into the garden. Quinn followed him.

"Are you sure this whole thing with Maya isn't a reaction to how things ended with Morgan? It would be totally normal for you to... attach yourself to someone kind of familiar like that."

Quinn hated it when her dad practiced his armchair psychology on her. Of course, he didn't know what had happened between his daughter and his neighbor ten years ago, and Quinn wasn't about to tell him.

"Yes, I'm pretty sure, Dad. As sure as I can be at this stage." She dramatically huffed out some air. "I'm in love with her and I'm pretty sure she's in love with me. It could just be as simple as that."

Her dad shook his head. "There's nothing simple about the whole thing. It's infinitely complex. I've been trying to get my head around it since you told me about Maya, but I can't figure it out, Quinn. Unless you're going through a mid-thirties rebellious stage. Although you rebelled plenty already when you were a teenager." He rubbed his full, gray beard.

"Dad, please stop doing that. Stop analyzing me."

"Then what do you want me to do?"

"Accept it," Quinn said.

Her dad sighed. "That's the thing, sweetheart. I'm not sure I can do that." He shot her a look that didn't inspire much confidence in Quinn that he might change his mind any time soon—despite what he had claimed when Quinn had first told him about Maya. "Shall we go in? Your mother will be wondering what we're talking about out here."

Quinn nodded. There wasn't much else she could do.

Quinn was lounging in a deck chair outside, enjoying the silence of Milbury and trying not to get too worked up about what her father had said before lunch. She heard noises coming from the house where Maya used to live—the house where it had all started.

"What's going on, darling?" her mom asked as she sat down in the chair next to Quinn's. "You arrive home out of the blue. You hardly ate anything at lunch. And there's this weird vibe between you and your dad that I can't put my finger on."

Great. An inquisition by her mother was all Quinn needed. She was still trying to digest what her dad had said to her earlier. For as long as she could remember in her thirty-four years alive, her dad had always given her his unconditional acceptance. No questions asked. Why couldn't he do it now? Was Quinn expecting too much of him? Or was it him not trying hard enough to give his only daughter the benefit of the doubt?

"All I can say is that... I disappointed him, and he disappointed me. Things are a bit tense because of that."

"Is there anything I can do to help?"

"Mom." Quinn shook her head. "I don't really want to talk about it."

Her mother took a deep breath. Then she said, "Is it about Maya?"

Every last one of Quinn's muscles tensed up. "What? Um, what are you talking about?"

"I know your father spoke to her on the phone earlier this week. He's been out of sorts ever since. You were with her when he talked to her. I'm just drawing the only logical conclusion that I can."

Quinn sat up and turned so she could get a better look at her mother's face. What did she know? Surely her parental powers of deduction weren't that mighty.

"I gave her your number when she moved to New York and told her to give you a call. I take it she has and that you've been in touch. What I don't understand is what has made both you and your father so upset regarding Maya."

Quinn relaxed a little. Her mother wasn't totally in the dark, but she was hardly in the know either. Right now, she was just fishing.

"It'll blow over," Quinn lied, because she didn't know how it could—unless her father relented.

"I sure hope so," her mom said. "It's hard to upset your dad like that, especially when it comes to you." Her mom tried to find Quinn's gaze, but it was impossible for Quinn to return it.

"You can talk to me as well, you know. I always have been and always will be your mother."

"Mom, it's just that..." What irked Quinn even more was that her father had lied to her when he'd told her he wanted her to be happy above all else. Maya had been right. He'd been telling her what she wanted to hear at the time. It made Quinn wonder how many times he'd done that in the past instead of telling her how he really felt.

She had come home to try and make some sort of amends but it was looking highly unlikely that was going to happen. Quinn regrouped. "My show opens on Thursday and that's a huge thing for me. I know this won't stop Dad from being there." Not even an out-of-season snowstorm would keep him from being there, Quinn believed. Or did she have to rethink that as well? "But..." Quinn had no idea how to talk to her mother about this. Not without telling her the truth. "Maya will be there as well. There's a picture of her in the exhibition. I want to enjoy my moment in the spotlight. But the way things stand right now, I'm not sure I'll be able to."

"What are you saying? You don't want your dad to come?" Her mom sounded horrified. To Quinn as well it was unthinkable that her father, her biggest champion since she was born, wouldn't be there.

"No, of course not. I want you both there, obviously, but... it's supposed to be a joyous occasion. I'll be nervous enough without having to worry if Dad's about to go off on one."

"But why would he do that, darling? That would be so unlike your father."

"Because..." Tears stung behind Quinn's eyes. Oh, what the hell. "I'm in love with her, Mom. I'm in love with Maya. Dad just told me he's not sure he can ever accept that. And earlier this week, when you heard him on the phone, he gave Maya a piece of his mind." Quinn pushed her palms against her eyes.

"Wait, darling. Can you repeat that? You're in love with... Maya? Our old neighbor? That's the Maya we're talking about?"

Quinn attempted to dry her eyes and braved a quick glance at her mother. "We fell in love. I thought Dad of all people would understand. But he doesn't. I do get that he needs some time to process, but that really doesn't give him the right to speak to Maya so disrespectfully. And... I just hate feeling like this. I don't know what to do about it. It's not as if I can will myself to stop loving her because of you guys. Because she used to live next door."

Her mother had gone a touch pale. She swallowed hard. "You and Maya?" She shook her head. "Are you pulling some sort of elaborate prank on us?"

Quinn tried to exhale slowly to regain her composure. "I'm sorry. This is really not how I wanted you to find out about this."

Her mom held up both her hands. "I don't want to know about this at all." She straightened her spine. "Don't tell me anything else." She stood. "You have a knack for pushing the envelope, but this time you've really gone too far." The ice in her mother's voice cut Quinn much deeper than she thought possible. Without saying another word, her mom disappeared into the house.

Quinn didn't hold back the tears any longer. Why would she? She was all alone out there.

Maybe her mother was right. Maybe she had gone too far. She sobbed into her hands until she felt she'd depleted all the moisture in her body. She skulked through the house, picked up her overnight bag where she'd dropped it earlier, and left quietly through the front door.

CHAPTER 39

This was not the Quinn Maya had come to know. She was even more obsessed with her phone than usual, hoping for word from Bill or Brooke. It had been two days since she'd come back from Milbury in tears. Maya was beginning to think she'd have to intervene. She felt like she needed to do something to help Quinn, not only because it was awful to see her suffer like that, but also because, professionally, this was the most important week of Quinn's life so far.

She was having a solo exhibition in a gallery of quite some repute—a surge or pride had coursed through Maya when she'd looked it up and found out about the esteem the gallery was held in for discovering the next big artist. Surely Bill and Brooke would come around by Thursday?

Meanwhile, Maya had been so focused on her own family's reaction to Quinn, she'd been so busy expecting the worst for herself, that she hadn't spent enough time trying to talk Quinn out of driving all the way to Milbury in a huff last Saturday. She'd had a hunch it was a bad idea, especially because Quinn was doing it out of anger more than a desire to reconcile.

Maya hadn't wanted to play the age card and tell Quinn that experience had taught her doing something out of anger was seldom a good idea, but, in hindsight, she should have done just that. Because now all four of them, Quinn and Maya but also Bill and Brooke, didn't know what to do with themselves.

Quinn sat at the kitchen island typing furiously on her phone. Maya had no idea what she did on that too-small device all day long, but Tommy and Beth were exactly the same. Maybe that was why neither one of them had even mentioned Quinn this weekend when Maya had gone over to babysit Ethan—they'd been too busy living their lives, their real ones, and also the ones that existed on their phones. No wonder they were so exhausted all the time.

Maya walked over to Quinn and put a hand on her shoulder. "Why don't you take a break from that thing?" she asked.

Quinn put her phone away as though all she'd needed was someone to tell her to do so.

"There's a surprising amount of press," Quinn said. "Imogen from the gallery is getting all excited about the pre-opening buzz."

"It's not every day you have Quinn Hathaway's art on display in your gallery." Maya squeezed Quinn's shoulder.

Quinn let her head fall back against Maya's belly. She heaved a deep sigh. "What if they don't come?" Her tone was defeated, as though her only choice was to accept that the worst might very well happen—that her own parents wouldn't show up for her moment of glory because they didn't agree with who their daughter loved.

"There's just no way." Maya spoke from her own experience as a parent again. Regardless of not having a rebellious bone in his body, Tommy had managed to get under Maya's skin quite a few times in his life, but it would never have stopped Maya from wanting to be with him when something significant happened. She couldn't think of anything he might do that could keep her away.

She understood Bill and Brooke's reaction better than she admitted out loud to Quinn, but she also knew that they loved their daughter no matter what and that they were the kind of people who would want to share this special moment with her. Bill would be there beaming with pride and Brooke would probably be going around the room telling everyone who wanted to hear—and everyone who didn't—that she was the artist's mother.

But Maya could presume all she wanted; people could still surprise you. She was especially surprised by Bill's refusal to call his daughter. Because he usually called her every day, it meant something when he didn't. And it hurt Quinn so very much. Maya hated being the source of so much suffering.

"I could try to talk to them," Maya offered. It would be awkward and horrible, but she would do it for Quinn. She would brave Bill and Brooke Hathaway's chagrin. Because at least this crappy ordeal had made something very clear to her: she wanted to be with Quinn and she was willing to fight for that. At least against the Hathaways. She would deal with her own family when the time came—one battle at a time.

"And say what?" Quinn asked.

"Just listen to what they have to say, for starters." Maya imagined Quinn had been too angry to really listen to her father's arguments.

"I don't want them getting into your head." Quinn slipped off the chair and faced Maya.

"That's the last thing you need to worry about right now." Maya cupped Quinn's cheeks in her hands. "They can't get into my head. It's not possible. It's too full of you." Maya smiled. "You have my word."

"People's word isn't worth that much to me right now."

"I hope mine is."

Quinn nodded. "Your word is sacred to me." She managed a wry smile. "I just don't know what to do."

"Then let me help you. I hate seeing you like this. You should only be nervous about your show right now, not about your family."

"I can't believe he hasn't called." Quinn's voice broke. "He must be so fucking pissed at me. Or maybe Mom's mad at him, although that has never stopped him before."

"Not hearing from them is driving you crazy." Maya's determination grew. In a way, she had caused this. Maybe she was the only one who could make it better. "What's the worst that can happen if I call your mother?" Maya shrugged, trying to look more casual than she felt. "She could hang up on me, but we already have her silence."

As the phone rang, Maya wondered which emotions were going through her old friend Brooke as she saw who was calling. Rage? Defiance? Unadulterated motherly wrath? Maybe Brooke was considering if she should pick up at all. Maya ignored her own emotions. If she didn't, she wouldn't be able to have this conversation.

When Brooke picked up there was a brief silence on the other end of the line before she said, "Maya?"

"Hi, Brooke. How are you?" It was an automatic question. It was what you asked the person you'd called. Maya hadn't prepared a bunch of arguments to support why it was okay for her to be with Brooke's daughter. She just wanted to break this wretched stand-off the Hathaways were in. She wanted joyful Quinn back, who showed her the tattoo on her side whenever she felt like it—which was often, Maya had learned, and not always in an appropriate environment.

Brook didn't immediately reply. It was both easier and harder to do this over the phone. Maya would have liked to be able to see Brooke's face but she was also glad she didn't have to deal with the possible disapproval plastered all over it. At least she had picked up and hadn't hung up instantly. Brooke probably wanted to find a way out of this as well, but pretending it wasn't happening wasn't going to solve anything.

Brooke's silence continued.

"Look." Maya decided to fill the gap. "I know you're upset, and I understand that very well, but Quinn just wants to know if you and Bill are coming to her show on Thursday."

"If Quinn wants to know something, she should call us herself." Brooke sounded clipped. "Or maybe she shouldn't have snuck out of the house like a thief in the night. She just left without saying a word to us."

"She was upset."

"So were we."

"I know, Brooke. But Quinn's miserable. Bill hasn't called her and she doesn't know what to do with herself."

"Maybe she should have thought of that before she took up with you. Or maybe you could have thought about the consequences, Maya. Why didn't you? That's what I'd like to know. Do you really expect us to simply accept that you and Quinn are a couple now? The whole thing is simply preposterous."

"I don't expect you to accept it just like that at all." Maya tried to keep calm, even though this was one of the most difficult conversations she'd ever had. And the question Brooke had just asked her was one she hadn't entirely resolved for herself yet either. "I know it's difficult to hear." Maya could hardly tell Quinn's mother that life was for living, not for judging your daughter with whom she'd fallen so madly in love. "It's awkward and hard to understand." It helped that Maya could genuinely empathize with Brooke on this. "It's most certainly not what you want to hear, but... none of that makes it less true. We can't change how we feel."

"I beg to differ," Brooke said drily. "Maybe Quinn is too pigheaded to even try, but *you*..." Brooke turned the accusation in her tone up a notch. "Why didn't you stop it? You're not even gay, Maya. Are you doing this to spite us for some reason? If so, why? What did Bill and I ever do to you except be good neighbors?"

It's got nothing to do with you, Maya wanted to shout down the phone, but that wouldn't get her anywhere. "I tried to stop it," Maya said truthfully. "I really did, Brooke. I didn't want this. Not at first. I felt exactly how you feel right now. Believe me, I tried so hard to stop it, but I couldn't. Quinn is..." Maya stopped herself. She wasn't about to explain to Brooke how amazing she thought her daughter to be. "I know I should have been the wiser one, but, in the end, we're two adults choosing to be with each other, and there isn't anything wrong with that." A ripple of unexpected pride coursed through Maya for saying that out loud—for standing up for their love.

"And we just have to accept it?" Brooke scoffed.

"Quinn and I are happy together," Maya said. She may as well play the happy card now—which mother could resist that?

"How long has this been going on?" Brooke asked.

"A while."

"A while?" Brooke shouted. "Is it even serious yet?"

It's very serious, Maya thought. She knew that in her bones, because of the ups and downs they'd gone through already. Because of her own doubts she'd had to conquer. But again, this was not something she should say to Brooke right now.

"If you could just be there for Quinn on Thursday. It would mean so much to her."

"I don't need you to tell me that. She's *my* daughter, damn it."

Maya heard a man's muffled voice in the background. Brooke had probably covered her phone with her hand. Had Bill been listening along all this time?

"Maya." There he was. "This is Bill." As if it needed saying.

"Hi, Bill."

"Tell Quinn that it goes without saying that her mother and I will be there for her. We will always be there for her."

Before Maya had a chance to say anything, the line went dead. She didn't know if she'd obtained a good result or not. But at least she knew they'd be coming to Quinn's show. For now, that was all that mattered. They'd take the next hurdle when it presented itself.

CHAPTER 40

"Ready?" Imogen asked.

"As I'll ever be." Quinn watched Imogen unlock the front door, but this wasn't a concert or exclusive club night and it wasn't as if there was a line outside, eagerly waiting for admission to the premises. Only Griff walked in as soon as the door was opened.

"Aaaah!" Griff squealed. "I'm so excited for you, Quinn."

"Thanks." Quinn followed Imogen to the corner of the gallery where they'd set up a bar.

"Here you go." Imogen handed them both a glass of champagne. "To a great opening and an amazing show of Quinn Hathaway originals."

They clinked glasses, after which Imogen excused herself to go and take care of something.

"Are you not nervous?" Griff asked.

"Not with you by my side," Quinn quipped.

Griff threw an arm around her. "I know it's been a tough week."

Quinn nodded. She'd been surprised by the emotional turmoil inside of her. Even as she stood here, at the cusp of one the most important evenings of her life, she felt like she could burst into tears at any given time. Or maybe that was just her nerves acting up. Because this was a big deal.

"When's Maya arriving?" Griff asked.

"Depends on traffic." Quinn looked at her watch. "She should be here any minute." Maya had offered to cancel her Thursday afternoon classes so she could be there with Quinn for the last preparations, but Quinn had assured her that was not necessary. Now she felt sorry she had wanted to be so independent. She couldn't wait for Maya to arrive. Her presence would calm her down, release some of the stubborn knot of tension in her stomach.

There was movement outside, but it was just a few people walking past. Nobody wanted to be the first to arrive. Quinn took a few more sips of champagne. She paused, then downed the entire glass. She was at the start of an evening of, hopefully, non-stop talk about herself and her work. Who knew when she'd get another chance for a drink? More movement outside. Quinn stiffened. That gray head of hair. That lanky, stiff silhouette. Even though Maya had assured her they would come, Quinn hadn't been able to shake off every doubt. But there they were.

Now that she actually saw her parents, Quinn wasn't so sure she'd be able to hold back those tears for much longer.

"Sweetheart." Her dad walked in with his arms outstretched.

Quinn all but ran into his embrace—once a daddy's girl, always a daddy's girl. Tears ran down her face as she pushed herself against her father's solid, safe chest. She felt her mother's hand against her back.

"What's all this?" her dad said, gesturing at the room. "Looks like you've been busy."

Quinn dried her tears. For a moment, she'd wished she could hide in her father's arms all night long.

"Darling." Her mother squeezed her shoulder and kissed her on the cheek. "You're quite something, but I've known that forever."

"Oh my god." Quinn exhaled audibly. "Up until you walked in, I really wasn't sure you'd come."

"We're here." Her dad pinned his gaze on her. "Got it?"

Quinn nodded, even though she didn't know if he meant anything else by that. But they were here and it was really all that mattered. She glanced at the door. No sign of Maya yet.

"Walk us through?" her dad asked, after he had said hello to Griff and had a glass of champagne in his hand.

Quinn steered them to the opposite side of where Maya's portrait hung. She'd wisely save that for last.

Quinn turned the corner, her parents in her wake. They hadn't mentioned Maya yet, but soon neither one of them would have a choice, because she had just walked in.

Quinn could feel tension crackle in the air. She heard her mother inhale sharply—as though she'd just seen a ghost.

Maybe they should have set up this confrontation somewhere else other than in this gallery, where more people were starting to arrive, but this was how things had turned out. Quinn thought everyone involved would be civilized enough not to make a scene at an occasion like this.

Maya walked straight toward them with that confident gait she had from a life of dance. She stopped in front of Quinn, a wide, undaunted smile on her face. Maya had battled so many doubts about them and to have her show up like this, tonight of all nights, unfazed in front of her parents, meant the world to Quinn. She reached for Maya and kissed her briefly on the lips.

"Congratulations," Maya said. "I could just burst with pride." Only then did she look sideways—did she turn her attention away from Quinn. "Bill and Brooke Hathaway." She gave a slight shake of the head. "I guess we have a thing or two to talk about."

Quinn watched her dad extend his hand, as if this was their formal first meeting and they hadn't been neighbors for decades. But she couldn't expect miracles to happen. Or maybe one had already happened. Maya had shown up unafraid to face her parents, which meant she was no longer ashamed of her and Quinn being together—of them.

"Oh, come on, Bill." Maya took his hand but, at the same time, pulled at his arm and drew him near for a hug. "The number of steaks you've cooked for me on that precious grill of yours and now you're just going to shake my hand?" Maya had a lifetime of performance experience and she obviously knew how to turn it on.

Quinn's dad embraced Maya, stiffly at first but then he relaxed, giving in to the affections of the woman he'd known for such a long time. But Quinn's dad was always going to be the easiest to win over. The true test would be her mother.

Once extricated from Bill's hug, Maya turned to Quinn's mother. "Brooke." Did her voice just break a little? Maya cleared her throat. Maybe hugging Quinn's dad had loosened some emotions in her. Maybe it made her think of Tommy—the next ordeal on their list. "It's so good to see you."

Quinn could easily tell how much Maya meant it and she could only hope her mom could feel it too. That despite the circumstances not being ideal, they could be a kind of family tonight. Quinn knew that her parents being here and socializing with Maya didn't mean they had suddenly, as if by magic, accepted that they were together. But maybe they could just start by pretending. By getting a feel for how things would be if they spent time together in this particular constellation.

"Oh, Maya." Her mom shook her head but then opened her arms wide for Maya. Their hug, no matter how swift, or perhaps even put-on, touched Quinn deeply.

"Say it ain't so," Quinn's dad said. At first, Quinn thought he was referring to Quinn's mom and Maya's embrace, but then he said, "Is that Tommy?"

Maya froze. So did Quinn. She looked at the door and that was definitely Beth Robbins who had just walked in.

"On my god," Griff squealed behind her. "Beth Robbins! I didn't know she was coming."

Neither did I. Quinn guessed, from the look on her face, this was a big surprise for Maya as well.

CHAPTER 41

What on earth were Tommy and Beth doing here? Maya didn't get it. She had mentioned Quinn's show to Tommy when she'd told him about having run into Quinn but she surely hadn't invited her son and daughter-in-law. Why would she have? Moreover, Quinn's name hadn't come up in conversation since Beth had caught her in Maya's bathroom.

Bill and Tommy shook hands while Quinn's roommate was going gaga over Beth.

Maya's brain frantically searched for answers. She exchanged a look with Quinn. "Did you know they were coming?" she whispered.

Quinn shook her head. "No idea. You?"

"None. Something's going on."

"Like what?" Quinn asked.

Imogen tapped Quinn on the shoulder. "Quinn, if I could just steal you for a moment, please."

"Will you be okay?" Quinn asked Maya.

"Yes. Go do your thing," Maya said, all the while feeling Tommy's intense stare.

"Hey, Mom," he said after he'd finished his catch-up with Bill.

"Tommy." Maya kissed him hello. "What are you doing here? Where's Ethan?"

"He's with Beth's mom." Tommy narrowed his eyes. "Something told me I didn't want to miss this event."

Maya was too stunned to reply.

"It was easy enough to find the details online," Tommy said. "There's been quite a bit of buzz about this show, actually, and..." He maneuvered Maya away from the small group they stood in. "When my mother mentions she's been spending time with our former neighbors' daughter, and my wife tells me she found that very same person naked in my mother's bathroom... I don't know, Mom. I guess my curiosity has been more than piqued."

Oh, damn. Maya had been prepared to deal with Bill and Brooke. Awkward as it might be, it would make good practice for when she would need to confront Tommy. But she hadn't expected to have to do that tonight as well. A chill shuddered along her spine. She took a deep breath, but she still didn't know what to say. It was an impossible situation because she'd just kissed Quinn on the lips in front of Bill and Brooke. She'd just shown them how she felt about their daughter. She couldn't rewind, nor could she hide her feelings for Quinn any longer. Most of all, she didn't want to lie to her son.

"Tommy," she started. "I—" How to say it, though? It was especially hard because Maya could feel Brooke's icy stare on her. She might have agreed to hug her for Quinn's sake earlier, but she didn't look as though she was going to make any more allowances now that Quinn had been whisked away.

There was only one way to say it—only one way to do this. "Quinn and I, we... we're together."

"I figured as much," Tommy said matter-of-factly.

Maya huffed out a breath. She needed to release some tension from her body. "There are many reasons why I couldn't tell you sooner."

"I told Beth weeks ago there was something different about you." He shook his head. "When she told me about Quinn in your bathroom, all the pieces of the puzzle slipped into place in my head." He cast his gaze about the room before it landed on Maya again. "But I had to see it for myself."

More and more people were arriving, filling up the gallery. Maya wondered what it meant that Tommy and Beth had taken time out of their busy schedules to be here tonight. It was hard to tell if it was a show of support or an opportunity to frown on Maya's choice of who she spent her time with. Beth wouldn't want to draw attention to herself like that and Tommy was usually such a discreet person. But still, Maya's mind was too frazzled for her to read her son, the person she knew best in the world, right now.

"I'm in love with her," Maya said. They were both the hardest and the easiest words she'd ever spoken to her son.

"You must be." Tommy released a deep breath. "Beth and I have talked about this beforehand and we didn't come here to make a scene. I just... wanted to know." He eyed Beth who was still talking to Griff. She looked about ready to be saved. Maya called her over.

Tommy gave her a quick nod, as though confirming their suspicions.

"I have a lot to say, but this isn't the place to say it." Maya braved their gazes. "Bill and Brooke are here and they aren't too pleased to see me, but there's one thing that I'm not going to do and that's apologize for how I feel. I've waited years to feel like this again and now that I do, I don't want to ruin it." She held up her hands. "That doesn't mean I won't take your feelings into account. I will listen to whatever it is you have to say, just not right now. I'm here for Quinn. It's her night."

"Mom," Tommy said. "It's okay." He looked her in the eye. "I've done some pre-processing about this, in case my intuition was correct. I just want you to be happy. That's really all I want." He briefly touched his hand against her arm.

Pre-processing—that sounded just like Tommy. It was something his father would say.

Beth, who was a much more tactile person, curled her arm around Maya's shoulder and pulled her near. "Don't worry about Tommy, Maya. You know I've got him whipped." She leaned in closer and whispered in Maya's ear, "You deserve to be happy just as much as anyone else. Who are we to stand in the way of that? We love you." Beth released her grip.

Maya wished she could be held a little longer.

"Evening, Mercers," Angus said. With all the commotion, Maya hadn't seen him come in. "Don't mind me. I have a knack for interrupting special family moments. Pretend I'm not here, if it helps."

"Yeah right." Maya was so happy to see a friendly face—someone she didn't have to explain anything to. "As if you would ever stand for not being noticed." Angus was wearing his most flowery suit with a mustard yellow shirt underneath.

Angus gave her a look before turning his attention to Beth, whom he adored. "How's that adorable little boy of yours, Miss Robbins?"

"Angus, please, call me Beth." They played the same old game every time they saw each other and the familiarity of it comforted Maya. She tried to find Quinn in the crowd, but she couldn't see her. She couldn't wait to tell her that, suddenly, everyone knew.

"Can I speak with you for a minute?" Brooke asked.

Maya was just studying—again, she had to admit—the blown-up portrait of herself. The one where she seemed to float on a cloud over the Acton Academy building.

"Quinn is so talented," Maya said, in case Brooke was refusing to look at the picture of her daughter's... partner? Girlfriend? Lover? Ever since her conversation with Tommy, Maya's elation had only grown. The free-flowing champagne might also have helped. It was only then that Maya noticed the red dot on the card next to the artwork. Did that mean someone had bought it? If so, could she find out who? She made a mental note to find the woman who owned the gallery later.

"Between us," Brooke said, "I don't think she gets that from Bill. Close as they are, art was never something they bonded over, although Bill always did encourage her to follow her dreams, no matter what they were. I guess that's coming back to bite him in the ass big time now." Brooke crossed her arms over her chest and took a step closer to the picture of Maya. "He's very proud of her for this. For the record, neither one of us would have missed this for the world."

"I figured as much."

"It may also surprise you that Bill is having much more trouble accepting this—or no, accepting isn't even the correct term yet. It's too soon for anything resembling acceptance. He just can't even begin to fathom it. I asked him who he was expecting given the women Quinn has dated in the past." She made a tsking sound. "At least that ghastly woman who broke her heart into a thousand little pieces isn't here."

"Morgan?" Maya asked.

"It went on for years and years. I just didn't understand how Quinn couldn't see that it was going to end badly. Up to the point that I started wondering what I had done wrong in raising her that she picked a woman like that to be with." Brooke sighed deeply. "It's always the mother's fault, you know."

"Then I'll take full credit for how happy Tommy is with Beth." Maya knew she sounded condescending, but she didn't care. She had an inkling she should arm herself for whatever Brooke would say next.

"They do make a dashing couple. And you're a grandmother now as well." She paused. "What does that make Quinn? Step-granny?"

There it was. "Just say what it is you really want to say, Brooke."

"Will Tommy be calling a woman who's barely older than him his stepmom soon?" The pitch of Brooke's voice rose higher as she spoke—as she got more and more agitated. "Why can't you see this is not right? You and my Quinn..."

"Quinn is never going to be Tommy's stepmother. He already has a mother and a father. Parents he has a great relationship with, for your information, because in my family we just want each other to be happy." Maya knew she sounded smug, especially because her initial fear of Tommy's response to their relationship had almost driven her and Quinn apart for good.

"Oh, come on, Maya. Put yourself in our position. What if Beth were twenty years older and your former neighbor. A woman you used to share confidences with because you were peers. Because you were *friends*."

"Do you mean to say if Beth were you?" Maya was having trouble staying calm—it had been easier on the phone because no one did the reproachful glare better than Brooke Hathaway.

"Yes, actually. That is what I mean to say." Thank goodness

Brooke didn't have the presence of mind to go same-sex on the comparison.

"I know it's not easy, Brooke. You're worried about your daughter." The problem wasn't that Maya couldn't see Brooke's point of view—she could see it all too well. Maya didn't have a defense at the ready for this. "As I would be about my own child if he were in Quinn's situation, but..."

"I understand why you would fall for her. Quinn is an amazing person, but what she sees in you." Brooke shrugged. "Worst of all, the fact that she's with you is keeping her from being open to other, more appropriate prospects."

Why don't you say what you really feel, Maya thought. "Newsflash, Brooke." Maya wasn't going to stand here and be insulted by Quinn's mother much longer. "Your daughter's been into older women for a very long time, so if that doesn't suit you, don't you dare lay the blame for that on me." Brooke would probably have a heart attack on the spot if she ever found out what had happened between Quinn and Maya ten years ago.

"Everything okay here?" Maya had never been more relieved to hear her son's voice.

"Tommy," Brooke said on a sigh, as though she'd been the one under Maya's verbal siege and not the other way around.

"Brooke and I have a lot to discuss," Maya said. "So much has happened since I moved to the city."

"Too much," Brooke said. Maya hoped she wasn't trying to gain Tommy's sympathies—or worse, trying to turn him against his own mother.

"It's okay to be a little bit upset, Mrs. Hathaway." Tommy had the uncanny ability to remain polite in any given situation —another something he got from his father. "But I was just talking to Quinn and, um, well first of all, as far as I can tell, she hasn't changed a bit since I last saw her, except that this time around she will actually have a real conversation with me."

Maya felt her eyes well up. This was her son's perfectly imperfect way of standing up for her. She wished she could have been there when he spoke to Quinn.

"Most importantly, she reminded me that, um, well, life is for living." He put a hand to his chest. "I could judge my mom for this, but, honestly, after all she has done for me, who am I to deny her even an ounce of happiness?" His voice grew stronger as his impromptu speech progressed. "I can only hope that, in time, you can feel the same way about it." Tommy put his hand on Maya's back. "By the way, Mom, Beth and I bought this picture of you." He gave her a quick kiss on the cheek and walked off, leaving Brooke, but especially Maya, in stunned silence.

CHAPTER 42

Quinn leaned her elbow on the bar and looked around the gallery. Most people had left. Response to her work had been heartwarming and supportive. Imogen seemed ecstatic. Over the course of the evening, she'd found Quinn's ear at regular intervals and whispered that they'd just sold another of her works—a sensation that most certainly didn't get old.

Maya had seemed tethered to the area around her portrait. Quinn knew Tommy had bought it. She also knew her parents had bought a large and expensive one that featured people doing all kinds of acrobatics on the Brooklyn Bridge.

Still hovering in the vicinity of her portrait, Maya was talking to Angus and Griff. Tommy and Beth had struck up a conversation with someone Quinn didn't know. Her parents were chatting with Imogen, but Quinn could tell from her mother's body language that she was about ready to get out of there—that she'd had enough of all that she'd been put through this evening. Quinn guessed it was probably a bad idea to invite them to the after-party she was having at her and

Griff's, but she had to ask. They were her parents. She walked up to them.

"Here she is," Imogen said, her enthusiasm powered by a battery that never needed charging. "It's always lovely to meet the artist's parents." She stood there beaming, oblivious to the tension between Quinn and her mom and dad.

"We're going back to our place for another drink," Quinn said. "You're all very welcome to join us."

"I have to close up here," Imogen said. "Make sure the place looks spic-and-span again by tomorrow." She smiled and moved away.

"It's late," Quinn's mother said. "And surely you don't want us there, darling."

"We should get back to the hotel, but let's have brunch tomorrow," her father said.

"And by 'we', you mean...?" Quinn was still on a high—and she needed to know.

"The three of us," her dad said. "We need to talk, Quinn. Find some sort of peace, because this strain between us is driving me crazy."

"That's not what you said last time you came to the city." Quinn's mother had been right when she'd said that Quinn always had to push and push—but she knew who she got that particular trait from.

Her dad took a breath. "Before it can be... the four of us, it needs to be the three of us. We need to discuss this as a family. I—" He shook his head. "I can see now that it's serious and that I need to work on adjusting my feelings about it, but I also need to say some things to you, father to daughter. Can you give me that?"

"Of course, Daddy." Even though most days they only spoke for a few minutes, Quinn had missed her daily interactions with her father. It was his approval she'd been seeking all of her life and that wasn't any different now. "I'll text you the address of a great place where we can meet."

"Hey." Her dad opened his arms to her the way he had done when he'd arrived. "I'm so proud of you, kiddo."

Quinn happily stepped into his embrace.

"I hope you're proud of yourself," he whispered as he held her close. "You should be."

Quinn wondered if he only meant about her show.

"See you tomorrow, darling." Her mother suddenly sounded much more mellow as well. Maybe she was beginning to realize that she only had one daughter—and Quinn only had one mother. Her mom took over from her dad's hug seamlessly, the way they'd done when Quinn was a toddler. They wrapped her in a fort of their arms so she could stay in their embrace as she went from one parent to the other.

Quinn had seen her mother in what looked like a rather heated discussion with Maya earlier, but she wasn't going to ask what they'd talked about now. Maya would tell her later. And it didn't matter in this moment, this all-too-brief instant in which all three of them remembered the love that existed in their family of three-for-now.

"Sleep tight." Quinn watched them leave. They only gave the rest of who was left—Maya included—a quick wave of the hand.

Quinn joined Tommy and Beth and asked if they wanted to follow on to hers.

"While I'd love to get smoke blown up my ass by your roommate all night long," Beth said, "I have to work tomorrow."

Quinn chuckled. If she'd known Beth was coming, she'd have given Griff a heads-up to prepare herself emotionally for coming face-to-face with her news idol. "Thanks for coming."

"I'm sure we'll see you again soon," Tommy said.

Quinn nodded. She was mainly happy for Maya, who had spent so much energy dreading her son's reaction. She could stop doing that now.

Quinn had made sure the place she was meeting her parents was more classy than hipster—the sort of restaurant she would take Maya to, instead of where she would go with Griff.

They were already seated when she arrived.

"I had expected you to look a lot worse for wear," her dad joked as he hugged her hello. He was still in full-on hug modus then.

Quinn was still too happy about how her opening had gone to let any signs of a hangover intrude on her buzz. And she'd woken up next to Maya, who had made it clear that she wasn't that fond of staying over at Quinn's but had made an effort because of the occasion last night.

"Morning, darling," her mother said. "Let's get you some coffee." Her mother had always shown her affection in more practical than emotional ways. She was already signaling a server. "This is a nice place."

They chitchatted about the hotel her parents were staying at and what their plans were for the rest of the day until the food arrived, all the while avoiding the elephant—or cougar, Quinn thought gleefully—in the room.

"Tommy looks very happy," Quinn's mom said during a lull in conversation. "A bit tired perhaps, but having a baby will do that to you."

"Have you met the little one?" her dad asked. "What's his name again?"

"Ethan," Quinn said, remembering the day Beth had arrived at Maya's unannounced with the baby. "He's so cute."

"But don't you want children, darling?" her mother blurted out. "Of your own, I mean. Not... I don't know what to call him. Tommy's son is hardly your grandchild now, is he?"

Maya had told Quinn about her mother's fixation on Maya being a grandmother—and what that might make Quinn.

"Of course, he's not."

"But Drew's new wife, what's her name..." Her mother waved her hand about. "She's Tommy's stepmom."

"Is she?" Quinn guessed her mother was getting so worked up about semantics because it was the easiest way to vent her frustration. She took a sip of coffee. "Look, I'm never going to be Tommy's stepmother, okay? That's not what this is."

"Your mother, like me, is concerned that you might not get out of this relationship... what you put into it," her father added.

"Because I'm younger?"

"Yes," Quinn's mom said.

"I've told you this before. I don't want children. I've never wanted them. I'm almost thirty-five. I don't think that's going to change."

"But, darling, you say that now." Her mother scratched her nose. "What if this thing with Maya goes on as long as your previous... affair," she as good as spat out the word, "with Morgan. You'll be almost forty. What if you change your mind then?"

"Why would I change my mind? I've never been the slightest bit broody. Some women simply don't want children. I'm one of them." It wasn't as if it would be so much easier to have children with someone her own age, she thought, but didn't think it wise to share. Maybe her mother was jealous of Maya because she was a granny more than she was angry about how it related to Quinn.

"I don't think wanting kids or not is really the point here," her father said.

"Look." A dull headache started throbbing at the base of Quinn's skull. "I know that me being with Maya is not what you want for me. I get that it's this parental instinct kicking in and that you need time to get past that. But I'm not with Maya just so that I can disappoint you or annoy you. I'm with her because... she makes me feel alive. She makes me feel like I can do anything. Because she's the only person I want to be with."

Her mother inhaled audibly through her nose. "It's not ill will," her mom said, her voice breaking a fraction. "It's not that I don't want to deal with this, but I don't know how. I tried to talk to Maya last night. God knows, over the years, we've spent many evenings in each other's company, chatting the hours away, but that shared history was all gone. It was like she had become a different person to me."

"It won't stay that way, Mom," Quinn urged. "You're still shocked. You're still processing. It's probably going to take some time to adjust to the idea of us."

"What struck me the most last night was how casual Tommy seemed about the whole thing," her dad said.

You and me both, Quinn thought. "Did you talk to him about us?"

Her dad nodded. "He's from the generation that finds it easy to accept things that for people our age are much harder to swallow."

"Maybe, but..." Quinn wasn't sure how to make the rest of her argument and whether there was an argument to make at all. Maybe they just needed some time. She'd had a chat with Tommy herself and he'd been much more fun than she remembered—it must be the influence of his hot semi-celebrity wife. "I'm not expecting you to invite Maya and me over for dinner next weekend. In fact, I have no expectations of you when it comes to this because I know that you love me and I also know that my unconventional choice of partner is not going to make you stop loving me. If that were the case, we would have become estranged a long time ago." Quinn allowed herself a quick albeit nervous chuckle. "And look at it this way: at least you know Maya. You know that she's a good person with her heart in the right place. Doesn't that count for a lot?"

"It counts for something," her dad said. "And let's not forget she's single." He flashed her the beginnings of a smile.

"Good grief," her mother joined in. "When did Maya even become interested in women? In all the years I've known her, she's never said a word about that being the case."

"I think you're going to have to accept that it was a later in life epiphany for her," Quinn lied, because some things could never be said out loud.

Her dad lifted his glass of water. "To time," he said. "That it may guide us well."

Quinn snorted at his attempt at adding gravitas to the conversation, although she did appreciate the sentiment.

"And always keep us together as a family, no matter who our daughter falls for," her mother added.

Quinn grinned at her parents. At their core, this was who they were. Practical. Forward-looking. Easily shaken perhaps when it came to their daughter's antics, despite loads of practice, but never willing to stew in their pessimism for too long. Above all, she knew they loved her, and they always would.

CHAPTER 43

"It's all going to be all right," Quinn said. "I know that now."

Maya had to get a move on if she wanted to be in Manhattan on time to teach. But she'd wanted to stay at Quinn's until she came back from brunch with her parents.

"I can't believe I actually entertained the thought that they wouldn't even show up." Quinn looked tired, but a lot more relaxed than before she'd left. "They were always going to. I also know that now." She walked over to Maya and, as though this was their custom, sat astride her lap. "It's like Tommy. He reacted the way he did because you're his mother. Because you being the person you are, made him into the person he is, which is a son who just wants his mother to be happy."

"Quinn, sweetheart." There was no way Maya could wiggle herself out from underneath Quinn when she straddled her like this. "I have to go. I'm teaching in less than two hours."

Quinn huffed out some air. "I think you should play hooky."

"I'm the teacher. I can't play hooky."

"When's the very latest you have to leave?" Quinn's big blue eyes looked down at Maya.

"Fifteen minutes ago."

"Oh, no way." Even though Maya had to leave, she loved it when Quinn spoke to her in a won't-take-no-for-an-answer tone of voice—as though, for her, it was simply not an option that she and Maya couldn't spend more time together. "Traffic isn't that bad." She curled her body closer toward Maya's. "And we haven't properly celebrated yet." She kissed Maya's neck.

"We can celebrate all weekend." Maya tried to push Quinn away but it was only a feeble attempt because she wanted Quinn as close to her as possible.

"If you stay ten more minutes"—Quinn kissed her way down Maya's neck to her collar bone—"I'll take you dancing tomorrow."

"Ten minutes? Will that be enough?" Maya was already prepared to stay much longer than that. Seeing Quinn in her element last night had aroused her. Watching her surrounded by her friends and family— and people who loved what she did—had been electrifying. And that string of kisses down her neck was helping as well.

"Do you have any idea how lucky you are?" Angus had asked her last night, with his gaze firmly planted on Quinn. "And how foolish you would have been if you hadn't listened to me when I talked some much-needed sense into you?"

Maya had hated doing it at the time, but she'd had to agree with him.

"Ten minutes will be plenty of time if we go into the bedroom now," Quinn said. "Griff doesn't appreciate it when I squirt lube all over the couch, especially during her 'year of no'."

Maya chuckled as Quinn hopped off her. She followed Quinn into her bedroom, not caring any longer that her bed was too narrow or her mattress too lumpy. She could see now that her frustration about those things had mostly been fear in disguise.

Quinn slammed the door shut behind them in case Griff came home, then wasted no time pushing Maya onto the bed. She came to lie on top of her, pushing her body into Maya's, kissing her deeply.

Maya held her tight and let the physical sensations, as well as all the feelings she had for Quinn, wash over her like an avalanche that swallowed her whole. She didn't resist anything—she'd done enough of that. Quinn was right. Everything would be all right. But Maya also knew that, from the vantage point they'd had before, it had been impossible for either of them to see.

Usually prone to whispering sweet nothings in Maya's ear during foreplay, Quinn was silent today. After they broke from their kiss she just gazed into Maya's eyes, leaving Maya to wonder what was going through her head.

Maybe it was the same thought that occupied most of Maya's brain—that she was so in love, she could withstand the wrath of Quinn's mother if she had to, the disappointment of her father, the looks they would get in the streets, the gaze of strangers upon them who were no doubt debating whether they were mother and daughter or something much more interesting. None of it mattered because they were together.

Now there was a thought Maya had never been willing to entertain because how could she? How could all those things no longer matter simply because she'd fallen in love with another person? At the time, she couldn't know what she now knew. That love did that to you. It took away the doubts and the fear and replaced them with something magical, something so delightful that it obliterated any remaining uncertainty.

Quinn kissed her again and Maya kissed her back even more ferociously. She slid her hands through Quinn's hair, grabbing at her, needing more of her. No wonder Maya felt like she'd been catapulted back in time to her teenage years, because despite her age, this all felt so new to her. The intensity of her desire. Her sheer need for Quinn. The quickness of her arousal. For years, she had wrongly believed she was beyond all that. She had secretly hoped her move to New York might change that—that she might find someone in this vast city who could make her feel like that again. But never in a million years had she expected that person to be Quinn Hathaway. And never had she expected it to be so all-consuming. So thrilling. Nor so devastatingly frightening at first.

Quinn reached for Maya's hand that was buried in her hair. She kissed her palm, looked into Maya's eyes, then pinned Maya's hand above her head. When Maya moved her hand, reaching for Quinn again, Quinn curled her fingers around Maya's wrist and placed it above her head again. She narrowed her eyes as she locked her gaze on Maya. Oh, so it was like that.

At least Maya still had her other hand to feel Quinn with, to cup her delicious breasts with. But Quinn swiftly reached for Maya's free hand and pinned that above her head as well. What would she do next? Tie her up?

"Keep them there," Quinn whispered. As if she didn't trust Maya to follow this simple instruction, she curled her fingers tighter around Maya's wrists. Maya looked above her head and saw a couple of letters of the word *Radical* from Quinn's tattoo. She'd become so familiar with Quinn's tattoos that her brain automatically added *Acceptance*. She might as well do that—radically accept anything that was happening and anything she was feeling. Not only because Quinn told her to, which was surprisingly arousing in itself, but also because the position Quinn now held her in left her tantalizingly vulnerable and exposed to Quinn's whims.

Quinn unbuttoned Maya's blouse with one hand, exposing her upper body. She kissed the swell of Maya's breast. By the time she had to let go of Maya's hands to hike up her skirt, Maya was more than willing to keep her hands above her head—she'd tie them to the bedpost herself if she could. She relished Quinn's easy power over her. Just as she relished all the new—or forgotten—sensations being with Quinn had brought her.

Quinn, who had never relented in her pursuit of Maya. Who had only needed one photo shoot with Maya to feel that spark again, to fan the flames they'd been forced to extinguish between them ten years ago. Maya had felt it too, but just like back then, she had to be the spark killer. Quinn was too reckless for that kind of responsibility.

And now, as it turned out, so was Maya. Because being with Quinn was reckless and mind-blowing and a touch crazy, but it was also the only way it could be for Maya now. Just like, right now, the only thing for Maya to do was lie on Quinn's bed with her hands above her head, her skirt wrinkling underneath her because Quinn had pushed it all the way up, with her panties nowhere to be seen.

It was all exactly as it should be, Maya thought, as Quinn's fully lubricated fingers slid between her legs. With her other hand, Quinn imprisoned Maya's wrists again, while she gazed into her eyes. More newness. More of Quinn's beautiful thought processes at work—maybe being under time pressure enhanced her creativity. Maya should have been in a taxi half an hour ago. She was going to be ridiculously late for her own class. In all respects, it was an utter disgrace, but she didn't care. How could she when Quinn's fingers slid inside her and made her feel like this? When Quinn looked at her like that, as if there was only one woman left in the entire universe that was important to her, and that woman was Maya.

CHAPTER 44

ONE YEAR LATER

"Win," Ethan uttered while he pulled himself up with the help of Quinn's leg.

"That child is as crazy about you as his grandmother is," Angus said.

"Come here, you." Quinn picked Ethan up and put him in her lap, knowing he would only stay a few minutes. A sixteen-month-old toddler, she had learned, didn't much care for staying in one spot for a long period of time. He always had places to be and new, exciting things to discover.

Ethan briefly put his head against her shoulder and everyone in Maya's living room cooed as though Ethan had just won the Nobel Prize for being a baby. Most people present here today would actually believe he deserved a prize, simply for being alive—Maya most of all.

"Feel free to hand him over if he's bothering you," Tommy said.

"How could this cute little man ever bother me." Quinn put her arms around Maya's grandson and gave him a cuddle. She'd done her fair share of babysitting over the past year and she had grown very fond of the child. In that respect, the year had not gone as planned at all. Not that Quinn ever had a grand scheme mapped out for her life, apart from trying not to get too heartbroken again and sell a picture once in a while, but for someone without a natural affinity to children, she had made a huge exception for Ethan. The kid had gotten under her skin and nowadays, when she didn't see him for a week, she got antsy. Sometimes, when Maya was teaching and Quinn was in Manhattan, she'd drop by Tommy and Beth's by herself just to see him.

"Tell me about it," Griff said. "He basically stole you from me." She leaned against Roxanne's shoulder. After her 'year of no' ended, Griff had wasted no time asking out the cute barista from the coffee shop on the corner. Quinn had never been able to establish whether Griff had actually waited until the clock had struck midnight on the last day of the year—she strongly suspected she might not have, but what did it even matter?

Roxanne patted Griff's head. "It's okay, baby. You have me now."

"I might move to Manhattan as well," Griff said. "Not because I can't live without my former roommate, but because the commute is killing me." When she'd needed a new assistant producer a few months ago, Beth had offered Griff the job. She had not merely taken it, but embraced it as though her life depended on it. "Have you ever tried writing a book on the L-train? Let me assure you, it doesn't work."

As predicted, Ethan wiggled his way out of Quinn's lap and waddled to the corner of the carpet where a bunch of his toys lay.

Quinn watched how her mother followed the child with her gaze. Brooke and Maya had taken Ethan to the Bronx Zoo a few weeks ago and no one had gotten hurt. Upon their return, Quinn had declared it a miracle, because they could joke about these things now.

"I'll get the grill going," Quinn's dad spoke the words Quinn had heard him say so often.

"I'll give you a hand." Tommy rose.

"Oh, for crying out loud," Maya said. "What is this? Men grilling outside on the deck while the women do the dishes inside?" She shook her head. "That's not how things are done these days."

Quinn's father looked confused. "You don't want me in charge of the grill?"

Maya huffed out some air and sipped from her champagne. "Oh, go on. Do what you like, just don't be too... manly about it."

Angus burst into laughter. "I would help, but this suit is simply too extraordinary."

"We're all just a bunch of clichés," Griff said. "Quinn's moving in with her girlfriend. Mine's moving in with me already after only a few months of dating. How lesbian can you get?"

Quinn watched her mother shuffle around in her chair.

"Griff's been a real asset to our team," Beth said. "What with her special powers of observation." She took a swig of soda water. "It's invaluable when you work in news."

Griff pulled a face. "You'd better watch out I don't take your job while you're on maternity leave."

"That's one cliché too far." Beth put her hands on her belly. "Besides, Griff, you're not just my co-worker. You're my friend. I trust you accordingly."

"We'll see when it comes to picking the new one's godmother how good a friend you consider me to be."

"Is it okay with everyone if I go out on the deck now?" Quinn's father stood there grinning. He slapped Tommy on the back in a faux-macho way. "My daughter's never taken a great interest in grilling, so all my hopes rest on you now, young man."

"Tommy's more a Good Housekeeping recipe kind of guy," Beth said. "His key lime pie is to die for."

"Come on, Bill, before the womenfolk get out of control," Tommy said and headed out with Quinn's dad in tow.

Too lazy to walk, Ethan crawled to his mother and pulled at the sleeve of her blouse. Beth took him into her lap.

"Another one of those in a few weeks," Angus said.

Quinn looked at Maya. She'd been over the moon about it for months. Sometimes she wondered if Maya had been so overjoyed with the prospect of having another grandchild that she'd asked Quinn to move in with her whilst in a state of delirium. While it was true that Quinn stayed over at Maya's a lot, sometimes not returning home for a full week, she hadn't expected the question. Ever since Rachel, more than ten years ago, Quinn hadn't lived with a romantic partner. Ironically, it was Rachel kicking her out that had brought her and Maya together for the first time. That she had just moved into Maya's condo was just another example of how you could never guess how life would play out.

"At least you'll have an extra pair of younger hands to help you," Quinn's mother said, surprising everyone. As the year had progressed, her quips had become less sharp and, most surprising of all, even a little bit funny at times.

"Bwook," Ethan suddenly shouted, leaving all of them in stitches. He held out his little arms in Quinn's mother's direction.

Quinn's mother melted on the spot. She might have railed against Maya being a grandmother when she'd first found out about Quinn and Maya, but she sure looked happy to have a small child in her life.

"This member of the womenfolk is going to get the salads together." Quinn stood. Since moving into Maya's luxurious condo with its swanky marble-topped kitchen, she'd been doing more cooking than she'd previously done in all her life.

Maya followed her into the kitchen. "Let's do it together," she said.

CHAPTER 45

On the actual day of the first anniversary of them seeing each other again—the day of that fateful photo shoot—Maya had giddily agreed to Quinn's suggestion. It had sounded like such a romantic idea at the time, but now as they stood outside the tattoo parlor she wasn't so sure.

Maya was in the second half of her fifties. What was she doing getting a tattoo? And a matching one with Quinn at that? When she looked at it from a regular, everyday kind of viewpoint, the whole thing was preposterous. But then she glanced over at Quinn, and pictured all of Quinn's existing tattoos, and then the whole thing made a lot more sense again.

"Ready?" Quinn asked, and took her hand.

"Hell, no."

"Sometimes it's better to jump before you're ready." Quinn pulled her inside.

"You have a motto for every situation," Maya muttered under her breath, but Quinn wasn't even listening anymore.

The tattoo artist greeted Quinn as though she were a long-lost friend. Quinn introduced Maya and the woman didn't so much as bat an eyelid—that was New York for you. Maya had learned as much. She'd been here over a year and a half now and during that time she had found out that it took a lot to perturb a New Yorker. Of course, they were met with a raised eyebrow once in a while and when she told Indira at Acton about her and Quinn, she'd seen her swallow as her brain computed that particular bit of information about Maya's personal life. But most people, Maya had found, like this tattoo artist, didn't care one iota about Quinn and Maya being together. It was a refreshing experience for Maya who had spent the best part of her younger years being judged in dance competitions and the time between then and now in a small town like Milbury where gossip spread like wildfire. Then again, if she'd stayed in Milbury, she wouldn't be on the cusp of getting a tattoo right now.

"I'll go first," Quinn said. She looked Maya in the eye. "You don't have to do this if you're not totally convinced. Lasering ink off your skin is a real bitch, babe. You'd better be sure." Quinn had always had an unflinching quality about her, even all those years ago, when she'd seduced Maya as though it was a well-practiced hobby to go after middle-aged women from the suburbs.

"I know." Maya couldn't keep the tension out of her voice, but she was allowed to be tense about this. This was a big thing. This tattoo, wasn't simply permanently marking her skin; she was also saying to Quinn that she was in this for the long haul. Although, as Quinn had told her when she'd first suggested this, it wasn't exactly like getting married either.

"Because divorce might actually be easier than getting a tattoo removed," Maya had quipped.

Quinn had shaken her head, and said, "Our tattoos will match because we're together. If something were to ever drive us apart, it doesn't mean we have to get the tattoo removed. We're not getting each other's name tattooed on our bodies. The text can work perfectly well on its own."

Quinn took off her top. Her tattoo would be on the other side of her body that said *Life is for living.*

Maya had once joked to Quinn that if she ever found herself somewhere without a book and needed distraction, she could always read Quinn's skin. She watched as the artist disinfected Quinn's side and prepared her equipment. Before she started, she studied the note with the text Quinn had given her earlier.

"Same font as the one on the other side?" the artist asked casually, as though Quinn was a piece of paper she was about to write on.

Quinn confirmed and the tattoo artist got to work.

Maya tried not to look at Quinn's face. If she really had doubts about getting a tattoo, she wouldn't be here. She would have stalled or simply said no. But she wanted it in the same reckless but unmistakable way she'd wanted Quinn, over eleven years ago and again a year ago. What scared Maya most was the prospect of physical pain. Having a needle jabbed repeatedly into your skin wasn't her idea of a fun afternoon.

"It's half an hour of pain in return for a lifetime of feeling connected to me," Quinn had said, with that silver tongue of hers.

Nerves coiling into a tight knot in her stomach, Maya watched Quinn get tattooed. The text wasn't long and it wasn't part of an elaborate artwork—Quinn saved that for her day job—so it was fairly straightforward and, indeed, didn't take much longer than half an hour.

"Do you want to take a look?" the tattoo artist asked Maya.

Maya nodded and walked to Quinn's other side.

It wasn't pretty—yet—but the words of Quinn's new tattoo were clear as day: *Some nights are unforgettable*.

When Maya's eyes fell on it, all her nerves melted like snow under the sun. She straightened her back, squared her shoulders, and said, "I'm ready for mine."

ABOUT THE AUTHOR

Harper Bliss is a best-selling lesbian romance author. Among her most-loved books are the highly dramatic French Kissing and the often thought-provoking Pink Bean series.

Harper lived in Hong Kong for seven years, travelled the world for a bit, and has now settled in Brussels (Belgium) with her wife and photogenic cat, Dolly Purrton.

Together with her wife, she hosts a weekly podcast called Harper Bliss & Her Mrs.

Harper loves hearing from readers and you can reach her at the email address below.

www.harperbliss.com

harper@harperbliss.com

Made in the USA
Middletown, DE
25 February 2022

61843072R00189